THE OUTLAW

JENNIFER MILLIKIN

Copyright © 2021 by Jennifer Millikin
All rights reserved.

This book or any portion thereof
may not be reproduced or used in any manner whatsoever
without the express written permission of the publisher
except for the use of brief quotations in a book review. This book is a work
of fiction. Names, characters, and incidents are products of the author's
imagination or are used fictitiously. Any resemblance to actual events, or
locales, or persons, living or dead, is entirely coincidental.
JNM, LLC

ISBN: 978-1-7371790-5-4
www.jennifermillikinwrites.com
Cover by Whiskey Ginger Goods
Editing by My Brother's Editor
Proofreading by Sisters Get Literary

ALSO BY JENNIFER MILLIKIN

Hayden Family Series

The Patriot

The Maverick

The Calamity

Olive Township Series

Penn

Hugo

Ambrose (Forthcoming)

Duke (Forthcoming)

Standalone

Preorder Hard Feelings (Dom and Cecily's story)

What We Keep

Here For The Cake

Better Than Most

The Least Amount Of Awful

Return To You

One Good Thing

Beyond The Pale

Good On Paper

The Day He Went Away

Full of Fire

The Time Series

Our Finest Hour

Magic Minutes

The Lifetime of A Second

— "LOVE IS THE ULTIMATE OUTLAW. IT JUST WON'T ADHERE TO ANY RULES. THE MOST ANY OF US CAN DO IS SIGN ON AS ITS ACCOMPLICE." - TOM ROBBINS

PROLOGUE

Jo - Eighteen Years Old

It's not as if I thought my life would ever be anything great. Cults that operate under the guise of religious sects don't exactly allow for a lot of independent thought or imagination.

But in my wildest dreams, this isn't what I would've envisioned for myself.

I should be happy. And I am. Sort of. How happy can one person be when the best day of their life coincides with their worst? You'd think maybe they would cancel each other out, but somehow, they don't. The negative is a boulder, the positive, a balloon.

She's leaving now, her car stuffed to the gills with their belongings. Her ankle-length skirts, her jars of dusty potpourri, and all the things a toddler needs.

She's walking through the apartment once more,

double-checking to make certain she has everything. She's taking with her a lot more than just her personal possessions.

"Say goodbye to your brother," she says, stopping a foot from me in the open doorway. Travis, twenty-seven months old and squirmy, leans away from her and holds his hands out to me. I hold tight to his top half, letting his soft yellow curls sweep my chest.

"Best get going," she clips, clearing her throat and gently pulling Travis from me.

I stand back, pulling myself up straight and staring at her. We are eye to eye, my height reaching hers this last year. As mothers go, she was young when she had me. Twenty-four. She looks older than her forty-two years now. And she never wears makeup.

It's the cult that won't let her paint her face. *Makeup is meant to tempt men, and temptation is a sin.* Of course, she's been living out from under the watchful eye of the leader, Magnus Markusen, for two and a half years. Still, no makeup. *Such a faithful servant.*

"You can come too, Josephine."

I rear back, her words a strike. She correctly interprets my flinching and says, "Having a child out of wedlock is a sin. I'll be lucky if they take me back."

"You don't have to tell me that, unless you're practicing your lie to make sure you sound convincing when you arrive and tell them how sorry you are and how lucky you feel."

Anger pulls at the muscles in her cheeks. Travis kicks his feet and bucks his body. She grips him with a second arm. No matter how much this cult likes to remove the need for sovereignty over oneself, they worship children. Children are loved, doted on, and cared for every hour of every day.

Travis will want for nothing until he is older, until he wonders why nobody leaves, why the adults look like replicas of each other. That was my downfall. I dared to question.

I follow my mom to her car and wait while she buckles Travis into his car seat. She steps back when she's finished, and I lean in, replacing her.

"I love you, little buddy." I kiss his forehead, his chubby cheeks, breathe in the scent of the dry cereal he ate earlier mixed with the smell of his skin.

"Dis," he says, pointing at me. "Dis, Dis!"

"Yes," I answer, smiling at him and touching my fingertip to his. "Sis."

"We need to go," my mom says quietly from the front seat.

I kiss my fingers and place them against Travis's chest, right over his heart. My eyes burn. I climb out of the car and back away. The passenger window is open, and she leans across the center, her head framed by the window.

"Make good choices," she says to me.

"Same goes to you," I instruct, my voice stern.

We share a final, long look, then the car begins to roll. I want to run after it, to chase it down and speak words that will make her stop, say things I should've said a long time ago, words that would've altered the course of everything.

Back then, I was too ashamed to speak up. Now, I'm too unstable.

Hot tears course down my cheeks, and I don't bother to wipe at them. I walk back into the apartment, knowing I have only two weeks left in it before the rent is due.

To pay rent, I need a job. And I can't find a job if I'm

sitting here on this sagging couch, crying about the fact that my entire life just drove away.

I wipe my eyes, blow my nose, and change my shirt. Our apartment is close to town. The walk is easy; it's each step that feels so overwhelmingly hard.

Once I reach High Street, two different people wave to me from their storefronts. Maia, from the Merc, and Wade, from Marigolds. I might've only moved to Sierra Grande a little over two years ago, but the small town took me in like a cactus absorbs every drop of rainwater, until I felt like I was here from the beginning, a native.

When I see the town's biggest and nicest hotel needs a server in its restaurant, I feel like I've hit the jackpot.

I get the job. I start shadowing the woman who has just put in her two-week notice, and when she's gone, I'm on my own. I do fine; eventually I have regulars, and I make enough to support myself.

The same cannot be said of my mom. God's Redeemers does not take her back into the fold. Apparently, she is not worthy of redemption. How ironic.

She stays gone for a year, trying to get hired at a hospital somewhere near the cult. They do not have openings for nurses, so she works in the gift shop. She's overqualified, but one day she saves a person's life when they go into cardiac arrest while picking out a gift for someone they've come to visit. Eventually the friend my mom and Travis are staying with gets married and moves, and my mom cannot support them without help.

Almost exactly three hundred and sixty-five days later, she returns to our apartment. We live together for seven years until my mom finds an opportunity to be a home nurse for a woman in Monte Vista, a town nearly five hours away. When she goes for the interview, she meets the old woman's son, Henri.

In no time her bags are packed, along with Travis's. It's the same scene from seven years ago, minus the pudgy hands and baby scent of his head.

The heartbreak is nearly identical.

1

WYATT

"He's coming home. Tonight. Right now."

It's loud in the Chute, the voice of the lead singer in the live band bouncing off the walls and ricocheting around me, but I can still hear the fear in Sara's voice as it travels over the phone line.

"I'm on my way." I end the call and push away from the bar, tucking the stool back under the bar with my booted foot.

Denny and Ham stare at me, quiet judgment plain on their faces.

"Stop," I bark, peeling off a couple twenties and stuffing them in the rocks glass that holds my tab.

"You can't save her for the rest of time." Denny's brave enough to say what he knows I don't want to hear. Around the longneck bottle poised at his lips, he adds, "Or him."

The muscles in my face flex. I know the truth as well as they do, but I'm not ready to face it. Sometimes a person needs to see something through, needs to bleed the situation dry before they can admit defeat.

I owe Mickey. Without him, I don't know where I'd be. He saved me once upon a time. Now I'm saving him. From himself, of all things.

I nod my head at my friends. "See you back at the ranch." Denny and Ham are cowboys at the Hayden Cattle Company, but they've been my friends for as long as I can remember. They're also Mickey's friends, but they've washed their hands of him. Or maybe they're showing him tough love. I don't know which it is, I just know I'm not doing either.

The Chute is busy tonight, hosting both a live band right now and bull riding later. I weave through bodies, stopping for a moment to say hi to Jackson and his younger brother, Colin. Colin sips from a bottle of root beer and smiles wide at me, his arms opening for a hug. Colin has Down syndrome, and he likes me for reasons that have nothing to do with my last name. I hug him, the same way I have for years. He steps back, his frame bulky in this tight space full of bodies, and bumps into someone's back. The guy turns around, pissed. The front of his shirt is wet with what I assume is the other half of the beer he's holding.

"What the fuck," he growls.

His eyes never get the chance to land on Colin because I'm there, stepping in front of him. It's possible the guy would've seen Colin's disability and chilled the fuck out, but now we'll never know.

"I'm waiting for your apology," the prick says. He's wearing black jeans, leather lace-up tennis shoes I know are expensive as fuck because I own boots by that brand, and a shirt with a hole near the neck. The hole looks too on purpose, like the shirt was sold that way instead of earning a tear with hard work. I dislike the guy immediately.

"You should hold your breath and wait to see if that happens," I tell him, pulling myself to full height, expanding my chest and lengthening my shoulders. Along with giving me a good life and emotional wounds, my dad showed me how to be physically intimidating. The first two are woven into the fabric of my life; the latter I call upon every now and again.

I don't have time for this shit with whoever this newcomer is, but I also don't have it in me to back down. Behind me, I hear Jackson tell Colin it's time to take a seat, and that makes me feel better. I push past the guy, giving him a good shoulder shove, and continue on through the crowd and out the door.

The truth is, I have no business driving right now. Laws are arbitrary to me, but there are a few I abide by, and drinking and driving is one of them. Despite this, I keep hearing Sara's voice. The fear. The dread.

I get in my truck. Turn it on. Sit back. Grab the bottle of water from the center console and down it. Sara's house isn't far from here. It's later on a Friday night. There won't be very many people out right now.

Just as I go to shift into drive, a tap on my window stops me. The lighting in the parking lot is dim, so I can't tell who it is very easily. I roll down my window.

"Fuck," I mutter.

"What are you doing, Wyatt?" Shelby Trask crosses her arms in front of herself. Her stiff uniform doesn't ripple, which is an accurate metaphor for her personality. She has definitive beliefs about right versus wrong. Let's just say Shelby and I have never really seen eye to eye.

"I'm just sitting in my truck, Officer Trask." I smile at her. It gets me nowhere.

"Wyatt, are you aware that it's against the law to sit behind the wheel of your vehicle when you are intoxicated?"

"Who says I'm intoxicated?"

She sighs. She knows I've got her there.

"It's not a huge leap to assume that when Wyatt Hayden emerges from the Chute, he's put back a few." She eyes me knowingly.

She's not wrong. But, of course, there's no way for her to confirm she's right. I'd pass any field sobriety test administered. I don't have the time to continue this with Shelby though. I need to get to Sara's before Mickey arrives. Give him something else to hit besides his wife.

"Officer Trask, it was great catching up, but I should be going."

"Not so fast, Wyatt. You see, I happen to have this handy little tool back at the station called a breathalyzer, and—"

Shit. This can't happen. If I'm waylaid, I don't know what will happen to Sara. Or Mickey. "Shelby, how long have we been friends? Since seventh grade?"

She frowns. "Save your words, Wyatt. Nothing you say will work. I am bound by law to bring you into the station."

Time for some serious cajoling. "We're the only two people in this parking lot, Shelby. Nobody will know if you let me go."

Her head is shaking before I finish my sentence. She points to something attached to her uniform. "See that? It's a body cam. It's recording, which means even though it's only you and I here right now, it's not only you and I who know you're intoxicated and behind the wheel of a vehicle."

Fuck. There's nothing more I can do, short of taking off and leading her straight to Sara's house. Which will create a whole host of problems, far greater than the one I was trying to prevent. Sara vehemently refuses to involve law enforcement.

I unbuckle. Hop out. Walk beside Shelby to her cruiser. She spares me the hassle of cuffing me. Small town and all.

We pass the turnoff for Mickey and Sara's house on the way to the station, and I wonder if Mickey has already made it home.

THE METAL CHAIR SHIMMERS DULLY IN THE BLUNT OVERHEAD light. I don't know why they've stuck me in here. I'm not being interrogated.

I was fine in the large cell with James Croft, the idiot who set off a bottle rocket earlier this evening when everybody and their senile grandparents know it's illegal. And the other guy, the one wearing obscenely tight jeans, was brought in for trespassing on Hayden Cattle Company land. He's probably still crowing about how his wandering was inadvertent. I didn't believe a word out of his mouth, nor did I tell him my last name is Hayden.

Like a watched pot never boils, a watched door never seems to open. I've glanced at my watch so many times I've lost count, the minutes ticking by at a sure and steady pace. Every minute in this place feels like an hour, and my mind is filled with the bruises that are most likely just beginning to take form on Sara's body.

Finally, the door opens. Sheriff Monroe steps in. He's getting on in age, thicker around the middle than he'd like to be, and has a zigzag scar on the back of his head from riding a horse into a barbed wire fence when he was a teenager.

The sheriff opts not to sit down, but stands behind the chair opposite mine, his hands gripping the back. His knuckles are hairy and he wears a silver ring with a piece of turquoise in the center.

"Where were you headed tonight, Wyatt? Before Officer Trask brought you in."

I don't want to say, but I know my compliance will make it more likely he'll be lenient with my punishment. "To help a friend."

His bushy, salt-and-pepper eyebrows draw together. "By any chance would that 'friend' be Sara Schultz?"

I'm not surprised he knows, but doesn't he have better things to do? Like, I don't know, protect the town of Sierra Grande? Then again, his wife is a terrible gossip.

Anger, and a healthy dose of injustice, bubbles up inside me. This town notices my truck parked outside the Schultz's home when it otherwise shouldn't be, but they don't see what's right under their noses. How did nobody else see it when Sara began wearing long sleeves in July? How was I the only one?

I tamp down the anger, hold tight to the sting of injustice, and answer. "Yes, Sheriff."

Emotion flickers in his eyes. He's not disgusted. Judgmental, yes. Probably confused about my morals, or apparent lack thereof. "Doesn't matter to you that she's married with kids?"

He waits for my reply, but I don't have much of one. It *does* matter to me that she's married with kids. It matters a whole hell of a lot. Just not for the reason the sheriff knows about. I nod at him. At least it's the truth.

He chews on his cheek and watches me. I know he's thinking about what to do with me.

"Who should I call, Wyatt? To come and get you?"

"I can walk."

He tells me no with a shake of his head. "You're still intoxicated. If I let you go in this state and you cause more trouble, it's my head on the chopping block."

My hands fist under the table and I let go of my final shred of hope that I can make it to the Schultz's tonight. Sara called, asked me for help, and I failed.

"Wes." My voice is rough, a rock scraped over sandpaper. "Call Wes."

AN HOUR PASSES. MAYBE MORE. I'M TORTURING MYSELF, running through scenarios of what could've gone down tonight at Mickey and Sara's. I pulled up memories of them as a happy family, like they used to be before Mickey lost his job and left to find work outside of town. When I'm sick of torturing myself, I run through a list of shit I need to do when I get out of here. The metal chair I'm sitting in started to feel like concrete about thirty minutes ago. My ass is asleep.

The sudden opening of the door startles me, and I sit up straight. The sheriff steps in, followed by my father.

My heart, my stomach, my whole body drops out of me, scattering on the cold floor.

Not my dad.

I'd specifically asked for my big brother, Wes. Not my

other big brother, Warner, because he has kids and his wife is pregnant. Wes has a baby at home too, but my nephew is sleeping through the night now, and a call to Wes isn't as disruptive.

Wes is tougher than Warner when it comes to me, but he was the next best alternative to my dad. So how the hell did I get stuck with the man who regularly fails to hide his disappointment when he looks at me?

Sheriff Monroe stops on the other side of the table. He holds on to the back of the chair like he did earlier and levels his gaze on mine. My dad, who could just as easily have at least stood on my side of the table, steps up beside the sheriff. Guess I've never really needed to draw a line to know what side my dad's on. It's whatever is opposite mine.

The sheriff says in a tired voice, "We're not arresting you, Wyatt."

I nod, close to telling him I know that already, but keep my mouth shut instead. I might have a quick wit and a smart mouth that's gotten me into trouble more times than I can count, but I know how to harness it. "Thanks, Sheriff."

I dare a glance at my dad. Nothing moves. Not his face. Not his stance. Not even a muscle tic along his jaw. Beau Hayden is a beast of a man, a local legend, and a damn living statue.

My chair scrapes its protest as I stand. In this cold, quiet space, the sound bounces off the walls. "Ready to go home?"

My dad's steely-eyed gaze doesn't leave me. "Can we have a minute, Sheriff?"

The sheriff doesn't respond, but his booted retreat speaks his reply. The door closes.

Now the muscles in his face twitch. When we were younger, he'd flick our ears with what felt like the strongest, meanest fingers in the state of Arizona. Misbehavior was avoided because nobody wanted to draw his anger. A lot has changed in twenty years. Somewhere along the way, I stopped giving a fuck.

"Where's Wes?"

He crosses his arms in front of himself, partially covering the HCC insignia on his vest. "Wes doesn't need to come to your rescue. He has a son to raise." He eyes me meaningfully. "And so do I."

I bristle. "I'm an adult."

"A person would be hard-pressed to know it."

I mimic his stance. The last thing I want is to hear from my father how I've managed to disappoint him yet again. "Can we go?"

His lips are drawn in a grim line. "You think drinking and driving is no big deal?"

"I wasn't actually driving. I was sitting."

A terse stream of air huffs from his nose. As sounds go, it's as ubiquitous as his flicking fingers. It means he cannot believe the sheer stupidity of the words you've just spoken.

"Quit playing cute, Son. If Shelby hadn't been there you'd have been driving."

"Does it even matter anymore? It's over."

"What was so important that you were going to do something you know damn well is illegal? Not to mention dangerous."

My lips tighten, an invisible needle and thread sewing a seam.

"Christ," my dad mutters, shaking his head at me. "I already know where you were headed, Wyatt. Just thought maybe you'd do me the courtesy of telling me the truth."

If I told him the truth, Sara would lose her husband, her

sole source of income for her and her two kids, and Mickey would go to jail. Should Sara keep absorbing Mickey's liquor-fueled fists? Hell no. That's what I'm for until I can think of a better solution. Until I figure out a way to help Mickey long-term.

He turns toward the door. "Come on," my dad growls, dissatisfied with me once again. What the fuck else is new?

My entire existence is a letdown for him.

He loves me because he has to, because it's hardwired. One thing I've learned though, is that while a person can feel love for someone, they can also feel a hundred other emotions, and absolutely none of them have to be good.

2

JO

"Mrs. Abbott?" My shoulder lifts to hold the phone against my ear so I can use my hands to pour the wine. I don't usually tend bar, but Lulu woke up to a feverish kid, and my job as manager is to be able to do everyone else's job when necessary. I place the two glasses of cabernet next to the ticket at the pickup station and pull the three new orders from the printer. "Is everything okay?"

"I tried calling your mom, but she didn't answer. Travis got into another fight today." She is tired of him. She grew tired of him months ago, and he knows it. I'm not sure how much patience school guidance counselors are supposed to have, but she seems to operate on less than what I remember when I was in high school.

I uncork the champagne bottle and line up three glasses. Who's celebrating on a Monday at noon? And can I join them? It's been a while since I had something to celebrate.

"Is he okay?"

A disapproving sound. That's what I get in answer to my question.

"Travis is fine. The other *child* is not."

I deliver the drink order and refrain from reminding her we're talking about high school freshmen, not kindergarteners. "Please put Travis on the phone." I finish the next two tickets while I wait.

"Hey." Travis's voice travels across the miles, sullen as all hell but also defiant. He is not sorry for what he did.

"Stop fighting at school," I hiss, ducking my head to make my own sliver of privacy.

"I didn't start it."

"What happened?" I don't have time for this right now, but I can't afford to push this aside. Travis needs someone to listen to him. God knows nobody else does.

"I had a presentation in class today, and I was really nervous. And..." His voice trails off, and my heart breaks a little. He doesn't need to say anything more. I see him in his favorite jeans, standing in front of all those pimply, expectant faces. I hear the snickering from behind cupped hands the first time he stutters. No doubt it only gets worse from there.

"Oh, Trav..." My arms ache to hug him.

"I tried to ignore it, Jo. Really. But they wouldn't stop teasing me after class. And I had enough."

The ticket machine screeches with another order. I round the corner of the bar and pull it up, reading. "Travis," I say calmly, taking a deep breath as I gather my glassware. "You can't solve your problems with your fists."

What I want to say is that the little shit who teased him had it coming, and maybe next time he won't have to learn his lesson the hard way.

"Thanks, *Mom*," he says in a petulant, sarcastic voice.

I sigh and keep pouring wine for other people.

"Sorry," he mutters.

"It's fine. I need to get back to work. Are you going to be okay?"

"You mean when Mom finds out? She probably won't even care." My heart breaks a little more. He's not completely wrong. She'll care, just not as much as she once would've. She's too in love to see straight, her eyes, judgment, and attention clouded by Henri, her French pot farmer boyfriend. Such a far cry from those cultish religion days, although not so far out of the realm of her personality. My mother is a person who wants something fantastical, something immersive, something so few others are doing. Still, Travis has had a good life with her, and I wonder what would've happened if I'd chosen to leave with her when I was eighteen. No sense looking in the rearview mirror, I guess. It doesn't do any good.

I wish my mother was better for Travis now, when the years are so important. She's taking her eye off the ball when the game is getting intense.

"She cares, Trav," I promise him. "I care."

"You're the only one who does."

"You're wrong."

"Whatever. Don't worry. I have to go."

The line goes dead. I look at my phone for a beat, then slide it back into my pocket. He won't call back. There's no need to.

It'll be summer break soon. Maybe Travis can come here to Sierra Grande for a few weeks. I don't have room in the two-bedroom house I share with my best friend Shelby, but we can make something work. Maybe I can get a discounted room for him and me at the Sierra. Then again, they're not exactly loving me over at the hotel right now. They weren't happy when I quit to come here to manage The Orchard. I may or may not have told them where to stick their attitude. I wasn't about to turn down a better paying job. Every cent gets me closer to my dream.

My stomach is in knots for the rest of the afternoon, thinking of Travis. I don't waste any time finishing up the paperwork for my shift and cashing out the servers. I hustle from the restaurant, already a few minutes late to meet Shelby.

***

Shelby doesn't want to tell me. I can't blame her for that, considering we both know what my reaction might be.

When it comes to him, I get a little mopey. Or angry. Sometimes, I get sullen. I broke a plate once, after I came home from a birthday dinner where I'd first heard about him and Sara Schultz.

"I promise to behave," I bargain, hoping this will be enough to make Shelby tell me what happened with Wyatt last night.

She watches me from her place across the table. We've been coming to this restaurant on Monday nights for years, eating our weight in chips and guacamole. It's busy tonight, and when she starts to speak I have to lean forward to hear her. "I was on patrol, which in this town is about as fun as watching paint dry, when I decided to pull into the parking lot at the Chute. I was going to grab a water and maybe some curly fries, because who wants to live without those blessed little darlings, when I saw Wyatt walk out. He wasn't obliterated, not like"—guilt floods her eyes—"well, you know…".

I wave my hand, trying to get her back on topic. Nobody needs to be reminded of that night in Phoenix eighteen months ago. Shelby is the only person who knows what happened. It's not lost on me how ironic it is that one of the participants of that night's sexual escapade doesn't remember, and therefore doesn't know. "Continue, please."

Shelby dunks her tortilla chip in the mashed avocado. "He was tipsy. And, to be fair, I only knew it based on circumstantial evidence."

I stir the ice in my drink and raise my eyebrows. "Circumstantial, meaning?"

"Meaning the circumstances are that it's a bar and it's Wyatt."

"Very nice, Shel."

She rolls her eyes but looks contrite. "I know. No benefit of the doubt given. Not that he didn't ask for it."

I laugh softly, picturing Wyatt Hayden. "He went for the friend card?"

Shelby nods. "Oh yeah." She clears her throat and adopts a deep tone of voice. "How long have we been friends? Seventh grade?" Her lower lip juts out in an attempt to imitate Wyatt's perpetual pout.

I compliment her on her accuracy. "You look just like him."

Shelby executes a small bow. "I took him in. He was carrying on about how he needed to get where he was going, and—"

"Where was he headed?" As soon as I ask the question, I wish I could take it back. It's the look on Shelby's face, the pity.

"He wouldn't tell me where he was going."

I nod once and look away. I could make a pretty safe bet about Wyatt's destination when he left the Chute last night.

And even if I can't see it, I hear it in her response. "Forget him, Jo. He has more problems than a pregnant nun."

Despite the uneasy feeling building in my stomach, I laugh. "Don't worry, Shelby. My feelings for Wyatt Hayden are long gone."

Shelby nods approvingly, even though it's obvious she doesn't believe me. "Right. And you have Jared now. Mr. Steady Eddy."

"Correct." Jared is Wyatt's polar opposite. An anti-Wyatt.

"I mean," Shelby continues, draining her tea. "Jared's probably more of an adult than me, and that's saying a lot. I bet he contributes to a 401(k) and does yard work on the weekends."

I can't speak for the financial part of what she said, but the weekend landscaping is spot on. Jared is a good guy. He opens doors, pays for dates, compliments me. The whole nine yards.

"Jared is a good person," I say, nodding as I picture his classic haircut and *aw shucks* grin. "I'm lucky to have him."

"Yes, you are," she replies firmly. Shelby would probably support me dating a rum-running pirate if it stopped me from pining over that arrogant, elusive, sexy as sin cowboy. "I wish you looked a little happier when you think of him."

I shake my head. "It's not that. Travis's guidance counselor called me at work today. I'm still upset about that."

Shelby makes a face and tips her head, listening to the whole story. "What are you going to do, Jo?" she asks when I finish. She knows how badly I want to get Travis back up here to Sierra Grande.

"I don't know. I'm not in a position to argue with my

mom about where Travis should live. She'd never move back here, not now with *Henri*"—I say his name in a hideous French accent—"keeping her there. And she'd never send him to live with me. My schedule is all over the place, and he needs stability." I stab at a cube of ice with my straw. "One day, I'm going to open that camp I've been talking about."

Shelby smiles out of one side of her mouth. "And until then?"

"I'm saving all my pennies." Opening up a camp for troubled youth has been my dream for the past few years, right after the first time Travis got in trouble. The first thing I need is land, which is in short supply around here. The second thing I need is money, which is also in short supply.

"This topic is depressing." I slide out of the booth. "I'm going to use the ladies' room."

"One day," Shelby calls out. I wave my hand above my head as I walk away. *One day* sounds a lot like *never*.

I'm standing at the sink washing my hands when she walks in, heels snapping against the floor. Jericho Barnett. Her phone pressed to her ear, she leans closer to the mirror above the second sink and fixes lipstick I'm positive isn't in need of fixing.

"I can't believe it either," she says. She sounds so pleased with herself, but I think she might live in a constant state of feeling happy about the various things she accomplishes in a day. "The Circle B is a prestigious listing, and they chose me out of all those other realtors." She frowns at whatever has been said by the other person on the phone. "I know it's for a reduced price, but I'm looking at it as a résumé builder."

I tap on her arm. She turns, looking at me like she had no idea I was in here when she walked in. She knows me from The Orchard. Her favorite wine is a red blend, and the cooks call her Jeri-No because she modifies the shit out of every food order she places.

"I have to go," she says into her phone, then ends the call and looks at me. "Hi, Jo."

"Hi, Jericho. Did I overhear you saying the Circle B is on the market?"

"Not yet. Not officially, I mean. I'm going to list it tomorrow. The sellers chose me an hour ago." The same slow, luxurious look of content slides over her face. Maybe she was facing a lot of competition to be the listing agent, and can't control how pleased she is to have won.

"Congratulations," I say. It's obvious this is what she wants to hear. "So," I start before she can say anything. I take a deep breath. This is it. My chance. It's now or never. I don't know what I'm doing, but since when has that ever stopped me? I'm an expert at learning on my feet. "I want it."

Jericho blinks. Squints. "I'm sorry, I don't think I heard you correctly."

"You did."

She stares at me. "You want to buy the Circle B?"

"Yes."

Her hair swishes around her face as she shakes her head, confused. "What for? You're not a rancher. It's a *ranch*."

"A wilderness therapy camp. For troubled youth."

Jericho laughs. I think I'd prefer real laughter to this disbelieving cackle coming from between those overly made-up lips. She sees my straight face and stops laughing. "You're serious?"

I nod.

She crosses her arms and leans a hip against the bathroom counter. "I already have people calling me about the property. It's hot, and it's not even live yet. Do you know what that means?"

I didn't graduate from business school, but I know it means there's competition. Demand. And demand drives up price. I think of Travis, and square my shoulders. "I want it."

Jericho makes a face. "I'll add your name to the list."

The bathroom door opens. Shelby walks in, gaze darting between me and Jericho. "You've been gone for a while. I wanted to make sure you weren't sick."

Jericho walks to the door, and Shelby steps aside. "She's not sick," Jericho tells Shelby. "Just crazy."

Shelby makes a face, and Jericho looks at me. "I'll be in touch, Jo."

Jericho leaves, and Shelby stares after her. "What was that about?"

I wash my hands again, because I need something to do with them. They shake with nerves as I run them under the water. "I either did something really great, or incredibly stupid."

3

JO

I hear her before I see her. It's those sky-high heels she wears, slapping the floor like quarters hitting tile.

Dakota, the owner of The Orchard, nods slightly and looks over my shoulder, watching Jericho approach. I turn around, ready to welcome her into the restaurant, but she tosses her expensive handbag onto the bar and looks me square in the eye.

"Josephine Daniella Shelton, I cannot believe I'm telling you this, but you got the ranch."

The air in my lungs disappears. Dakota grabs my hand, squeezing it. All I can see is her wide smile and Jericho's stoic face. A million thoughts race through my head at once, but none of them stay long enough to form anything coherent.

I gather enough air to murmur, "The ranch?"

"The ranch, Jo. Do you remember it? Abandoned, out of order—"

Dakota shuts her up with a stare. "I believe your listing called it 'a charming property waiting for a special touch'."

Jericho stares back. "Realtors' creativity."

Dakota makes an irritated sound and looks back at me. "They accepted your offer, Jo. I told them what you were planning to do with the place, and apparently they have a thing for do-gooders. This is huge." Her strawberry blonde hair tickles my shoulders as she hugs me.

"Yeah," I say slowly when she lets me go, still processing what this all means. I thought my offer had a greater chance of being laughed at than accepted. Jericho had made certain to inform me of who I was up against. Big name ranchers, commercial developers, even a home developer. Why did they choose little old me, with the shallow pockets?

"Congratulations." Jericho takes her purse off the bar top and threads her arm through the straps. "I'd thought I'd seen it all, and then this. Getting a ranch for pennies on the dollar." Her ponytail moves with her headshake. "It's a steal. You're practically a thief."

It's not the first time I've heard this passive-aggressive comment from her, and I know it's in reference to a lower commission thanks to a lower sale price. I want to remind her that you shouldn't bother crying over what was never yours. A lesson I learned the hard way, courtesy of a certain Hayden brother.

Dakota glances at her watch. "It's too bad you can't stay for lunch, Jericho. If only it were eleven and we were open."

"If only," Jericho replies, offering a fake smile. "Jo, the title company will be in touch to schedule the signing."

She waves and walks out, leaving us with her perfume.

"She's a piece of work," Dakota says. She grabs a bottle of wine and uncorks it.

"What are you doing?"

She pours two half glasses and hands me one. "Congratulations, Jo. You once told me you dreamed of opening a place for troubled youth, and here you are, making it happen."

Our glasses make a tinkling sound, and Dakota squeezes my shoulder.

"I really have wanted this for so long." Ever since the first time Travis got in trouble, when I saw signs of the anger and emptiness brewing inside him. His behavior changed. The lens through which he looked at the world was fractured. And now... Can I really do it? Put together a ranch that can help not only my brother, but other kids too? Would my mom be willing to send him to a ranch, a real place where he could live and enjoy himself? It wouldn't be my couch in my living room, but a real home. How much could she argue with that?

For the first time, it seems possible. The pieces are falling into place, fitting together like a choreographed kick line.

I might actually be able to pull this off.

"Jo?"

Shelby's calling my name from the living room. I'm in the bathroom, swiping mascara with an unpracticed hand. A dinner to celebrate me signing all the paperwork earlier today deserves a little makeup.

"What?" I yell back.

"Your phone is ringing. Should I answer?"

I open my mouth to respond but stop when I hear

Shelby say *hello*. I finish my second eye while I listen to her muffled voice, followed by footfalls. Shelby walks with purpose, so I never have to wonder where she is in our shared home.

She steps into my bathroom, shoulders shaking excitedly. "It's Alison Stein," she mouths, pointing at my held-out phone.

"The reporter?" I mouth back.

She nods, shoving the phone at me.

"Hello," I say, taking it from her and bringing it to my ear. "Josephine?"

"This is she," I answer, making a silly face at Shelby. I feel uncharacteristically giddy. "You can call me Jo."

"Great, Jo. This is Alison Stein, I write for the Sierra Grande Gazette. I heard you bought the Circle B and have some big plans for it. Would you be interested in letting me interview you? As news goes in our small town, this is pretty big."

"It is?"

She laughs. "Yes. A ranch with a history like the Circle B is deserted and remains empty for fifteen years except for high school keggers and a movie filmed there recently, and then it's suddenly purchased by one of our own residents. Sounds big to me."

I'm confused. What history is she talking about? I've lived here for a long time and I know nothing about the Circle B's history. The way she said it, it gives the impression that whatever happened before is sordid.

In an effort not to come off as clueless as I so clearly am, I return her gentle laugh. "What can I say, I have big dreams."

"Is right now an okay time to ask a few questions?"

I glance at Shelby. She gives me a thumbs up and goes back to whatever she was doing.

"Sure," I answer, putting the phone on speaker and leaning it up against the bathroom mirror. I finish my makeup and hair while explaining to Alison why I bought the ranch.

"This is all preliminary, because as you know I just bought the ranch. Ultimately, I plan to turn the Circle B into a therapeutic ranch that serves troubled youth."

"That's very altruistic of you. Is there a personal connection?"

I see Travis's face in my mind, and say, "No. I happen to think a lot of the world's problems could be solved by investing in our youth." Not a lie, just skirting the truth a little. "Ranching is a beloved part of the Sierra Grande community, and we all know nature is incredibly healing. There are young people out there looking for their place in life, struggling, and vitamin nature might be a large part of what they need. I plan to use outdoor and ranch activities, coupled with equine therapy and perhaps some still unknown to me concepts to facilitate a more casual approach to therapy." I'm making this up on the fly, but it's true. Maybe some troubled youth need serious therapy and strictly regimented schedules, but I happen to believe a lot of wayward kids just need space and something to be responsible for, work they can take pride in. And an adult who shows them kindness and respect.

Alison goes on to ask me questions about forthcoming job openings and the construction. I make all that up on the fly too. I've had ideas and rough sketches for two years, ever since I had the idea for a place like this, but now that it's actually happening, it all feels bigger than what I've been imagining. I'm going to need help. A whole lot of help. And to be perfectly honest, I don't know exactly what I'm in for, so I'm not yet sure what kind of help to ask for.

We finish up the interview, and Alison tells me it will probably be in the paper in two days, that tomorrow's paper has already gone to print.

I find Shelby parked on the couch, watching TV. She presses the pause button when she sees me, gazing at me expectantly. "How did the interview go?"

"Good." I pinch my bottom lip with two fingers. "I was feeling glowy and hazy, like I was walking through a gold-tinted cloud or something, but now..." I shrug. "Alison's questions made me realize how out of my depth I am. I can have all the good intentions in the world, but"—my shoulders lift and drop—"they won't do me any good if I don't know what the hell I'm doing."

Shelby gathers the blanket around her midsection. "Nobody knows what they're doing. Do you remember when I bought this place?" She gestures around at the house. "I wasn't even through the academy. I had no idea if I'd be able to afford it. But we needed a place to live, and you needed cheap rent." She smiles at me, and it prompts me to return one in kind. "Sometimes you have to close your eyes, and leap."

I keep thinking about Shelby's words while I finish getting ready. Jared shows up on time, of course. He opens the passenger door of his silver sedan, closing it behind me when I'm safely tucked inside. We chat on the drive, him telling me about his day, and me telling him about the day shift at The Orchard following my signing at the title agency. I don't know when my last day at work will be, but it will have to happen eventually. Dakota knew when she hired me that I wasn't going to stay for long. In fact, that was how we bonded almost two years ago. Me telling her about my big dream of running a ranch for troubled youth, and her opening up about her relationship with Wes. At the time I'd just returned home from that weekend in Phoenix, the one where Wyatt and I shared a night only one of us remembers, and I told Dakota what had happened. Sort of. I edited the part about who it was I slept with.

And then—

Oh my God, there he is. As if thinking about him has made him appear out of thin air, Wyatt Hayden is walking along High Street. Not walking. Striding, in that overconfident Hayden way. They all do it, but Wyatt has something extra. Swagger.

I've learned my lesson. I stay the hell away from Wyatt, because I know what's good for me. And that would be Jared. My hand slips over the center console, resting on his thigh. I meet his eyes, match his smile, and internally double down on what he's offering.

Reliable, secure, a safe bet.

I don't look back at Wyatt, and soon he's nothing but a speck in the rearview mirror. Literally and figuratively.

Jared and I go to dinner, a fancier place in the next town over. We eat decadent French food I can't pronounce, drink champagne, and later, when Jared's inside me, I close my eyes and remind myself that this is where I'm supposed to be.

4

WYATT

Finally, fifteen fucking seconds of peace. I glance back through the large front window into the homestead, where the rest of my family chatters like they haven't seen each other in months. It's been three days, for the record.

Tenley and Dakota can carry on a stream of never-ending conversation, and this morning is no exception. They gesture, their hands flying in the air, as one of them tells a story and the other interrupts to add to it along the way. Of course my brothers would end up with wives who become best friends.

"You come to me when you need a break from them, okay?" I whisper to my six-month-old nephew, Colt. His little body is heavy against my chest, sleep turning him into a lump of soft warmth. Dakota handed him off to me when she finished feeding him, claiming my talent for taming horses extends to human babies. She's not wrong.

Through the front window, I watch my family, everyone in the middle of conversation, their stomachs full of my mom's famous quiche. Wes and Warner shoot the shit, probably talking about the ranch. Wes is without a second-in-command right now, an absence created by Warner's career change that surprised everybody but me. Apparently nobody else noticed his lack of enthusiasm for the day-to-day running of the ranch, or the amount of time the guy spent holed up in his office. In all fairness, I'm probably the only person with a view of his office. I live the closest to him, and my bedroom window faces his office window, and I can't count the number of times I saw him at his desk, working. Come to find out, he was earning a master's degree. Now he's doing what he really loves, teaching at the local college. I think his ultimate goal is to teach at a university, but that's just speculation. Once again, this is knowledge I've gleaned by watching and listening to what's left unsaid.

Jessie, my younger sister, has joined Tenley and Dakota. Jessie is a spitfire, as my grandpa likes to refer to her. Looking out for her has been my job, because Wes was gone in the military for twelve years. After that he was here but still absent, an ill-tempered shell of his former self. We all have Dakota to thank for whipping his ass into shape.

As for Warner, well... he was present physically, but he had his own shit going on. A seemingly perfect marriage to his high school sweetheart that imploded. Two kids caught in the crosshairs. He was pulling dual-parent duty by himself for a while, but things have evened out for him. He's remarried, to an unofficially retired movie star, of all people, and happier than I can ever remember him being.

Looking at my big brothers' track records, you'd think I'd be next in line for my own happily ever after. I don't see that happening. I think I'll end up being the fun uncle, the one the kids all come to when they have questions they're too embarrassed to ask their parents. I'll teach them how to throw a mean right hook, and the wisdom to know when to use it.

I cradle Colt in my arms and watch through the large front window as my dad walks into the living room. He steps up beside my mom, and they look at each other with unfettered pride, silently saying *look what we created*.

The picture is ideal for them, because I'm not in there to ruin it.

Turning away from the scene, I focus on the stable in the distance. The round pen behind it. Cowboy House, where all the cowboys live, including Denny and Ham. Maybe I'll hand off Colt to Dakota, and go over there. Sometimes I feel closer to the cowboys than I do my own brothers.

"Wyatt?" My dad steps from the homestead. The look of pride on his face when he gazed upon his family is gone now.

I bring a finger to my lips, signaling to be quiet, and turn so my dad can see Colt's sleeping face.

Everything about the hardened Beau Hayden softens, like ice cream in the sun. You'd have to see it to believe it, but the guy is a puddle when it comes to his grandkids. And to his daughter. Jessie's the miracle my mom and dad gave up on when they cast their eyes on me and saw I was a boy. Who knew a newborn could disappoint an adult? Three more attempts after me, all ending in miscarriage. They thought they would never get their daughter, and then *surprise!* For different reasons, I'll never forget the day she was born, but mostly because I watched my dad kiss my mom's forehead and heard him whisper, "We finally got our girl." My first heartbreak came not from a woman, but courtesy of my dad. I know now how many different ways a heart can break.

In a low voice, my dad says, "Sheriff Monroe called. He wants to see you at the station."

I sigh, turning my head so the stream of air flowing from my nose doesn't touch Colt. "Alright. I'll come inside in a second."

Dad looks at me like he wants to say something, then changes his mind and goes inside.

I look down at the sleeping baby, brushing my lips across the top of his head. Who knew I could love a kid so much, and he's not even mine?

I hand off Colt to Wes, say goodbye to my family, and try not to laugh at my ancient grandfather, snoring loudly from his seat by the fireplace. I swear the guy takes more naps than Colt.

Dad meets my eyes on the way out of the house. Judging by the fact that nobody has mentioned my police station debacle, I'm guessing my dad didn't mention it to the rest of the family. Surely this has more to do with his embarrassment of me than his respect for my privacy.

I hop in my truck, make a quick stop at my cabin just a mile away on the HCC property, and grab my wallet. Wouldn't want to be caught driving without a license.

I PULL INTO AN OPEN SPOT IN FRONT OF THE STATION AND park. No doubt there will be talk about why a Hayden Cattle Company truck was parked at the police station. Lucky for me, my recent presence here wasn't marked by my truck out front. It was safely parked at the Chute, while Shelby gave me a ride. In her cop car. In the back seat.

I walk in, letting the admin know that my presence has been requested by the sheriff. He picks up the phone, has a brief conversation, then hangs up and tells me to sit, the sheriff will be with me shortly.

Behind him, I see the rest of the station. Shelby ducks behind the computer at her desk, probably because she doesn't want to meet my gaze. I smirk and look away. The next person to meet my eyes is Dan Howard. He's the last person I'd have chosen to be a police officer. The guy can't tell his ass from a hole in the ground, so how the hell does he plan to uphold his promise to serve and protect?

He stares me down, only because his blue uniform gives him a false sense of courage. He likes me about as much as I care for him, and that's exactly how I prefer it. He's the first to break our stare.

After a few minutes, the sheriff emerges from his office and motions for me to come back. I make sure to pass Shelby's desk, and offer an overly friendly hello. She narrows her eyes at me.

"Wyatt," the sheriff greets me, leading me into his office. "Sit down. I'm waiting for one more person."

I don't sit. One more person? "Who?"

The sheriff ignores my question, keeping his eyes trained on the front door. "There she is now."

I turn to look. *Jo Shelton?*

Jo and I used to be friends, at least in the general sense. I've known her forever, we've been running in the same social circle since she moved here and showed up as the new student when she was sixteen and I was seventeen. And then, sometime in the last year or so, she froze over, at least where I'm concerned. She doesn't speak to me, meet my eyes, *nothing*. I am officially persona non grata when it comes to her.

Like he did me, the sheriff waves Jo back. I'm watching her approach, her blonde, light pink tipped hair brushing her collarbone, so I see it the moment she spots me. Her shoulders stiffen, her eyes turn to steel. I don't know what I did, but Jo hates me. She glances down at Shelby as she passes. Shelby shrugs quickly, shaking her head back and forth as if to say she doesn't know why Jo's been called in.

"Come on in, Jo," the sheriff directs. He motions for her to sit at the chair in front of his desk. "You too, Wyatt."

We both take a seat, and we both do it reluctantly. It's the closest we've been to each other since that weekend a big group of us went down to the valley for a couple days away. I sat next to her at dinner one night, and I remember liking the way she smelled. Like citrus and flowers. Kind of how she smells right now.

I spare her a quick glance. Her entire body is rigid, her back perfectly in line with her seat. She's beautiful, no man would disagree. My eyes linger for one extra second, roving over her defined cheekbones. I'm hit with a feeling that doesn't make sense… her skin under my touch, my fingertips trailing over her cheek.

I'm thrust from this moment, from this office, and into a place I don't comprehend. What I just felt was my imagination, I know it. So why is it that it feels more like a memory?

"Wyatt, are you with us?" Sheriff's irritation slams into my consternation, breaking apart my thoughts and delivering me back to the present.

"Here," I answer, tearing my eyes from Jo's profile. She still has not spared me a single glance.

"This"—the sheriff picks up today's paper—"was interesting today." He opens it and looks at me over the top. "Did you know that Jo here has purchased the Circle B?"

I shake my head. "I did not know that." Why would anybody want that place?

Sheriff Monroe smirks. "Did you know she's hiring?"

Jo frowns. "I'm not hiring yet. I'm not doing *anything* yet. It's only been final for two days and I'm figuring out the next steps."

Sheriff turns his attention to her. "What would you say is your first next step?"

"Clean up. Demo. Figuring out what's salvageable."

Sheriff nods. "And do you have people to help you with that?"

Jo looks like she's about as tired of this conversation already as I am. "Not at the moment."

"I have your first helper. Unpaid, of course." His gaze flickers over to me.

Wherever the sheriff is mentally, I haven't yet joined him. He may as well be talking in riddles. Apparently Jo isn't quite there either, because she says, "What are you getting at?"

Sheriff Monroe doesn't even try to hide his shit-eating grin. "It just so happens Wyatt here is in need of some community service."

"I am?" I was really hoping my last name worked in my favor and the whole situation had been dropped.

He nods. "You are." His words are followed by a look that tells me in no uncertain terms am I to even think about challenging him. I get the message. I have the feeling he wouldn't hesitate to lay my shit bare right here in front of Jo, and I don't particularly want that occurring.

"Crook," I say under my breath.

He chortles. "Takes one to know one."

He has me there.

"Excuse me," Jo cuts in, her voice tight and her volume higher than it was before. "Do I get a say in this?"

"Sure," the sheriff answers.

"Good. Because I don't want Wyatt serving his community service at my ranch."

I glare at her profile. "What's your problem with me?"

Finally, for the first time since we both arrived in this office, she turns her gaze on me. And I'm hit again, another figment of my imagination masquerading as a memory. *She is small underneath me, allowing me to push her back against the wall, running my hands through her hair.*

What the actual fuck is wrong with me?

Jo's in the middle of a sentence. "...and you're unreliable. And you're not even listening to me now!"

"I'm hearing you," I tell her. Turning back to the sheriff, I ask if there are any other community service opportunities available. He folds his arms across his stomach and shakes his head back and forth slowly. "This is it for you, my friend."

I turn back to Jo. "Please, Jo?" Her eyes widen when I say her name, and not in a good way. She looks ready to rip my head off. "I promise you won't even know I'm there."

Jo unclenches her jaw. "Fine," she nearly spits the word.

Sheriff loudly claps his hands once, and both of us jump. "Good, good. Glad that worked out." He's obnoxiously proud of himself. "If you two don't mind, I have other problems that need solving, and I can only hope they go half as well as yours."

Jo stalks out of the office, and I follow, glancing at Shelby as I go. She already has her phone in her hand, no doubt texting Jo about everything she overheard.

We get out front, the warm Arizona sunshine spilling over us, and Jo turns on me. "Just to clarify, I wasn't the one with the problem. In fact, all Sheriff Monroe did was *create* a problem for me." The air around her buzzes with her intensity.

I point back at myself. "I'm a problem?"

She says nothing, but her expression doesn't waver. "Be on time. Be sober. Be ready to work. Think you can handle all that?"

"What was that last one?" I mean it as a joke, something to lighten the mood between us because I'm uncomfortable with how much she hates me when I don't even know why, but her response tells me how unappreciated my attempt is.

"Don't fuck with me, Wyatt Hayden, or I will kick you off my ranch and you can have whatever alternative punishment you are surely deserving of."

Jo turns around, gets in her car, and drives off.

I stand there, stunned. I have somewhere to be, and still, it takes me nearly a full minute to be able to climb into my truck and drive.

I've never been told off like that by a woman. And, if I really think hard about it, I've never seen Jo exhibit that much emotion before.

5

JO

18 MONTHS AGO

Now I understand it firsthand.

Coyote ugly.

Except Wyatt's about as far from ugly as it's possible to be. He's lying beside me in the hotel bed, that dark hair of his messy and sexy, one section dipping down over his forehead. The fancy, down-filled duvet comes up to the middle of his torso. He is hard muscle, rippled abs, generous and well-defined shoulders. His nose has a slight bump in the center, like it's been broken. Day-old scruff darkens his face.

My skin prickles at the thought of that scruff scraping along my body last night.

Which is why this is a coyote ugly situation. It won't be Wyatt's looks that'll make me gnaw off my own arm to slip out of his room undetected.

I'm afraid of what I'll see in his eyes when he wakes up and remembers what happened between us last night.

If I can get out of his hotel room without waking him, I won't be here for his initial response. I can remain blissfully unaware of whether he thinks it was a happy accident that we ended up in bed together, or a colossal regret.

I've liked Wyatt Hayden for so long, I can't bear to watch.

Inch by brutal inch, I lift one section of my body off the bed. I'm sore from last night's sexual antics, so holding my various body parts aloft while I attempt this silent rising from the bed is painful. On tiptoe I gather my clothes, search for my bra and finally locate it on the lampshade of all places, and pull everything on, waiting to zip my jeans until I step into the hall.

I suck in a huge breath and sag against the wall. I made it.

I send a thank you to the man upstairs when I don't run into any of my friends in the halls, and slip into my own room as quietly as I left Wyatt's. I could use a few more hours of sleep, especially considering the two-hour drive we have back home to Sierra Grande, but I'm due down at breakfast in forty-five minutes. Last night, before all the cocktails took root in our bloodstream, we made reservations for the hotel's Sunday brunch. If it weren't fancy, and I hadn't put down a deposit to reserve a table for a group as large as ours, I'd cancel. In total there are eleven of us. A few couples, the rest of us singles, and all of us have known each other since high school.

After a long hot shower, I dress and towel dry my hair, pausing to study myself in the full-length mirror in the bathroom. I don't look any different after last night, but everything inside me feels tilted. The world I knew yesterday is not the world I know today. I've waited years for Wyatt to notice me, no exaggeration.

Mercifully I didn't have to sit around watching him notice other women. As far as I can tell Wyatt doesn't date. At least not seriously. Maybe after last night that will change.

I'm the first to breakfast. Everyone trickles in, grimacing and making jokes about needing a little hair of the dog. I feel like shit too, but I'm holding on to a secret so delicious it overrides my hangover.

Wyatt is the last to join. His eyes are bloodshot, he's yawning, and wearing last night's shirt. He takes the only available seat, about four down on my right.

I'm willing him to look at me, meet my eyes, share a furtive glance, *anything* to silently acknowledge what went on between us.

He doesn't look up from his menu. And when he does, it's only to order from the server. She bends over like she's trying to hear him better, giving him an opportunity to look at her ample cleavage. To his credit, he doesn't take the bait.

Nor does he take any of *my* bait. Not that I'm any good at setting it. I can't flirt, or manufacture opportunities, to save my life. Which is what makes last night's encounter a miracle.

Kyle leans back in his seat and wraps an arm around Corrine's shoulders. Gaze directed across the table at Wyatt, he asks, "What did you get up to last night? You left the pool and that was the last we saw of you."

He went to the little sundry store that was two minutes from closing for the night. Bought a bottle of Gatorade. Ran into me. Pulled me behind an ivy-covered wall and kissed me senseless. Told me he could already tell I was going to be the best thing he ever tasted, and I melted like the ice in my tea on an August afternoon.

Wyatt shrugs. His full bottom lip juts out slightly, the tiny line that runs down its center becoming more pronounced. "Not much. Went to my room. Passed out."

Kyle shakes his head. "You were hitting the liquor pretty hard last night."

Wyatt grimaces. "Little too hard. I'm lucky I made it to the right room. I don't remember much past leaving the pool."

Conversation moves on around the table. Laughter, discussing the funny things that must've happened after Wyatt and I left. Nobody seems to piece together that Wyatt and I were missing at the same time. Not that anybody would find it suspicious. I'm known to be the first of us to leave, and Wyatt is known to do whatever suits him at any given moment. He is an enigma, as equally perplexing as he is interesting. I've spent years in Wyatt's orbit, but never really crossing. Until last night, when we finally collided.

Breakfast continues, and Wyatt looks my way only once. He does what he always does when he sees me. A lift of his chin, eyebrows raised. Fleeting recognition of my presence. No warmth in his eyes, no barely perceptible smirk, literally nothing that implies he knows what I look like without clothes on.

He doesn't remember last night.

My heart sinks. Anger bursts into my chest, coming from some combustible part of me. I'm mad at him, and I'm even more upset with myself. I knew he was hammered. I didn't sugarcoat the situation, thinking our hookup would instantly make him fall in love with me. I knew there was a high probability this wouldn't be all roses. But when you love chocolate cake, and someone serves you the most decadent, moist slice you've ever seen, how do you pass that up?

You don't.

Good thing learning my lesson the first time is my specialty. Wyatt will never get under my skin again.

My longtime infatuation with the annoyingly handsome, infuriatingly mysterious, emotionally unavailable cowboy is officially over.

6

WYATT

In a little old house, almost at the edge of town, lives a little old woman I've come to love.

Carol Calhoun.

She's funny. Feisty. Sweet as pie, and she doesn't take shit from anybody. Telemarketers beware, because Carol Calhoun won't be fooled by anyone.

Or so she says. Mrs. Calhoun's health has diminished rapidly. The time she used to spend in her front yard gardening is now spent sitting in her front porch chair. Words that came easily sometimes struggle to find their way into a cohesive thought.

I've been trying to figure out a way to get her the help she needs, but all I can think to do is hire a nurse. I can't put her in a home, where her needs can be met twenty-four hours a day, because I'm not family.

As far as I know, Mrs. Calhoun doesn't have much in the way of family. Her son isn't alive anymore. Neither is her grandson.

Thanks to the Hayden family.

That's not to say either one of the Calhoun men were innocent. Especially her grandson. Mrs. Calhoun being left without family was collateral damage. Doesn't make it okay, though. And that's why I'm here, and why I've been coming around for a while. Reparation.

Mrs. Calhoun's in her tan wicker chair, like always. Her white hair is combed, her clothes are clean and ironed. If I walk into her house, it will be immaculate. Completely out of date, but cleaner than any room at the homestead has ever been.

I pull up and get out, walking to her. She smiles when she sees me. I've seen pictures of her from back in the day. She was beautiful. She is now, too, but in an entirely different way.

"Hi, Mrs. Calhoun."

She nods at me. "Hello, young man."

There hasn't been a day since I started visiting her a couple years ago that she didn't greet me with those words.

I stop a few feet from her. "Do you have a list for me? I have those plants you asked for in the back of my truck."

"Oh yes, yes. On the kitchen table." She gets up slowly, and I lean forward, ready to help her if she needs it. I learned not to verbally offer her assistance, so instead I act like I'm not even thinking about it when really I'm paying close attention.

I walk in front of her and open the door. She may not like help, but she appreciates gentlemanly behavior.

Like she said, the note is on the kitchen table. She makes herself a cup of tea while I read her scrawling cursive.

"Shorter than a couple weeks ago," I comment, holding the slip of paper in the air.

She places a tea bag in the steaming water and smirks. "I'll make sure to think of more stuff for next time."

I laugh and get to work. Most of the work is minor, maintenance type things. A couple of trees are overgrown and need to be trimmed. Two of her wooden fence posts are broken and need to be replaced. I clean a few windows I know she cannot reach. When I see her bending down to weed her herb garden, I make a mental note to build her a planter box that is hip height, so she no longer has to bend over. I'll tell her I found it in a pile meant for bulk trash, otherwise she won't accept it, and I won't say a damn word about how she shouldn't be bending over like that anymore.

She's back in her chair on her front porch when I'm done. Like always, there is a crisp twenty-dollar bill on the table beside her. She picks it up and hands it to me.

"Thank you for helping me, young man."

"You're welcome."

"I'll be getting some company in a few days. Two of my grandsons are coming to visit."

Grandsons? I thought she only had one.

"That's nice, Mrs. Calhoun. What are their names?"

"Ricky and Chris Marks. Brothers."

"Good." I smile at her. "I'm sure it will be nice to see them. If you don't mind, I'm going to grab a drink of water and I'll get out of your hair."

I walk into the house, get a drink, and slip the twenty back into her wallet where it came from. Like always.

Later that night, when I'm by myself in my house, I search the internet for Ricky and Chris Marks. I don't like what I find.

The brothers, twenty-two and twenty-four, were found in possession of meth and sentenced to three years in prison.

Everybody makes mistakes, I know that more than anybody, but something about the photo that accompanies the story rubs me the wrong way.

Maybe it's that they look so much like Dixon, if not by physical characteristics than by facial expression.

Arrogant. Entitled. Like the world stole something from them, and they're planning to get it back.

The date on the article is from just over three years ago.

I could give them the benefit of the doubt. Maybe prison changed them. Maybe they got degrees while they were in, or found Jesus.

Either way, I'll make sure I pay close attention when they get to town.

7

JO

I have a teensy bit of a headache. After meeting with the sheriff yesterday, I stewed for the remainder of the day. And, as soon as it was reasonably acceptable, I opened a bottle of wine.

A few years ago, the idea of forced proximity with Wyatt Hayden would have sent me into a tailspin of hearts and flowers. Now it drives me to drink.

I could've said no to him helping on the ranch, as Shelby pointed out last night. And I wanted to, I really did. But even as much as I'd like to make him squirm, I couldn't say no. I don't know what was awaiting him if not for community service, but I didn't want to deliver him straight to it.

Dakota's on her way to meet me here at the Circle B. I'm standing outside my car, looking around.

I knew what I was getting into before I signed the papers. The ranch has been empty for almost two decades, and I've seen it enough over that time period that I thought I knew what to expect. When I'd mentioned an inspection to Jericho during the purchasing process, she laughed and told me all the other prospects wanted this property so much they'd offered to waive the inspection. What she was really saying was *don't fuck this up by asking for more than the others*. Message received.

I haven't been by the Circle B in a while, not since before Tenley Roberts showed up in Sierra Grande to film her movie and they used the ranch for some of the scenes. Tenley Hayden, I guess, but professionally she kept her maiden name.

A long line of Bald Cypress trees runs parallel to the far side of the backyard. The house is a sprawling one-story, with a river rock façade. The siding used to be red, but now it's faded and dull, peeling from all sides like tendrils of baby hair. The stairs leading up to the front porch don't look like something to be trusted, and the porch flooring sags in the center.

Jericho had said the family who deserted this place hired a person to take care of property management, but from the looks of the outside I'd say they paid him for a whole lot of lip service.

Tenting a hand over my eyes, I turn and look out to the valley opposite the house. Gently sloping hills give way to flat land. None of it is green, and I'm not sure why. It doesn't rain much, but there should be a water table somewhere, providing water to the land. It's not a huge concern right now, because this won't be a working cattle ranch, but it's something that has to be dealt with eventually.

A few hundred yards from where I stand sits a large barn and stable. Thank heavens for small miracles. I don't have the money to build that.

The round pen looks salvageable. It's going to take me a while to get the right kind of horses, the kind that are dead broke and wouldn't bat at a fly. Off to the side is what looks to be a very new trailer, forgotten by whoever it is that's in charge of trailers on a movie set. I'll run it by Tenley, but hopefully she'll let me use it as a makeshift office until the main house is livable.

Dakota pulls up in a ranch truck and climbs out. She calls out a greeting, then opens the back door and reaches in, coming away with Colt. She straps him into a carrier she wears on her chest, and walks over.

"Hey there," she gives me a side hug.

We spend a few minutes chatting about the baby, but Dakota eagerly changes the subject back to the Circle B. "First off," she says, pointing at the sign, "what's the new name?"

"Add it to the list of things I need to do." I frown as I think of how long the list is, and its steady growth rate.

"I know it can seem overwhelming," she says, rubbing a hand on my shoulder. "I felt the same way when my dad put me in charge of building The Orchard." She looks at the main house. "And that didn't even include demo."

"Am I going to need to demo?"

"My guess is that you'll have a decent amount of work to do. You said someone has been looking after the place, right?"

"That's what Jericho told me. She said the house needed some TLC, but it wasn't in the state you'd think it'd be in after sitting empty for so long. Apparently they had a caretaker come once a month and check in. Make sure the pipes didn't burst and flood the place, that kind of thing." I bite my lip as I recall the name on the papers I signed. "It was odd, honestly. The seller wasn't a person, but a company."

"Ohh, sounds like you have a mystery to solve."

"No thanks. I don't plan on looking a gift horse in the mouth."

Dakota threads her hair through an elastic hair tie and asks, "You ready to figure out what you're in for?"

I grab a pad of paper from my purse and a pen. "Lead the way," I tell her.

We go all around the property, Dakota shielding Colt's tender skin from the sun. Dakota points out various things, some obvious (broken windows) and some I would've not thought of until the problem smacked me in the face (electrical work).

By the time we take a break, I have a list of repairs, demos, and the names of who to call that's longer than my arm. Dakota instructs me to open up her back seat, and I find a full lunch from The Orchard, including my favorite sandwich, a pesto, artichoke and Havarti grilled cheese that was her mother's recipe.

"There's an extra cookie for you, too." Dakota comes up behind me. She's nursing Colt as she walks, the house framing her as she approaches, and I'm hit with a sense of disbelief. I can't believe this is really happening. All of this seems so out of this world.

We settle on the bottom front step of the main house, on the section that isn't rotted.

Colt makes noises as he eats, gulping and swallowing audibly. Dakota peeks down at him. "He's a noisy eater."

"Doesn't bother me." I take a bite of my lunch. "Do you remember that first night you came to Sierra Grande?"

She laughs. "The restaurant at the hotel. Your hair almost skimmed your lower back." She reaches over, playing with my hair. "I like it this way too, though. You're a natural beauty."

A year ago I cut off seven inches, so that now it falls to the middle of my chest. I kept the pink tips, though. I'm a play by the rules kind of girl, but the color makes me feel a bit like a person who doesn't have to be so serious *all* the time.

"Thanks."

"Do you want to know what I remember more than those first few times we met at the hotel?"

I nod, sucking a drip of pesto off my thumb.

"Running into you at The Bakery. When we shared that wine I had in my purse and a lemon bar. I feel like that's when our friendship really started."

I remember it exactly. I was sitting at a little table, sketching ideas for the very place I'm sitting in right now. Dakota walked in and ordered dessert like a woman who needed a sugar spike, stat. "You looked so confused about Wes."

She bops my shoulder gently with her own. "You looked pretty confused yourself. Are you ever going to tell me who made you feel that way?"

I look out at the flat, brown fields in the distance. "It doesn't matter. It's long over."

Dakota switches subjects. "How's Jared?"

"Really good." I nod enthusiastically. "He's so nice."

Dakota's silence draws my attention. Her lips are pressed together.

"What?" I ask, picking up a fallen piece of artichoke and popping it in my mouth.

"Nothing."

"Just say it, otherwise I'm going to read your body language and what if I'm wrong?"

Dakota laughs. "You're good." She uses one finger to

push a wayward piece of lettuce back into her sandwich. "Every time I ask you about Jared, those are the two words you use to describe him."

I think back to our past conversations, but nothing sticks out. "Good and nice?"

She nods, chewing and brushing away crumbs that have fallen onto Colt's shoulder.

My eyebrows pinch together. "They're not inaccurate."

"Of course not."

"What aren't you saying?"

"I just wonder why you don't have other adjectives to describe him. People aren't 'good' and 'nice' all the time."

"He kind of is." It's true. I've never seen him raise his voice, or even grow frustrated.

Dakota smiles. "As long as you're happy, I'm happy for you."

We finish lunch and Dakota leaves. I review the list she helped me create, trying to prioritize the to-do's in the order they must be done, and then get started on the trailer. Dakota told me not to worry about asking Tenley about using it, that she wouldn't care. I start by opening up all the windows to release the stale air, then clean it top to bottom using the supplies I threw in my car before I left. My headache is long gone, but the pain in my ass, by the name of Wyatt Hayden, persists.

8

WYATT

"Wyatt, answer the door." Dakota's standing at my door, knocking for a second time. "I know you're in there."

"Actually, I'm right here."

Dakota jumps a mile, whipping around to face me with a hand on her chest. "You're such an ass."

"You're the one who was banging on my door."

"I was coming to tell you about the Circle B. Jo needs help."

"I'm aware."

She cocks her head to the side, her eyebrows pulling together. "How do you know that? I literally just came from there."

"A little bird told me." There's no way I'm telling her about the meeting with the sheriff yesterday morning, because that would only lead to more questions. My dad hasn't told anybody, aside from my mother, about my near arrest, or the consequences of it.

Dakota knows there's more to it, but she also knows she won't get anywhere with me if she keeps pushing. "So, I was thinking, you should help Jo get the project started. I didn't tell her because she seemed very overwhelmed, but she's probably bitten off a bit more than she knows how to chew."

"That's not how the saying goes."

"I'm aware, but think about the words. I mean it. She can't chew because she doesn't know how to chew what needs to be chewed."

I shake my head at her. "Let's not say 'chew' for a while."

Dakota laughs and comes down the two steps to where I'm standing. She playfully bats my arm. "Agreed. So will you help her?"

"Why me? You think I have nothing else better to do?"

"No. I think you're smart and strong and really good at helping people."

Her compliment makes me uncomfortable, and I'm not sure what to say next. I'm rescued from having to respond when Wes emerges from the trees that separate my cabin from the homestead, his eyes zeroing in on me and Dakota. "There you are. I've been calling you."

My eyebrows lift as I palm my chest. "Who, me?" Obviously I know he's talking to Dakota, but I can't pass up a chance to give my oldest brother a hard time.

Wes shoots me a derisive look and wraps his arms around his wife. Dakota smiles and tells him her phone is in the truck, along with Colt.

Wes panics. "Colt is in the truck?"

"The truck is on. The windows are halfway down. I am right here. The truck is ten feet away. Everything is fine."

I wonder how many times a day Dakota calms Wes down when it comes to their son. I've seen her do it plenty of times. Wes won't tell any of us, but something happened in Iraq, and I'd bet all the money in my bank account it has to do with a kid. I've never seen him act so hyper.

He allows himself to be calmed down, but he still breaks away to go put his own two eyes on Colt. "Hey Wes," I call after him. "Your wife thinks I'm smart and strong. Sorry about your luck, pal." The only way I know to accept a compliment is to joke about it.

Wes flips me off without looking my way.

"Are you going to help her?" Dakota asks when I turn my attention back to her.

I'll be there no matter what, because I'd like to avoid legal action, but I don't tell Dakota that. What I end up saying is a form of the truth. "I don't think Jo wants me there."

Dakota makes a face. "Why do you think that?"

Because she said it. Out loud, I tell her, "It's a vibe I've been getting from her for a while. We've always been friendly, but I think I did something to upset her. A bunch of us went to Phoenix about a year and a half ago, and she's been cold-shouldering me ever since."

Dakota squints, and she tents a hand over her eyes to shield them from the late afternoon sun. "Cold shoulder since a trip to Phoenix?"

I shrug. "It's the only thing I can think of."

Dakota nods slowly. "Right. I'd keep going with that. Maybe there's something more to it."

Her voice has a weird lilt, kind of like excitement she's trying to tamp down. I start to ask her, but she interrupts me.

"Oh, sorry, can't talk. Colt needs to eat."

I point at the truck, where Wes sits in the open back seat. "He's not even awake."

Dakota stares at me. "Would you like me to tell you how my body lets me know it's time for Colt to eat?"

I huff a laugh. "Not really."

Dakota goes back to her truck, turning once to remind me that the sooner I can start at the Circle B, the better.

"It needs a new name," I shout after her.

"She knows," Dakota shouts back.

I wave goodbye to my brother and his family and go inside to eat yet another dinner by myself.

I'M WORKING FROM A LIST DAKOTA TEXTED ME LAST NIGHT. And I'm still on the first task.

General cleanup.

It's hard to know what's salvageable on the Circle B because everything needs attention. Everywhere I look there's some form of debris. Fallen branches, pine straw, pine cones, trash from parties past, even shit I'm guessing was left by the movie people. Dakota told me someone came to check on the property every so often, and it looks to me they did a half-ass job.

I'm here and ready to work with a giant paper to-go cup of coffee from the diner, an even bigger bottle of water, and at this exact moment I'm pretty damn grateful I thought to grab my work gloves. At this point I have a decent pile going, trying to consolidate as much of the stuff I identify as trash. I'm sure Jo's opinion on what's trash isn't totally the same as mine, but she's not here to direct me, so I'm doing the best I can on my own. I stick my earbuds in and get to work.

It doesn't take long for the sun to burn off the cool midmorning air. Sweat streams down my back, and since nobody is out here except me and the two blue jays I spotted thirty minutes ago, I take off my shirt and tuck it into my back pocket.

The work is hard, honestly a little harder than I'm used to. On my family's ranch I stick to jobs that have to do with horses, and that doesn't include cleaning stalls. That chore goes to the lowest man on the roster, and in the summers we hire a high school kid looking to earn some money.

So this? This is hard work. All because I was going to help Sara and Mickey. In hindsight, I should've walked to their house. Or jogged, actually, to get there in time. I saw Sara in town yesterday after I left Mrs. Calhoun's. She was carrying groceries, bogged down by how many she was trying to carry at once. I pulled into an open spot and took a few bags off her hands, and her long sleeve rode up enough that I saw the new bruise on her wrist. My presence could've protected her, that's for damn sure.

I know something more needs to be done, I just don't know what. If I step aside, if I involve the police when I know Sara won't, that'll be it for Mickey. The state can press charges all on their own, they don't even need Sara to do it. If they see evidence of abuse, it's game over. I'd hate to see that happen, but I'm afraid that's the road they're headed down.

Surprisingly, this hard work is good for me. My muscles are screaming, but I like it. I break only to drink from my water. I finished the coffee an hour ago. As much as I'm actually enjoying the labor, I'll have to quit soon. I'm almost out of water.

I'm bending down, trying to pry two old boards apart,

when I hear it. A crash, a scream, coming from the trailer three hundred feet away. I run toward it, completely confused, not understanding how such a thing could even happen when I thought it was deserted out here. Jo comes tearing out from the trailer, hair whipping her face.

She runs straight for me, then realizes it's me and skids to a stop. "What are you doing here?" she demands.

"Working. What the fuck happened in there?" I look over her shoulder toward the trailer, but all appears to be in order. No chainsaw-wielding madman chasing after her.

She wipes a hand over her forehead, where tiny beads of sweat have accumulated in her hairline, and ignores my question. "You're working? I haven't even told you what to do."

Wow. Jo really thinks I'm an idiot. Looking around here and figuring out where to start isn't exactly rocket science. Plus, you know, I had a list. "I'm a self-starter."

Jo frowns. Not shocking, considering that seems to be all I make her do.

I drop the act. "Dakota gave me a small list. Asked me if I could help you."

Jo's frown deepens. "So now you're a Good Samaritan? You get to come out of this smelling like roses, acting like you're helping me out of the goodness of your heart, when you're actually avoiding a DUI?"

The muscles in my neck and upper back coil. "You know."

She sighs and stabs dead grass with the toe of her sandal. "Shelby is my roommate."

I scratch an itch on my chest, and it isn't until my fingers meet bare skin that I remember I'm shirtless. I stand up a little taller, knowing it makes my muscles swell. It's not that

I'm trying to impress Jo, but I'm not trying to *not* impress her either. "There's probably something she signed somewhere about not telling people certain aspects of her job."

Jo shrugs. I bet she wouldn't be so cavalier if it was her private business being shared. "It's a small town. Word will get around eventually. It always does, Wyatt."

A small shiver curls around my spine. "You said my name."

"So?"

"It's the first time you've said my name since the sheriff called us in."

"Do you have a point?"

"Maybe you like me after all."

Her chin lifts, eyes blazing. "Don't count on it."

I look back at the trailer. "How long have you been here?"

"A few hours. I've been listening to music and researching. You?"

"Same." I look around. "Where's your car?"

"My boyfriend dropped me off."

I don't like the way she says *boyfriend*. Like she's pointing it out, or rubbing it in. Like she wants to make sure I know.

It works. A hostile heat spreads through my chest. "Does your boyfriend have a name?"

"You wouldn't know him," she says, but what I really think she means is *you aren't the type of person he'd be friends with.*

I make a face. "Come off it, Jo. I know everyone."

She folds her arms. "I highly doubt that."

I fold my arms too, ready to retort, but I'm stopped by what Jo's doing. Correct me if I'm wrong, but I think Jo Shelton, good girl extraordinaire, just checked out my bare chest. And my arms.

I'd love to tease her for it, but I know how badly that will go, so I call upon every ounce of willpower and keep my words to myself. I allow myself a smirk though, and I make sure she sees it, because I can't let her get away with it completely. Pink blooms on her cheeks. *Good.*

She turns around, muttering.

"What was that?" I ask.

"Put a shirt on," she snaps, walking back to the trailer.

I laugh, then remember what started all this. "Why did you scream and run out?"

"Massive spider."

"Do you want me to come kill it?"

"I already did."

"Then why did you run out?"

Her cheeks pink even deeper. "It's what I do when I kill a big bug. It's my, uh..."

Never in my life have I seen Jo fumble for words. She's so confident, so careful, so...contained.

"Just say it," I coax.

"It's my battle cry."

I try not to laugh, but it can't be helped. "Battle cry?"

"It gives me the guts to kill it. Otherwise I can't do it."

"Battle cry..." I contemplate the idea.

"Don't tell anybody I told you that."

I nod. She goes back into the trailer. I resume what I was doing, working until I'm not just out of water, but also parched, because she's still here.

I stop only when a newer model sedan pulls up. A guy steps out, her boyfriend I'm assuming. He's tall, but not as tall as me. He's thin, and nowhere near as muscular as me either. As pissing contests go, I'm winning.

I don't know why I think we need to have a pissing

contest. We don't. Jo is his girlfriend, and she hates me only slightly less than she hated me yesterday. *I think*. Progress.

Jo comes out of the trailer. She greets her boyfriend in a pleasant but subdued way. Probably because I'm nearby.

It would be awkward if I completely ignored them, even though I want to, so I come over and say hello. Jo starts to make introductions, but I cut her off, not to be rude but to prove a point.

"Hi Jared, from the bank." I stick out my hand and give her a pointed look. She narrows her eyes.

Jared grips my hand harder than is necessary. "Hayden, right? Wes, is it? Or Warner?"

Well played, fucker.

I match his grip. "Wyatt, actually."

We let go. He wraps his now free arm around Jo's waist, leaning down and kissing her. At first she's surprised, then a flash of irritation jets across her face.

I want to laugh, but decide not to. I'm on Jo's bad side enough as it is, and it's cold over here.

"Are you ready, baby?"

Jared's sentence earns him another look of irritation from Jo, and I'm guessing it has something to do with that nickname he just used on her.

"Sure, let me grab one thing I left behind." Jo turns and goes back into the trailer. I don't feel the need to stand here and make painful small talk, so I head back to my empty water bottle. I can hear Jared walking behind me. He stops when I do.

"She's in a relationship, you know."

I drag my hand over my forehead and turn around. "Did something about the way I shook your hand and introduced myself give you the impression I'm after your girlfriend?"

Jared's hands slip into the pockets of his pressed slacks. "No."

"Then what is it about me that's making you stake your claim unnecessarily?"

"I've heard about you. You obviously don't know how to keep your hands off what's not yours."

When I was younger, a comment like that would have ended one way: my fists flying. As I've grown older, I've learned better how to harness my temper. Also, he wouldn't be talking like this if he wasn't threatened by me. That's another lesson I've learned as I've grown older. People often operate out of fear.

I raise my eyebrows. "Guess you know who I am after all."

One corner of his lip turns up. "Stay away from Jo, and I'll make sure she stays away from you."

I laugh. "You're planning on telling her what to do? Here's your chance. She's right there." Jo stands a few feet away, and she's heard every word. I know because I watched her approach.

"Let's go," she announces, whirling around. Jared follows after her, his bravado curiously missing.

I wait for them to leave, toss my empty coffee cup on the huge pile of trash, and head for home.

On my way, I call my mom and ask her if I can have dinner at the homestead with them. She does her best to cover up her surprise, and I do my best not to notice it's there.

9
JO

"I wish you would've recorded it," Shelby says, taking a bite of the pasta she picked up on her way home from work.

"Me too. It was quite a sight." I sit down beside her on the couch, a plate balanced on my hand. "I've never seen Jared act like that."

"He was posturing. Marking his territory."

"But why?"

Shelby stares at me. "Have you *seen* Wyatt?"

I roll my eyes. "Once or twice, yes."

"Then I don't need to explain why."

"Jared doesn't have anything to be worried about," I say around a bite.

"Maybe not." She shrugs. "But strictly from a biological standpoint, there was one superior male there today, and it wasn't Jared."

I pause with a forkload of pasta. "Thanks," I say dryly. "I'll be sure I don't mention that to him."

Shelby laughs. "You know what I mean. Animal kingdom, nature, yada yada."

"Want to hear something interesting?"

"Always."

"Wyatt was working with his shirt off today."

Shelby pauses mid-chew. "I'm guessing you didn't record that either."

I reach over and wipe sauce from her upper lip. "I thought you didn't like him?"

"I don't like him, but that doesn't mean I can't appreciate the gifts God gave him."

I laugh. "I think you might be insane. Or really hard up."

She nods, agreeing with both, and keeps eating. "What are you going to do about Jared?"

"What's there to do? I already explained to him that he won't be *telling* me to do anything." He was embarrassed I caught him saying that. I think he let the blatantly obvious pissing contest get the best of him.

I told him I'd eat dinner with Shelby, because I already promised her I would, and that I'd be over later. He apologized for how he acted when he saw Wyatt, and I explained Wyatt wasn't going anywhere for quite a while. I could tell he wasn't happy about that, and he didn't understand it, but I'm not going to air Wyatt's dirty laundry just to make Jared feel better.

I'M STANDING IN FRONT OF THE COPPER PATINA CIRCLE B SIGN, playing around with new names for the ranch. I haven't landed on the right one yet. I need something unassuming. I don't want to be basic and obvious, like *Jo's Ranch for At-Risk*

Youth. The point is to be a place where these kids want to go, not rub their noses in their mistakes.

I study the list of possible names I've written down in my notebook, my thumb skimming the page. Maybe I'll show it to Dakota later and see what she thinks.

I head back over to the trailer and check my phone. Dakota should be here any minute, and Wyatt too. I texted him last night asking if he could come back. I had a giant Dumpster delivered early this morning after seeing the pile Wyatt had going. We need to transfer it all into the oversized bin before they come back for it. I've also called the numbers Dakota gave me, and have meetings over the next few days to get some estimates from a general contractor. I have plenty of ideas, and very little money, but I at least need to know what I'm getting myself into. At the very least, I need to make the main house livable enough for Travis to come and live with me if he wants to.

Dakota pulls in, and Wyatt's in the truck behind her. He waves hello to me, then goes to help Dakota get Colt out of the car. Instead of handing the baby to his mom, Wyatt keeps him. He strides away, his head close to Colt's head, and he's talking to him.

Dakota watches them with open affection as she comes my way. "He's a bit of a baby hog. Nobody has a chance if Wyatt's around." She drops a diaper bag at her feet. "You wouldn't believe the amount of stuff a tiny person needs."

I remember it all from when Travis was a baby. How often his diaper needed changing, and trying various ointments to help with his diaper rash. I don't mention it to Dakota though. She knows I spent two years with Travis before my mom moved away, but I haven't told her how involved I was in his day-to-day care.

I study Wyatt with Colt. He dips his face down, talking softly about who knows what. I've seen Wyatt in various situations over the years, but watching him care for an infant is probably the sexiest thing I've ever seen him do. And he doesn't even know he's doing it.

I groan silently as I recognize the first breath of my old crush awakening. Growing legs. Standing up from the place I banished it to. Stretching.

Absolutely not. I told Jared he has nothing to worry about and I meant it. Those old feelings are nothing but memories, so I push them down, turning away from the sight of Wyatt holding a baby.

"I figured it out," Dakota whispers.

"Figured out what?" I stage-whisper back.

"The person you slept with in Phoenix was Wyatt."

My stomach tightens. "I-I... Please don't tell anybody."

Dakota reaches for me. "Of course not. But if I'm remembering our conversation from back then correctly, you said he doesn't remember, right?"

I nod. Tears prick at the backs of my eyes. I feel stupid. I turn away so Dakota doesn't see me, and the feeling passes.

"You really care about him, don't you?" Her tone is kind. The lack of pity makes me feel better.

"Cared. Past tense. I'm over him."

"Sure, of course. You're dating Jared now."

"Right. And he's—"

"Good and nice?"

I give her a dirty look. "Stop."

"I'm sorry, it was too easy."

I shake my head and allow a small smile. I don't tell her those words were about to come out of my mouth.

Wyatt brings Colt back to Dakota. "He's rooting," he informs Dakota.

Dakota grins proudly at Wyatt, then turns to me to explain. "Last night I taught him what rooting means. Wes and I stopped by the homestead for Juliette's pie."

"There wasn't enough, but that didn't stop you," Wyatt grumbles playfully.

Dakota takes Colt from Wyatt. "Wyatt thinks he's the only person who likes cherry pie," she teases, elbowing Wyatt. He doubles over, pretending to be injured.

I've never seen this side of Wyatt. Bantering with family, being an uncle. It paints him in a different light and makes me uncomfortable. I need him to be an asshole, so I can operate firmly in the safe world of being over him.

Dakota pulls a cover from her bag, slipping it over her head and covering Colt, almost like an apron. She reaches under the fabric, adjusting her top, and peeks down to look at the baby. The cover must be for Wyatt's benefit, because she has nursed in front of me before. "So listen, Jo," Dakota starts, while Colt's happily eating. "I think your last day at The Orchard should be sometime soon."

"What? No. I'm on the schedule all next week." Not to mention my savings account was recently bled dry so I could put money down on this place, and my checking account isn't exactly flush with cash.

Dakota gestures out. "This should be your priority. It's your dream."

She's right, but also... food. Shelter. "I need the money, Dakota. Fixing this place up isn't going to come cheap."

She nods. "I understand, believe me. You can work at The Orchard for as long as you need."

After Colt's finished, Dakota takes Wyatt through the

place, pointing out things we talked about yesterday and put on our list. She takes off after that, saying she needs to get back to go over the wine order at the restaurant, and it's just Wyatt and me.

"Ready to get started?" Wyatt asks, slipping his hands into work gloves.

I stretch out my fingers and look down at my bare hands. "Um, yeah. I just need to run into town quickly. I'm sure the Merc carries—"

"No need." Wyatt walks to his truck and reaches into the bed, coming away with a second set of gloves.

They'll be too big for me, but I don't mention it. "Thanks," I say, taking them. A tag dangles from the outer edge.

Size small. Definitely not Wyatt's size. I tell myself they're probably his little sister Jessie's, but in my heart I know they're not.

I meet his gaze, and he holds it there for a moment before looking away.

With my hands sheathed in the gloves, we get started. Biggest stuff first, he says, and then down in size from there. The smaller stuff will fall into the cracks and crevices created by the bigger pieces.

We work side by side, falling into a comfortable silence. It's impossible not to notice the swell in his forearms, his T-shirt clinging to his swollen biceps, the way he works with a singular focus. Maybe I was wrong about Wyatt. At least a little.

After a while we take a break, sitting down on the open tailgate of his truck and gulping water. Sweat rolls down my rib cage, the back of my neck, even the insides of my thighs.

"Are you thinking about changing the name of this

place?" Wyatt asks. He swings his foot back and forth, regarding me as he waits for me to answer.

I look out at the Circle B sign in the distance. "Definitely, I just need to figure out the right name. I have some ideas."

"Do you want to share them?"

I stare at him. I don't mean to, but his kindness disarms me. "Um, sure." I go get the notebook from my car and hand it to him.

He reads, his lips twisting as he considers what I've come up with. "I think you should have the word 'ranch' in the name, for sure. Maybe something to indicate what the person is getting into. Like 'Relaxation Ranch' or something."

"That would work if I was building a spa."

Wyatt chuckles. "You get my drift. Make it obvious what it is."

"A place to send your kid when you can't get them to behave?"

He smiles. "Yeah, that."

I shake my head. "I can't make it so obvious that no kid will agree to come here. *The Ranch Where The Bad Kids Go,*" I say in a mock tone.

He huffs and grins like he finds me amusing. "Good point." His eyes look back out at the work in front of us for the day. "You about ready?" Wyatt asks, hopping down. He turns around and offers me his hand.

I don't need the help jumping down, but he's being nice, and I don't want to discourage that by declining. We're so back and forth, awkward one moment and only slightly less awkward the next. I place my hand in his and feel it immediately, the way my heart lifts and soars. I slide down off the tailgate, but when I go to take back my hand, Wyatt holds fast. He's looking down at me, but it feels as if he's not seeing me at all.

"What?" I ask.

His eyes squint as he studies me. They are dark, like all the Hayden men, but streaked with gold. I remember the way his eyes drank me in that night as he hovered above me, but the stab of pain rockets me back to reality.

"Nothing," he answers softly, dropping my hand and leading me back to our work.

We keep working, and it turns out Wyatt likes to chat. Add that to the new and surprising things I'm learning about him. Is it possible he has grown up a little since we slept together? The realization is striking, causing discomfort to unfurl inside me.

"Do you know the history of this place?" he asks, using the inside of his shirt sleeve to wipe sweat from his forehead.

I shake my head and push the hair back from my face. "The Gazette reporter mentioned it, but I forgot to look into it."

"I have to warn you," Wyatt starts. "I don't know how accurate this all is. It may just be Hayden family folklore."

"I like folklore."

He grins. "You asked for it."

I lean on the handle of my shovel and nod at him. "I'm waiting."

Wyatt pushes hair back from his forehead and begins. "When my gramps and my dad ran the ranch, there was a family who came in and started the Circle B. I was young and I don't remember any of this, so none of this is firsthand. The Circle B family tried to sell their beef for less money, undercutting not only the HCC but the entire

Arizona industry. We hadn't yet differentiated ourselves with pasture-raised beef, so we were selling the same beef but for more money. My dad couldn't figure out how they were selling beef for so much less and staying afloat, and eventually he gave up trying to figure it out, and took matters into his own hands." Wyatt breathes a laugh, and I wonder why his admiration sounds reluctant. He points behind us. "My dad bought up the land north of the Circle B, then had the stream that fed the ranch rerouted. The Circle B has a well, so you shouldn't have a problem, but they needed more for a herd as big as the one they were carrying."

It all clicks into place. "He dehydrated them."

"Essentially."

"It's like war, on a smaller scale."

"I suppose it is, in a way. My dad had to protect the HCC. Wes would do the same."

I have no doubt Wes would eliminate anything or anybody who threatened his ranch. "And you?" I ask.

"I'd protect the HCC." I like the way he says it, with quiet strength.

"I heard what Warner did. Stepping down like that. Why didn't you..." I grasp for the right words.

"Step up?"

I shrug. "For lack of a better term, yes."

Wyatt's lips press together as he thinks. "I would, if I had to. But I don't know that I can be the kind of person who shows up, day after day, doing the same job. I need something more." He gives me a look. "As you can imagine, it's not a popular opinion at the homestead."

"I bet not."

"I think my dad should be happy he at least got one boy

who loves the family business almost as deliriously as he does."

Something about the way he says it makes me think there's a lot more to his words. "He's not happy?"

"No, he's really happy. With Wes. And Warner too, despite the fact he left everyone high and dry to pursue his passion."

"And you?"

Wyatt shifts, and he looks uncomfortable. "It's complicated."

"Been there," I say, trying to make him feel better. "My relationship with my mom is complicated."

"What did she—" His phone rings. He sends me a look of apology. "It's an HCC cowboy. It might only be a minor question, or it could be that a hunter is on the property and won't leave, you never know."

"Answer," I urge. Now I'm curious what he'd do about a hunter who refuses to leave his land.

"Denny?" Wyatt says in lieu of a greeting. "What's going on?"

He listens, his posture shifting as the moments tick by. He stands straighter. His entire face hardens. "Where did you see her?"

I look away. Who is *her?*

It's so quiet out here, I can just barely make out Denny on the end of the line saying the name Sara. And even though I know better, something inside me plummets.

Sara Schultz. The married woman Wyatt's been sneaking around with. I didn't forget about her, but I put it out of my mind on purpose. It hurts to think about, more than it should. Wyatt's business is Wyatt's business.

And, once again, I am in a relationship. A happy relationship.

In my peripheral vision, I catch Wyatt's gaze sliding over to me. I keep my eyes fixed elsewhere, so I don't appear interested.

"Thanks for letting me know about... that," Wyatt says, and I get the feeling he's choosing his words carefully, knowing he has an audience. He ends the call and slips his phone back into his pocket.

"I have to get going," he announces, glancing at the pile of trash. "I'll be back to finish up in the morning."

He walks away on fast feet, and I refuse to watch him go. Resentment builds inside me until it's all I can feel.

She's *married*. It's his best friend's wife, for God's sake. What is he doing?

And why did he never want to do it with me?

10
JO

Wyatt doesn't show up for two days.

How many times have I had my finger poised to dial Sheriff Monroe and call this off? Too many to count.

How many times have I placed the call?

Zero.

11

WYATT

I'M GOING TO TELL HER THE BRUISE CAME FROM A BAR FIGHT. She'll believe it. She already thinks the worst of me, I can see it every time her eyes roam my face.

Just when I thought I'd made some progress with Jo, Denny called. I played my part, driving to intercept Mickey like the damn Calvary.

Remember when we used to spar? he'd asked, putting up his fists to protect his face, hunching his shoulders.

I laughed it off, hoping to dissuade him. But when he's in that state, Mickey won't be dissuaded. And he turns mean. Sparring in high school is nothing compared to what Mickey does when he's whiskey soaked.

Of all things, right in the middle of the fight with Mickey, I thought of Jo. And then I got clocked in the face because I lost my focus.

Jo comes out of the trailer when I pull up. She stands right outside the door, arms folded, and stares at me. Her ripped jeans mold to her curves, and dirt covers the lower corner of her white T-shirt, like she wiped her hand on it.

An apology is in order, not that I needed to see Jo's obvious anger to know that. The first thing I say when I'm close enough is "I'm—"

"Save it," she orders. "You're lucky I didn't call the sheriff."

I know better than to ask her why she didn't, but I'm curious. It would get me out of her hair, and she seems like she wouldn't mind having me gone.

She comes closer. Stops a few feet from me. Her eyes are bright and sharp, a blue I've only ever seen in an Arizona sky before a heavy rain. "What happened to your face?"

I swallow. For what is probably the first time in my life, I feel guilty lying. "Bar fight."

"Typical."

Ouch. I knew it was coming, and still it stings. "I'm sorry." I wish I could tell her why I was gone, explain about Mickey and Sara.

"I told you to save it."

Indignation swells in my chest. I know it wasn't cool that I didn't show, and I wish I could've come up with a more altruistic reason, but that doesn't mean I'm going to be Jo's punching bag. Maybe we just need a little space to cool off.

"What do you need me to do?"

Jo inclines her head toward the house. "Knock down the wall between the formal dining room and the living room. The last thing I need is a formal dining room."

I go inside, making certain I avoid the rickety stair and sallow section of the porch floor, to see what she's talking about and figure out which tools I'm going to need. The rooms are tall, the ceilings vaulted, and I'm going to need a ladder, which I don't have because I didn't anticipate needing one today. It would be nice if there were more people working on this job than just me and Jo. I'm not sure what her endgame is, because nothing much is going to get accomplished if she doesn't have the right people.

I go find Jo in the trailer. Her back is to me, but her laptop is open. She's on another camp's website, scrolling through a list of activities. "Are you ever planning on hiring more labor?" It comes out harsher than I intend.

Jo turns around. She has a pencil shoved through hair that's knotted on top of her head, bringing to mind sexy librarian fantasies where she removes the pencil and her hair comes swirling down. The expression on her face kills that idea in its tracks.

"You can leave anytime you like. I know how you shy away from hard work."

What the fuck? A few days ago it seemed like we were edging back toward friend territory, and now she's insulting me?

"What's that supposed to mean?"

"You said it yourself. Wes is running that ranch without help."

"Because I'm here, helping you, in case you haven't noticed."

"And if you weren't here, you'd be where? At the HCC?" She laughs and shakes her head. "Sell your lies elsewhere. Maybe to Sara Schultz."

My teeth grind together. Of course she thinks what everyone else in this town thinks. For the most part, I don't care, but knowing Jo shares the assumption upsets me. And it's showing in my tone and volume. "You don't know a damn thing."

Jo's entire body is rigid, but her eyes don't match. There's something in them I can't decipher, but I'm certain it's not anger.

I wipe my forehead on my sleeve. It's really fucking hot in this trailer. "I know you need the help, and I need the community service hours. But I'm not a plumber or an electrician, and I don't have ten arms. So start thinking about adding to this crew of two." I gesture back and forth between us. "Or your dream of opening the ranch will do what a majority of dreams do: die."

I push open the flimsy door, and behind me in a soft, defeated voice, she says, "Fuck you."

"Right back at you, sweetheart," I mutter.

My anger gets taken out on the wall after I get back with a ladder and a sledgehammer. Jo stays away from me, and I can only imagine how hot she must be in that makeshift office she has set up for herself. Once, when I sneak a look at the trailer, I notice all the windows have been opened.

I don't know what it is about that woman, but she drives me insane. I've never met another woman tougher than my mother, but I think that has officially changed. I've always thought of Jo as shy and quiet, existing on the periphery. She's always been beautiful, but it was the kind of beauty that's too good for me. Too pure.

But this woman I'm spending all this time with? I can't connect her to the girl I used to know. Maybe I never saw her straight before. Maybe I needed to grow up and clean the dust off the lens through which I viewed her. This woman is strong and firm, intelligent and sexy as hell. She's calling me on my shit.

I like it.

And that, I fear, is a problem.

The Outlaw

Tonight is my parents' fortieth wedding anniversary.

I invited Jessie out to dinner, to give them privacy. Not that it matters, because Gramps is at the homestead with them. It's the thought that counts, right?

There's a restaurant in town that Jessie likes, a little Italian place. I know she has a million restaurants to choose from when she's back at ASU in Phoenix, but she swears she craves this place when she's away at college.

We're seated next to the wall, where there's a mural of an Italian countryside. Using my menu to block my mouth from view of the rest of the place, I ask, "Is it me or is the hostess twelve years old?"

Jessie looks at me like I'm hopeless. "The older you get, the more you think younger people look like babies."

I put my menu down on the table. "That's not true."

She glances at me, her gaze on the fading bruise on my cheek, then back to her menu. "It's totally true."

I make a face and tap the underside of the menu. "You already know what's on here."

She grins. "I know. I like to peruse."

I lift an eyebrow and she laughs. "You miss me when I'm gone."

"Maybe. Maybe not."

She pokes my cheek with a fingertip. Our server comes over, takes our order, and leaves. I sit back and look around. Sierra Grande is starting to feel new, like it's been asleep for a long time and recently awakened. New faces everywhere I go. I have my sisters-in-law to thank for that. Dakota, for building The Orchard and bringing in out-of-town visitors with her local wines and once a month local vendor fair. And Tenley, because she's as famous as the president and more popular among those in both political parties. Tenley put Sierra Grande on the map. To some, that's a good thing. To others, it's not.

The Hayden's are no stranger to controversy, so none of this really matters.

I've got my hand on the back of my neck, kneading a knotted muscle, when I see her. In a corner booth, her hair hanging down like a curtain, his fingers slipping through it.

The same feeling from the sheriff's office comes over me once again. *I know what it feels like to slide my fingers through that hair.*

It can't be, and yet... it is. Inexplicably.

Jo tips her head back and laughs, deep and throaty. I swallow against the overwhelming desire to press my lips against the hollow of her neck.

"Uh, Wyatt?" Jessie waves a hand in front of my face. "You there, big brother?" She turns around, following my gaze to the cozy little corner. She settles back in her chair and waits for me to say something. I'm not sure what to say, and I know Jessie will talk anyway, because she has the perpetual need to fill a silence.

"Do you have a thing for Jo Shelton?"

I prop an elbow on the table, pressing the side of my fist against my lips. "I'm helping her with her ranch."

"Which is weird," Jessie points out, dipping a piece of bread in olive oil. "Why are you doing that again?"

"Out of the goodness of my heart." I lean my head back slightly and tip it to the side. From this angle, I appear to be looking at Jessie, but I can see Jo too, like one of those soft focus pictures where the subject in the foreground is the only thing in focus.

Right now, soft focus Jo is sipping a glass of wine. Setting it down. Fingering her necklace. Toying with the napkin on her lap. Soft focus Jared's mouth is running at an impressive rate of speed. He's missing all of Jo's non-verbals.

"Since when do you do anything out of the goodness of your heart?" Jessie asks, biting into the bread.

"Thanks," I deadpan. She laughs.

"Kidding, Wyatt." She waves her hand in the air between us, a gold bracelet with a four-leaf clover charm glinting in the overhead light. "You're the best of the bunch."

"Right." I take some bread.

She chews and swallows. "You are. I'm not kidding. Wes was always so single-minded, and, you know, *gone*. And Warner was great too, don't get me wrong. But he was always wrapped up in his own thing." She smiles shyly, and I see the little girl she once was. I remember so much of her childhood, because of our age difference. She's the reason I love kids. "So when I say you're the best of the bunch, I'm not kidding."

"Thanks, Jes." My chest tightens. Nobody tells me I'm the best, their favorite. Wes is my dad's favorite, it's clear as day. Jessie is my mom's favorite, for reasons so obvious they're not worth listing. Warner is the entire town's favorite because he's fucking Warner.

Warner and Wes would tell you I'm my mom's favorite, but I think she has a soft spot for me because it's so obvious how much my dad prefers everyone but me.

Sometimes I wonder if everyone knows. Does this entire town, my whole family, know that my parents wished desperately for a girl and got me instead? And if they don't know, do they guess? The signs are all there.

Fucking depressing. I don't want to think about this anymore. I sit up straight, making it so I can't see Jo anymore, and put all my attention on Jessie. She tells me about school, the classes she's signed up to take for her junior year starting in August, and a guy she met. I don't really want to hear about the guy, but I do my best to listen and not make a face. I ask her where she got her lucky charm bracelet, and she tells me it's from the new guy.

Our dinners arrive and we tuck in. All the hard work on Jo's ranch has made me into a starving teenager. I eat everything and finish Jessie's. There's movement in the corner booth, shifting, and Jo slides out, making it impossible not to see her. She's wearing a skirt, black and short, tight around her thighs, with one of those T-shirts she favors tucked haphazardly into the front of one side. She adjusts the skirt, her eyes sweeping the room and landing on mine. She stills. Her lips part. She recovers, swallows. If I pressed my nose to the skin by her ear, I'd smell citrus and flowers. *Impossible.*

She comes my way. Jared slips an arm around her, guiding her. She halts for the shortest second, and our gazes meet in the pause. Then she's gone, passing me by, leaving behind an earthquake in my heart that's immeasurable by the Richter scale.

"Wow," Jessie murmurs, drawing out the vowel. "I felt that."

It takes me a moment to climb from my state of overwhelm. When I make it out of the fog, I ask her what she means.

Her hands flit through the space around her head. "The air. It's thick. Serious vibes."

I make a dismissive sound with my mouth. "Right. Hate vibes. Jo doesn't have a very high opinion of me."

One side of Jessie's face scrunches. "You sure about that?"

I thank the server when she drops the check and reach for my wallet. "Pretty sure. If you'd seen the way she looked at me yesterday, you'd agree."

We're on the way out after payment is complete, but Jessie hovers near the front door. "I see something happening with you and her."

"Are you suddenly prophetic?"

She plucks a red and white mint candy from a bowl on the hostess stand and unwraps it. "Yep. Just call me 'the prophet' from now on."

I sling my arm around her shoulders and steer her out the door. "Nah, little sister. We call you Calamity, and for damn good reason." As a little girl, she was walking chaos and cursed like a sailor.

She shrugs me off when we get to the sidewalk. "I don't think I deserve that nickname."

I give her a 'come on' face, and she laughs. "Okay, maybe I do."

I go toward my truck, but Jessie grabs my arm and tugs. "Let's bring dessert to Mom and Dad since they wouldn't let us do anything fun for their anniversary." She leads me down the street, but I'm not sure where we're going because The Bakery is closed, and so is Marigolds. I don't think our parents want bags of candy from the Merc. Maybe we can talk Tenley into giving up one of those jars of spicy peach rings she's so stingy with.

I put on the brakes and turn back, saying, "Let's go back

and ask Ten..." The remainder of my sentence dies on my lips. Across the street, in the glow of a streetlight, Jared stands with Jo, his lips on hers.

"Wyatt, come on." Jessie tugs on my arm.

I look down, meet her gaze, and see that she's not at all surprised to see Jo and Jared. She was trying to keep me from seeing them.

What's happening across the street is like a car accident. I don't want to see it but I look again anyway. The kiss breaks. Jared lifts his head. Looks straight at me.

Motherfucker.

The instinct is there, strong and pungent, to stalk across the street, grab him by the throat, and stake my claim. But this isn't the African savanna, I'm not a male lion, and Jo isn't territory to own.

He's holding her in his arms, keeping her facing away from me. I keep my eyes fixed on his, and without conscious thought, my chin lifts.

Jessie tugs me once more, harder this time. I allow her to pull me away, breaking eye contact first. It feels like I've lost. I don't do well with losing.

And, in a turn of events I don't fully understand, I'm learning how badly I don't do well with losing Jo.

As if I ever had her to begin with.

12

JO

I know I wasn't ready for how fast everything happened with the ranch, but at this point I'm positive all the time and preparation in the world wouldn't have made me ready. None of this is going the way I want it to.

In the past two weeks, I've met with multiple general contractors, walked the ranch with each and every one, and most of them have told me what I'm trying to do here is crazy. They don't tell me no, just that they'll send me an estimate of how much they think the job will cost, and each one reminds me that "this is just an estimate". I hear their meaning loud and clear. Expect it to run higher than what they quote.

It's me who has to say no. No to every contractor, no to Wyatt every time he reminds me he isn't a jack-of-all-trades, and just like he warned me, my dream is fading, slip-sliding into that dark place where dreams take final, raspy breaths.

I'm meeting one more contractor this morning, though I honestly don't see the point. He won't be any different than the rest.

His name is Mike, and he shows up in a shiny truck, which I don't like. In my opinion, work trucks should reflect the work they do. Shiny truck equals clean hands.

Wyatt's here, working inside the main house. For someone who explicitly says he is not knowledgeable, he seems to know an awful lot. He's been working on refinishing the cabinets in the master bathroom. Sometimes I get the feeling he might be one of those people who inherently knows how to do things.

Wyatt seems to come and go as he pleases, which fits with his personality. Aside from those two days when he didn't show, I don't have a single thing to complain about. We don't talk much, both of us avoiding the other after our fight, speaking only when necessary and always about the job. I mention when contractors will be here, and Wyatt always manages to be here during those times.

I'm certain it's on purpose, and while my inclination is to remind him I'm perfectly capable on my own, it does make me feel safer to know he's nearby.

Mike is nice, very much like a grandfather type, and I see that it's his age that probably keeps him from working in a labor-intensive way. He's chattier than the other contractors, remarking on the property, how nice it will be once it's all fixed up. I explain how it will be used, and he tells me he has seven grandkids and hopes none of them will be needing the services of my ranch. I smile and agree. Maybe Mike's children are all good parents, and his grandchildren are happy, well-adjusted, and they never make a bad choice. Not everyone is so lucky.

We pass Wyatt as we walk through the main house. He's wearing a tool belt, an honest to God leather tool belt, and he looks like something out of a porn film. His T-shirt sticks to him in places where his sweat has soaked through, and his jeans are tight, his dark hair mussed like his hand has run through it recently. His muscles ripple and flex, popping under the physical labor. Everything about him screams sex, and I have firsthand knowledge.

All of which I can't think about right now, not with Mike the grandpa beside me.

I nod at Wyatt as we go by. Mike spouts his thoughts, and I write them down almost by rote. He says the same things most of them say.

I tell him there's one more thing I want to ask him about, then lead him to where I need to build the bunkhouses for the campers and camp counselors. I show him the plans, drawn by an architect at Dakota's dad's firm, and if they cost anything she isn't divulging. I don't even want to consider where I'd be with this project if it weren't for her.

Mike looks at me with the tenderness only a grandparent can, and asks me if I've obtained a permit to build on the property.

"It's my property." I have the giant loan in my name to prove it.

"You might own it, but that doesn't mean you can do what you want with it."

My lack of knowledge makes my neck heat up, and I pray the flame doesn't sweep across my cheeks. "What should I do?"

"Visit the county recorder's office. Get the parcel map, the APN—"

"What's that?" My pencil pauses on my notebook.

"Assessor's parcel number." There's a touch of astonishment in his tone, and not the good kind. "You need to make sure you can build on this land."

What I want to say is something along the lines of *I will do what I want on this land and I will do it when I want to do it.* What I actually say is, "Thank you for your time and guidance."

On the walk back to his truck, he informs me he will work up a bid, on the assumption the land is buildable and I am able to obtain a permit. He pauses in the open door of his truck, and I can tell it's on the tip of his tongue. He wants to tell me I'm crazy, that this undertaking is too great. He says, "I hope all this work you're going to put in turns out to be worth it."

What he means is that he doesn't think troubled teens are worth the effort. Maybe I wouldn't feel so offended if it weren't for Travis, but it digs into my skin like a burr. So I tell him, "For your sake, I sure hope your grandchildren never need what my ranch has to offer."

With a polite smile and a nod, I turn around and walk into the house.

I FIND WYATT IN THE MASTER BEDROOM WHERE I LAST SAW him. One day it will be mine, the bedroom will be where I sleep. With the wall Wyatt knocked out between the formal dining room and living room, I can create one large seating area where campers can eat. The previous owner must've liked to cook because the kitchen is enormous. Oddly, they left behind an impressive amount of cookware and other various odds and ends, including a gigantic hutch full of intricately detailed china and a single serving tray. The china is intact; the serving tray is more rust than silver.

For right now, the master bedroom and en suite bathroom look as torn apart as the rest of the house. Wyatt has the cabinet fronts off their hinges and leaning against a wall. He's using a makeshift work table to sand down one of the cabinet doors. He flicks off the machine when I walk in, the high-pitched sound decreasing until it's quiet.

He looks at me, waiting to hear what I've come to say. This is the way it's been between us since the day he showed up and I let him have it. I was mad about Sara, jealous of the way he'd run off when someone called and said her name. I know I'm not supposed to care. I have Jared, who has made it very clear to Wyatt that he's my boyfriend. Something I don't like, but understand.

I'm used to Wyatt being the center of attention. Arrogant in that cold, stiff upper lip kind of way. Hell, his indifference is probably what made me like him so much. *Oh, you don't pay me any attention. Makes me like you more!*

And then I moved on. I think it would be easier if Wyatt was the same guy I'm used to him being. This Wyatt, this tentative, considerate, watchful man, is turning my world upside down. I don't know how to be around him. It's far safer, to my heart and my current romantic relationship, if Wyatt would stomp around and act like an entitled prick.

"Jo?" He tips his head, surveying me. "Did you need something?"

I lean sideways until my shoulder hits the wall with a thud. "They all think I'm crazy."

Wyatt glances out the bathroom window, but Mike's truck is long gone. "Is that what he said?"

My head shakes and I turn so my whole upper back rests

on the wall. "He didn't have to. It was obvious. And he also doesn't think the people I'm building this place for are worth it."

Wyatt's voice has an edge as he repeats his previous question. "Is that what he said?"

"Not in those exact words, but yes."

Wyatt taps his head. "Small mind."

"Mike has a small mind?"

"Why else would he say young people who need help aren't worthy of receiving it? The future of our species depends on the next generation, and it's *small-minded* not to want to give them the best chance."

I love that Wyatt can see beyond his own little corner of the world. "I told him that for his sake, I hope his grandkids won't ever need this ranch."

Wyatt laughs and winks at me. "That's my girl."

The smile on my face dies. My entire body turns to ice, and somewhere deep in my core, a little fire ignites.

Wyatt forces out a fake cough. "What's next for this place?"

I find my voice. "A visit to the county recorder's office. Followed by a permit, hopefully."

13

JO

The trip to the Verde County recorder's office was far less eventful than I thought it would be. The woman who helped me, Nina, is brisk but friendly. She gives me what I need and tells me my next stop will be the zoning office, just to make sure there are no restrictions that would prevent me from building.

"I'm not building a skyscraper beside a runway," I say, genuinely perplexed at all the red tape. Nina gives me a withering look and points me where I need to go.

The zoning office gives me the all clear. Warm tears prick the inner corners of my eyes, the relief so tangible I can taste it. On my way out of the building I pass framed pictures of wildflowers, and suddenly I know what to name the ranch.

Wyatt is there when I get back, working on the cabinets. Apparently sanding and refinishing cabinets is more time-consuming than it looks.

I feel light, buoyant, for the first time in weeks. I have cleared my first hurdle.

"Hi," I say brightly to Wyatt when I stick my head around the open door into what will be my bedroom. Wyatt has set up a workstation for himself. He stills, his hand on the sander.

Surprise flares in his eyes, and he regards me cautiously. I guess I have been a bit grumpy.

"I have good news," I continue, coming all the way into the room. "Everything is good to go. I can build on the land. And I've decided to name it Wildflower."

A grin fills up his face. "That's great, Jo. Congratulations."

His excitement mingles with mine, coaxing it out from where I've been keeping it. Before now, it wasn't safe to feel excited. I look around, seeing the same layers of grime and dust and not hating them quite as much. "I know I've done this in the wrong order." My hair falls into my eyes and I push it back. "I've done everything in the wrong order. I wasn't ready when the Circle B came up for sale. It was sudden, and Jericho said she had a lot of interest already, and... I couldn't stand the thought of someone besides me buying this place. I felt like it was supposed to be mine..." My voice trails off. The back of my neck grows hot. "Anyway. Here we are. I don't know why I said all that."

Wyatt smiles crookedly. "You don't have to explain yourself to me."

I rub the toe of my boot into the rough blanket Wyatt has laid down to protect the wood floor. "I know."

"Jo?"

Wyatt's tone is tentative, like he's dipping a hand in bathwater to test its temperature.

My blue eyes lock onto his brown. I wonder if he knows he has gold flecks in them? "Hmm?" I ask, the sound vibrating my throat.

His gaze searches mine, and it feels as if he's reaching into me. My chest heats and the tops of my thighs pulse as memories of our night together flood my brain. When he speaks, I'm positive they aren't the words he planned to say. "Do you like the finish? Of the cabinets?"

I come closer until I'm standing beside him. It's a mistake, I think, to be so close to him. The air is thick with the scent of him, something male that's difficult to describe. It mixes with the earthy sawdust, the alpine air from the open window.

I force my gaze down to the workstation, and the three cabinet doors lined up there. My fingers are poised to touch them when I realize I probably shouldn't in case he has recently applied something to them. "Did you stain them this color?"

"That's what was underneath when I sanded them down. You can touch it."

My fingers drag the length of one small, square door, bumping over the ridge leading into the design cut into the center. "I can't believe how pretty they are under that paint." They are a beautiful medium brown, the ugly green paint stripped away to reveal the wood beneath.

"Layers."

"Layers?" I can't help it. I turn my head to him, even though his nearness transforms my breath to honey, makes it stick in my throat.

"It seems to me most things are made up of layers. People, too. We layer on the primer, the paint, the protective coatings. But under it all, we're just ourselves. As natural as this wood started out."

I watch him speak, his mouth forming these words that don't seem like they should be coming from him. Was he always this deep? This reflective? Did I just miss it? Was I too busy seeing his protective coating to notice what lay hidden beneath?

I turn back to the cabinets. "I love them. Thank you."

"You're welcome." His response is warm and deep, a caress I'm not supposed to want.

To put space between us, I walk away from him and into the master bath. The space is large for having been built thirty years ago. Large bathrooms and expansive kitchens weren't in style three decades ago, according to Dakota. This house has both. The master bath is missing a bathtub though, which I find odd. And disappointing. I say as much to Wyatt, calling out to him. He answers from a few feet away, startling me.

"I thought that was weird, too. It's almost as if there should be one over there." He inclines his head to an open space by the second window. "There's a spot for plumbing."

I picture a clawfoot tub, a crimson and burnt orange sunset, a glass of wine. "That would be perfect. Baths are kind of my indulgence, but it's been a while. My bathtub at Shelby's is really small."

Wyatt's looking at me now, doing that thing where his eyes darken, his thoughts bundling together and staying inside his mind. He has so much to say, but keeps it tucked away. I've always thought that about him.

I look out the window at my property. *My land.* I came here with nothing when I was sixteen. I scraped and saved from eighteen on, serving tables and taking on odd jobs so that I'd never have to ask my mother for anything. Here I am, almost thirty, and I finally have something to show for it all.

"Do you want to get some candy?" I thumb outside, toward my car. "I feel like celebrating."

Wyatt raises an eyebrow. "With candy? I can think of other ways to celebrate."

My throat tightens. "How?"

A smile tugs one corner of his mouth. "Champagne comes to mind."

"It's only mid-afternoon."

He frowns. "You shouldn't let the clock tell you what to do and when to do it."

My lips twist as I face him. Me, with my sensibilities, my basic ideas of propriety. Him, with his propensity to challenge any rule set forth.

He wins.

Why? Simply because his way sounds a hell of a lot more fun.

I walk past him, leaving the bathroom, taking great care not to let my shoulder touch his. "Champagne *and* candy, Hayden."

***

The Merc carries an assortment of very random items. Small things, like basic groceries. Bananas, apples, milk, those sorts of things. Also, napkins with funny sayings. Individual bags of chips. Candles made by a local woman, who also sells her wares at The Orchard on Local Sunday. But the really special part of the Merc is their candy selection. They have everything, from Lemon Drops to that bitter dark chocolate that's become popular.

Wyatt is acting like the candy decision is on par with being the one and only person who gets to vote for the next governor of Arizona. "I just don't think you can go wrong with Twix," he says, holding up the shiny wrapper.

"Cow Tales all day," I announce, extending the fistful of candy.

"Pshh," he responds, the sound making his lips splay.

A young kid, maybe eleven, at the end of the aisle glances at us. He reaches for a candy bar and slips it into his pocket. I elbow Wyatt.

"That kid just put a candy bar in his pocket," I say under my breath.

Wyatt looks over. The kid meets our gazes, shrinking with guilt. "Come here," Wyatt whispers to him.

The kid gulps and glances around, then decides it's safe. He walks closer.

"Listen," Wyatt continues whispering, clamping a hand on the kid's shoulder. "Stealing is wrong. But, if you're going to do it, never put the candy in your pockets. They'll ask you to empty them. You have to put the candy in your underwear."

The kid makes a face. I can't even imagine what kind of face I'm making. Wyatt is seriously giving stealing lessons to a child?

"I know, it seems weird," Wyatt assures him. "Put it in the waistband. Nobody is going to ask a kid if they can look in their underwear."

The kid nods, staring at Wyatt like he can't believe his lucky day. He moves to grab at his pocket and Wyatt stops him. "It's too late to change now. You have to commit. Go."

Like a frightened animal, the kid senses his chance to flee and takes it.

"Are you fucking kidding me?" I hiss when he's out of earshot.

"Don't make it a thing."

"Uhhh... how can I not? You just taught a kid to steal."

"That kid already knew how to steal."

"You improved his method."

"Nope. Guaranteed he gets caught sometime and learns the lesson the hard way. I could've told him not to steal, and he wouldn't have listened."

"So teaching him was your next best alternative?"

"I didn't teach him." He gives me a look that says 'we've been through this already'. "Come on, let's go buy all this."

"Why not just steal it?" I mutter as I follow him down the aisle.

His shoulders shake with a quiet laugh.

The teenage boy behind the register rings up our stuff. He announces the total, but instead of paying, Wyatt leans forward. "So"—he glances at the name tag—"Carson, a young boy about ten or eleven just walked out of here with a candy bar in his pocket. I want you to pay for it."

Carson's lip curls. "What? No way." He starts around the counter, like he's going to go after the kid.

Wyatt's arms shoot out. "Hold it. I said you're going to pay for the candy bar."

"Like hell—"

"Take it out of the twenty bucks I saw you steal from the register when I was in here three days ago."

Carson freezes. Stares at Wyatt. Wyatt returns the stare, doesn't blink.

"I don't know what you're talking about." Carson's voice wavers.

"You sure do," Wyatt says evenly, removing the cash needed to pay for our transaction. "But if me telling Maia is what's needed to jog your memory, then—"

"No, no," Carson hurries. He looks down at his hands. "I'll take care of it."

"Good. Thanks, bud." Wyatt grins affably and grabs our things from the counter. "No need for a bag."

I follow Wyatt to the door, which he holds open for me. I'm in a daze, trying to fit together the pieces of everything that just happened.

Automatically my hand dips into my purse for my sunglasses, but before my fingers find them I realize I don't need them. The sky has changed from sunny to cloudy while we were in the Merc, and in the distance, dark clouds gather.

Wyatt looks out. "Thunderstorm headed our way." He pulls his phone from his pocket and checks his weather app. "Yep," he says, confirming what was already obvious.

"You needed an app to tell you about the weather you can see with your own two eyes?" I tease.

He squints playfully. "You got jokes, Miss Shelton."

"I got jokes for days," I answer, doing a saucy headshake. Wyatt laughs. We come up to the little corner store that houses a surprisingly good selection of wine. "I'm going to duck in here and grab our champagne."

"I got it." Wyatt starts for the door, but I stop him with a hand on his arm.

"No, let me. You've been working for free. At least let me buy some bubbly."

"I haven't been working for free," Wyatt argues. He palms his chest, directly above his heart. "I'm repaying my debt to society."

I smile and shove him aside playfully. "I'll be right out."

Inside, I go straight for the champagne. Not prosecco, but the good stuff. The stuff that came from Champagne,

France. I don't have a lot of money to spare, but I'm celebrating. I cleared a hurdle I didn't know was a hurdle until someone told me it was a hurdle. The thought makes my brain hurt, and so does thinking about all the hurdles I've yet to clear.

I select a bottle and move toward the register. Two women stand in front of me in line. I don't recognize them, but it's not like I know everyone in Sierra Grande, the way Wyatt claims to. It's a small town, but it's not *that* small. Still, I get the feeling they aren't locals. Or at least, they haven't been for long. For one thing, they both wear designer flip-flops, an impractical choice of shoe. All the dust, paired with the heat and sweat, is going to make a paste between their toes, and anybody who's been here for a while knows this.

They turn around, smiling perfunctorily at me, both of them casting a glance behind me. I see the shimmer of recognition in one woman's eyes, and the lingering look on the other woman. I already know what has captured their interest. There's nothing behind me but bottles of wine, and out the front window stands Wyatt. I don't think it's the wine sending that flush across their cheeks.

"I told you my friend's mother-in-law has lived here her whole life, and she has some stories to tell about him."

I lean closer to hear them better.

"Spill," the friend instructs.

We all move forward one space in line, and neither woman thinks this should stop them from gossiping.

"She said he's been carrying on with his best friend's wife."

A gasp from the other woman. A second glance, right past me, and directly out the front window. No doubt Wyatt is standing there, completely unassuming, probably checking his weather app.

"Do you think he's interested in taking on any more bored housewives?" They laugh quietly, and the second one says, "Save a horse, ride a cowboy."

My eyes roll up to the ceiling. That comment was low-hanging fruit, and I would've bet a hundred bucks one of them was likely to make it before they paid.

They continue. "He'd be the perfect distraction. Barry is so busy with work, he wouldn't even notice. All I need is a cowboy like that to come in, get me off, and ride away on his horse after. I bet he wouldn't even mind. My friend's mother-in-law said he's from a big cattle family around here, but he's the black sheep. He doesn't do much except mooch off the family teat and use the last name to do what he pleases."

"Excuse me?" The women turn around. It takes two full seconds for me to realize it's *me* who has spoken. My heart hammers against my breastbone. "The person you're so openly talking about is an actual person, and he doesn't exist to service you or be a source of entertainment."

The brunette smiles like I'm funny. "Are you his sister?"

"His boss, actually."

"Ri-ight." She turns back around, ending the exchange. The person in front of them has finished their transaction and they step up to pay.

Adrenaline courses through me, just at that small exchange. Confrontation isn't something I do well with, at least not confrontation with women. I never could stand up to my mother, could never say the simple *no* I'd needed to say.

My brain floods with all the things I could say to these

women before they leave, and then the cashier is calling my name and the woman are leaving and it's over.

I pay for the champagne. Smile my thanks at the cashier, and decline the paper bag he's offered. When I turn around to leave, Wyatt is there, inside the small shop.

"Oh," I say, jumping.

"The thunderstorm is moving in quickly." He holds out a hand. I assume it's for the bottle I'm holding, so I hand it over. He takes it, then holds out his other hand. This time, I place my hand in his. He squeezes, ever so lightly, and I squeeze back. He leads me out of the store, breaking contact with me the second we're out on the sidewalk.

If it weren't for that small squeeze, I wouldn't have understood the point of him taking my hand. Is it possible he overheard what I said to those women?

Was he thanking me?

14

WYATT

The storm rolls in like a hurtling locomotive as Jo and I drive back to the Circle B. A sky that was clear before we walked into the Merc is now bruised deep blue and purple. Lightning flashes behind the clouds, lighting them up for less than a second.

Jo bites the side of her lower lip, peering at the ever-darkening sky through the passenger side window.

"Worried?" I ask her. I would be, if I were her. I know she hasn't had the roof inspected yet, and there's no way to know if it will hold through a summer monsoon. Arizona thunderstorms are unrelenting, the open skies creating a wide lane for thunder to travel, for wind to whip and rain to drive.

Jo spears me with a clear, fearful gaze. Her celebratory mood from earlier has disappeared. "What if it all comes crashing down?"

"The house?"

She shrugs, just the tiniest movement. "Everything. The house, my plans, my entire life."

I run my palm over the short, spiky hairs across my jaw. "Let's play a game."

"I'm not in the mood for I Spy."

I huff a laugh. "Let me rephrase. Let's talk hypotheticals. *Hypothetically speaking*, what would you do if the house came crashing down?"

"Run out of it."

"Assume you're not in it."

She releases a heavy breath. "Get it fixed, I guess."

"And what if your plans came crashing down?"

Jo shifts, pulling one leg up onto the seat and tucking it into her chest. "Live at the Circle B. Have the world's biggest mortgage. Put it back on the market."

"And your life? What if your whole life fell down around you?"

She taps her knee. "Reinvent myself."

"What would you be?"

"A princess on a Disney cruise."

I look at her from the corner of my eye as I make the turn into the Circle B. "You said that without any hesitation."

Jo smiles. "It's a secret dream of mine. Don't go telling anybody."

"I'll take it to the grave." A crack of thunder splits my sentence in two, and the sky opens up. Rain batters my windshield.

I come to a stop in front of the main house, and Jo shoves the bag holding the candy under her shirt. "Good luck to you in the deluge," she calls, then hops from my truck.

I'm laughing as I reach for the champagne. Jo is funnier than I remember. And she defended me just now. I'd come in to get her and overheard her. I don't know what those women had said, and I didn't know it was me Jo was talking about until she called herself my boss. What I do know is how it makes me feel, to be someone who she thinks deserves defending.

I reach into the back seat, grab the bag I forgot to take inside with me when I got home yesterday, and grip the neck of the champagne bottle. Rain pelts me as I run to the house, where a laughing Jo waits for me under the safety of the covered porch. We are both soaked. My shirt sticks to my skin, and drops of water roll down her face.

"I wonder if there'll be flash floods," Jo muses, looking in the direction of town, even though we can't see it.

The rain smacks the ground and bounces. The ground is hard, and it's been so long since it last rained. The clay is not yet soft enough to absorb the torrent, so it forms streams and, luckily, flows away from Jo's house. At least she has that going for her.

We toe off our shoes and go inside. From the bag, I produce a plastic-wrapped bag of plain white T-shirts, the kind that go under the work shirt I wear on the HCC.

"Here," I say, ripping open a bag and handing her one.

She takes it, shaking it out. "Thank you."

She disappears around the corner to change, and I trade my wet shirt for the dry. My jeans are wet in places, but not soaked. Even if they were, I can't remove them.

Jo walks back through the living room and into the kitchen. She holds her shirt over the sink, wringing out the water then draping the shirt over the faucet.

We walk through the place, checking for leaks. In total, there are five. I warn her there could be more, some may not develop until it's been raining for a while. She frowns, and I choose not to tell her entire sections of the roof can collapse.

I don't want her to fear our hypothetical conversation from the truck coming to fruition.

In the kitchen, we find a cabinet loaded with pots and pans. "Isn't that bizarre?" Jo asks, holding one up by the handle. She opens more cabinets and finds other kitchenware. "Why would they leave this stuff behind? They took the furniture."

"Maybe they hated cooking," I joke. We move through the house, placing pots under the leaks to catch the water.

We go back to the living room and she takes a notebook from her purse. "Roof," she says out loud as she writes. "My list just keeps getting longer."

Briefly I consider asking her why the roof wasn't on her list, then change my mind. The more time I'm spending here the more I see that Jo needs someone to guide her on this project. I'm thinking of how I can rope Dakota into helping more when Jo says harshly, "Quit it."

Her tone jolts me from my thoughts. "Quit what?"

Jo tosses the candy to me. "I know what you're thinking." She drags over an empty crate and flips it upside down, using it as a seat. I watch her gather her hair into a ponytail and secure it with the hair tie she had on her wrist. She has a graceful, slender neck. A tiny mole just below her left ear.

I unwrap my Twix and take a bite. "No, you don't," I argue pointedly.

"You're thinking I don't know what I'm doing here. You're trying to figure out how a person who hasn't yet had the roof inspected could possibly pull off the rebuilding of a ranch and the opening of a business." She points her full-size Cow Tale at me, the end hanging limply.

"Not true," I insist, pushing the last of the Twix into my mouth.

"Then what were you thinking?" Her eyebrows raise in challenge.

I don't think it would go over well if I tell her I was trying to keep myself from imagining what her rain-moistened skin would feel like against my tongue. "I was thinking it's pretty great what you're doing out here."

She narrows her gaze. "You're a bad liar."

I snort. "That's the first time I've heard that." I grab the champagne from where I set it on the counter before we walked through the house looking for leaks. "But you're right, that's not what I was thinking. That doesn't make the sentiment any less true, though. And I think what you're doing out here should be celebrated."

I hold out the bottle for her to take, but she points back at me. "You do the honors."

I pull off the foil and ball it up, tossing it aside. I position two thumbs on the side of the cork, then think better of it. Barometric pressure might make it come shooting out, and although it sounds fun, it also sounds like a mess. Instead, I twist the cork until I hear the *pop*, and a tiny amount bubbles over.

Holding the bottle out to her, I say, "To you, Jo, and your big dreams."

Jo smiles shyly, her eyelids fluttering closed for a brief moment. A flash of time takes over, as if I've lived another life. I see Jo in a dimly lit hallway, the walls stucco, two oversized plants on either side of her.

I blink against a memory that cannot be my own as Jo takes the bottle from me. She drinks straight from it and hands it back to me. I sip, and we're both quiet, listening to the rain and thunder. Jo rubs at her bare forearms and says she feels like she should be cold, even though she isn't. It's probably almost eighty degrees in here right now, and it feels even warmer from the humidity the storm has brought with it.

"Wyatt?" Jo says, looking up at me. I sit down beside her so we're on the same level. She continues. "How do you justify what happened in the Merc?"

I fully expected her question, and I'm ready with an answer. "That," I say, taking a sip and passing her the bottle. "Is what I like to call outlaw logic."

Jo gives me a reproachful look. "You're a scoundrel."

I smile and wink. "No, darlin', I'm an outlaw."

Jo throws up her hands. "You're also a flirt."

"Me?" I point back at myself. "I don't know what you're talking about. But," I stand up. "Since you leveled such an accusation, I might as well ask you to dance." My voice is calm, my furiously beating heart is anything but.

She stares at the hand I've extended. "You know I have a boyfriend."

"Yes, I know. Jeff, was it?"

She shakes her head at me. "You know his name."

I nod at the hand I'm still holding out. "It's just a dance Jo. I'm not asking you to run away with me."

But if you want to, let's go. I'd drive her right out of this storm, to whatever destination.

She sets the bottle beside her and stands. "I wouldn't even if you did."

"I'm aware," I tell her, as she places her hand in mine.

She lets me pull her in, our clasped hands resting on my chest. My other arm wraps around her waist. A crack of thunder causes both of us to jump, she presses herself into me, then pulls back.

"I don't even like you," she asserts, keeping her eyes

trained on my neck. It's the safest place for them to be. If our gazes met right now, I'm not sure what might happen.

"I know," I answer. If it wasn't for the hitch in her voice, maybe I'd believe her.

"Where did you learn to dance?"

I push her out, pull her back in. She's surprisingly good at letting me lead. "My mom. She gave me dance lessons in the living room when I was growing up."

"You're good."

"It's not hard." Not when you have the right partner.

The rain bullies the house, pelting it relentlessly, and though the roof holds up, everything inside me is collapsing.

I'm falling for Jo, and isn't it just like me to find the person who's already taken?

Maybe I am a scoundrel like she said, because right now, with Jo in my arms, her relationship status is the last thing I'm thinking about.

15

JO

I'VE MET WITH FOUR DIFFERENT ROOFERS OVER THE PAST TWO days, and they all say the same thing. Total replacement. Between the main house, the sleeping quarters, and the stable, I'm so far over my budget. There isn't much left in my savings for renovations, and there's no way I can take out a personal loan, even if they would loan me the amount I need, which they probably wouldn't.

There's one more possibility, a last ditch effort to save my dream.

Jared's on his way over now. I've made spaghetti and meatballs, his favorite, in an attempt to smooth things over. He wasn't happy when he learned I waited out the storm with Wyatt. I reminded him I had no choice. The storm was powerful enough to uproot three of the mature trees that line High Street. He changed the subject after that, telling me about a man who'd come into the bank that day and opened a checking account. He was dressed in a well-cut suit, and told Jared he's thinking of moving some business to Sierra Grande.

Tonight, my plan is to find out that guy's name. If he's thinking of moving 'business', whatever that consists of, to this town, maybe he'd also be interested in investing in a local business. Bonus points if this business partner would prefer to remain *silent*.

Jared arrives at seven precisely. He wears a light blue button-down tucked into crisp khakis, and a contrite smile.

"I've missed you the last few days," he murmurs into my hair when he hugs me.

"I've been busy meeting with roofers." My answer presses into his shoulder.

"Even at night?"

I bristle at the light admonishment. This is a new side to Jared, this possessiveness, and I don't care for it. "The noodles are probably boiling over." I step away from him and dart to the kitchen.

My mother didn't give me any good advice except for one piece, and it's something that's always stuck out to me. *"If it feels wrong, it probably is. And that, Jo, applies to just about everything in life."*

Jared's reaction to Wyatt feels wrong. I can understand him feeling threatened, because Wyatt is the kind of person who could take a thin shred of insecurity and magnify it. But what Jared says and does after he feels that emotion is up to him. And he's not painting himself in a good light.

I finish the spaghetti while Jared leans against the counter in the kitchen and watches. We talk about his coworkers at the bank, about the scene Waylon Guthrie caused when he was drunk at the park yesterday, and the way the uprooted trees on High Street make it look like a grin with missing teeth. There's a tiny dip in conversation after the trees are mentioned, and I know it's because Jared is thinking about the storm.

Dinner is ready, and Jared opens the bottle of red wine I've set out on the table. He compliments the meal and raves about the homemade meatballs. I tell him about the general consensus of the roofers, and how it's going to sink me if I don't get an investor. "So I was wondering," I hesitate, swirling my spaghetti into a nest. "If you can tell me who that mystery businessman was who opened an account at the bank? Maybe he'd be interested?"

Jared swipes a napkin across his lips. "Sawyer Bennett."

"Sawyer Bennett," I repeat, letting the name roll around on my tongue. "Why does it sound familiar?"

Jared shrugs. "I think it's just one of those names, you know?"

I grab my wine, pressing the cool glass rim to my bottom lip. "Do you know where he's staying?"

"The Sierra." Jared leans back, pressing a hand to the top of his stomach. "But he did say he loves the blueberry muffins at The Bakery—"

"Duh," I interrupt, and Jared smiles knowingly. There isn't a person in this town who doesn't wait impatiently for the once-a-week delivery of the best blueberry muffins from a neighboring bakery in the town of Sugar Creek.

"Stake out The Bakery, and I bet you'll find Sawyer."

"How will I know it's him?"

Jared chuckles. "You'll know."

We finish eating, and Jared joins me in the cleanup. I'm washing the bowl I used to mix the meatballs when he brings up Wyatt.

"I know this is a sore spot for you, but I need to ask you something. It has to do with Wyatt."

I keep cleaning, making sure to wash the bowl twice because it housed raw meat. It's giving me a great excuse not to look at Jared for more than a cursory glance.

"Okay," I say.

Jared takes the bowl from me and rinses it, then places it on a dish towel beside the sink. He turns off the water, leaving me with soapy hands and the next dish in line to be cleaned. His move forces my gaze to meet his.

"Jo, I want you to fire Wyatt. I can tell he likes you, and I don't think it's good for our relationship."

I stare at him, absorbing his sentence. My eyes flicker over his straight nose, his long eyelashes, the tiny dot of a scar on his earlobe from the time he let his cousin pierce his ear with the help of an ice cube and an apple. It didn't go so well.

The idea that Wyatt likes me is absurd. Wyatt is a flirt. He blankets his charm on everyone in this town, with very few exceptions. I've lost count of the number of times I've seen him chatting up the two old women who sit outside Marigolds and gossip about the town.

I take a second dish towel from beside the sink, curling it around my fingers. "Wyatt's not a paid employee. I can't fire him."

"Great," Jared says quickly. "Makes it easier to let him go."

Irritation pricks at my shoulder blades. "I can't do that, Jared."

His voice hardens. "Why not?"

I'm not going to tell him about Wyatt's agreement with the sheriff, so I say, "Wyatt needs to help on the Circle B. And he's free labor, which you know I need more than ever right now. So please, trust that I know what I'm doing."

"Have you seen the way he looks at you?"

My head shakes as I brush aside the nonsense question. "It doesn't matter how Wyatt looks at me, Jared. I'm a grown woman and my jeans and panties aren't going to go flying from my body just because Wyatt looks at me a certain way."

Jared, who isn't usually so stubborn, slips his hands into the pockets of his pants. "I hate to do this, Jo, but if you're not going to kick Wyatt off the job, then we're through. I can't keep spending my days at the bank knowing you're alone with him at an abandoned ranch, doing God knows what."

God knows what? Is this man serious? My hands tighten around the dishcloth I'm still holding. "I've given you no reason not to trust me."

Jared looks at me for a long moment. "I'm sorry to make you choose, Jo. It's either me, or it's him." Jared brushes a kiss on my cheek, then he walks out of the kitchen, and a moment later the front door closes.

I pour another glass of wine, sit down on the couch, and call Jared. He answers on the second ring. His window must be down while he's driving, because the air makes it hard to hear him.

"Hang on," he says, and in a few seconds it's back to normal. "Are you calling to tell me to come back?"

I blink. "No, Jared. I'm sorry, I'm not. I'm calling to tell you it's not necessary to drag this on. I think you and I are better off as friends."

He sucks in a breath. "Classic. Wyatt Hayden stole my girlfriend. I don't think anyone will be surprised by that."

I bristle. "That's not what happened, Jared. We aren't right together, and it has nothing to do with Wyatt."

"I've never thought of you as a liar, but here you are, lying."

"I'm going to go now, Jared, before you say something you regret."

The line goes dead.

My head falls back against the couch. A small tear rolls down my cheek. If I am lying, it's not to Jared. What I said to him was the truth.

But when it comes to Wyatt? He seems to be able to coax strong emotions from me.

Emotions a person just might lie to themselves about.

16

WYATT

I take the lumber off the cart, sliding it into my truck bed and taking care not to give myself any splinters. Normally I don't drive so far for lumber, but I wanted to make Mrs. Calhoun's raised planter out of cedar, and for that, I had to travel.

Since I was here, I also grabbed everything I'd need to replace Jo's sagging front porch and the stairs. I don't want her having to avoid the weak spots like she has been. What if she forgets one day?

I finish loading, then hop in my truck, shifting into reverse and immediately hitting my brakes.

"What the fuck is this?" I say to myself, staring at the sight in my rearview mirror. Dan Howard, also known as the useless Sierra Grande police officer, is one lane over, working with two other men to fill their trucks with lumber.

It's a fuck ton of wood for people who don't drive work trucks. Dan is dressed in plain clothes, a basic T-shirt and jeans, but the guys he's with look like they've seen better days. I can't see details from here, but my hackles are raised. Something about this is off.

Dan glances around, trying way too hard to be nonchalant. He climbs into a sedan, the other two guys get into their respective trucks. Dan leaves first, and almost five minutes later, the first truck pulls out, followed by the second.

Followed by me.

ALL THE WAY TO SIERRA GRANDE THEY GO. THEY SKIRT THE town, taking the turnoff that will eventually lead them to the HCC if they stay on the winding road leading up in elevation. But I have a feeling that's not what's going to happen.

I'm right. Up ahead, at a small bend in the road, they ease their trucks onto a nearly grown-over side road. It'd be easy to dismiss it as a relic of days gone by, a place nobody goes because how could anybody get there?

Except I know where it leads.

A few years ago, I'd watched Dixon drive this same path. I was on horseback, taking Wes's horse Ranger out for exercise because he was too busy. I'd been hidden by trees when a beat-up truck went driving by, turned off the road, and ambled up the gently sloping hill.

I already knew who it was, and the red warning flags were flying. I pointed Ranger in the same direction as the truck, and we traveled parallel, hidden from view. The truck didn't have to go more than a quarter mile through that thick brush before the foliage cleared. It was as if someone had maintained the road but left the entrance overgrown to keep it from being something anybody would notice. Eventually, the dirt road ended and the driver got out.

Dixon didn't even bother looking around, so sure that nobody had followed him. He took off on foot, due north. I stayed stock still and watched him until he disappeared from my sight. I waited another ten minutes, then went back the way I came. The next day, I retraced my steps, this time with Warner's horse, and when I found no sign of Dixon's truck, I continued on in the direction he'd walked. Eventually I came upon a clearing, with a shitty little house built into the middle. The windows were painted black, so I couldn't see in, and I knew better than to open the door. By then I'd surmised it was a meth lab, though I couldn't be sure it was operational.

This is how I know where these two sketchy looking guys are headed now. And the lumber they're toting tells me they're rebuilding the structure that exploded one night two years ago, with Dixon inside.

I keep going until I find a section of road wide enough for me to turn around. When I pass back by going the opposite direction, I look at the little turnoff. It's so tucked in, you'd miss it if you didn't know it was there.

I want to know what they're doing building up there. And I want to know who they are.

It's late afternoon by the time I finish with Mrs. Calhoun's garden bed. I have enough cedar leftover I can make a second one for my mom. I don't have time right now though. I'd like to get this one delivered to Mrs. Calhoun and get back here so I can work on Jo's porch and stairs.

Speaking of Jo, I haven't seen her today. Usually she's here somewhere, either working alongside me or researching various topics about building structures, running a business, and marketing. Her tenacity is admirable, but I don't particularly like coming up against it. I think we've made progress though. The afternoon of the monsoon felt like a step in the right direction.

Where the right direction is, remains a question. Friendship, I suppose. As much as I'd like to make Jared nothing but a memory, I can't. He is obviously good for Jo, in the way like attracts like. What do I even have to give her? My daddy issues? A slice of the chip I wear on my shoulder?

Sighing, I lift the garden bed and lay it on its side on my tailgate, gently sliding it all the way in. I close the gate, and gather my things, but leave the sawhorse and my tools out. I won't be gone long.

Like always, Mrs. Calhoun sits in her chair on the front porch. She waves when I pull up.

"Hello, young man," she calls.

"Hello, Mrs. Calhoun," I greet her, going to the back of my truck and lowering the gate. "I found something on the side of the road. It's bulk trash week in town." It most certainly is not, but she won't know that. Removing the garden bed, I carry it toward her.

She stands up and puts her hand to her chest. "Is that what I think it is?" Her hands clap in front of her. I open my mouth to answer but she says, "It's a trough. Where my horses can eat."

I stumble over my words and recover. "Mrs. Calhoun,

this is a garden bed, so you don't have to bend over to garden on the ground. See?" I set it down and stick my hand in the deep space. "Fill it with soil, toss in your seeds, and when it's time to tend, everything is right in front of you instead of being on the ground."

She holds onto the rail and walks down the few stairs. "Well, I'll be. Look at that. I can't wait to tell my sons."

I pause for a beat, not sure how to move forward, then ask, "Your sons?"

"My grandsons, I mean. Here they come now."

She's right. A truck pulls into her driveway. It's followed by a second.

The trucks, I already know. It's the men driving them who are a mystery to me. But that's about to change.

"I'm going to get everyone some iced tea," Carol tells me, going back into the house.

Both men get out. They are about the same height, but where one is thin, the other is overweight. Pretty quickly I figure out who's the leader of the twosome, judging by how one keeps looking to the other for guidance on how to behave right now.

The thinner of the two steps forward. I do the same, striding across the small grass yard to meet him.

I hold out a hand. "Wyatt Hayden." He shakes my hand, realization dawning in his eyes.

"Ricky Marks." We drop hands. He nods back toward his brother. "That's Chris, my brother."

He comes forward, and we repeat the handshake.

"Hayden, huh?" Ricky says, rocking back on his heels. His teeth are tinged yellow with brown stains spreading out at the gum line.

I shrug. "That's what they tell me."

"Interesting. Did you know my cousin, Dixon?"

I shake my head slowly back and forth. "Can't say that I did."

"Huh." Ricky crosses his arms, and I don't miss the pockmarks dotting his pale skin. "Could've sworn someone in town said he died on Hayden land."

"Well, they were mistaken. Dixon's meth house exploded just a ways off my family's land. We cooperated with authorities, and they determined the explosion was a result of your cousin's activities." I make a regretful sound with my lips. "Too bad. I'm sure he was a nice guy before he got into that stuff."

Chris is quiet, looking around, like he's not tuned in to the conversation. The lights are on in his head, but nobody is home. Ricky is a different story. He has a cunning air about him, sly like a fox and just as intelligent. Wes thought the same of Dixon, and he wasn't wrong.

Behind me, the screen door slams. Mrs. Calhoun stands on the porch, looking at the three of us with happy surprise. "Well, when did you all get here? I didn't even hear you pull in." Her animation, her cheerfulness at seeing us, does nothing but make my stomach sink. She's getting worse.

"Grandma, can you make us some tea?" Ricky calls.

"Sure can," she answers, retreating into the house.

"How is it you know my grandma?" Ricky asks. Suspicion rings in his tone. This is what I mean by intelligent. He senses I'm here for a reason others might overlook.

"Small town, you know? Everyone knows everyone. She's been on her own out here, and I drove by once and noticed some things that needed fixing. I asked around and nobody could tell me if she had any family, so I drove out here and asked her myself. She said she didn't have anyone, so I offered to help her out."

"That's awfully nice of you." Ricky picks at a scab on his arm, then realizes he's doing it and stops.

"It's funny, your grandma only talks about her one son and grandchild. She never mentioned either of you."

"Yeah, well," Ricky looks at Chris, finding nothing but a blank stare. He lowers his voice and says, "We did some time. Petty theft. We were down on our luck and made some bad choices. I think Grandma's a bit embarrassed by it, not that she would ever admit that."

I nod. "Right, right."

Ricky walks around me, stopping to turn back. Not shockingly, Chris copies him. "Thanks for helping out when we weren't around, but I think we can take it from here."

I give him a hard look, which he returns with a lifted chin. "No problem," I answer.

The brothers are walking toward the house when I say something else. Ricky turns back around sharply. Chris stumbles when he turns. "What was that?" Ricky asks sharply.

"I asked if you've been cutting down trees. You smell like lumber."

Ricky's eyes narrow.

I smile and raise a hand. "Have a good day."

17

JO

I woke up to an email from my mom.

Travis has been difficult recently. Maybe it runs in the family. This is the age when you started making life hard for me.

Sometimes, I dream about strangling her.

"Travis?"

"Yeah?"

I switch the phone to speaker and place it on my dresser. "Normally people say hello when they answer the phone."

"Very funny," he says, sullen. Not abnormal for a fifteen-year-old.

I snap my bra into place and pull a shirt over my head. "How are you?"

"Fine."

One-word answers aren't atypical for his age range either, and I'm used to it. "Are you sure about that? You don't sound fine."

"What do you want me to say? Life is great, it's so wonderful here, Mom and Henri are delightful."

"Can I assume the opposite of everything you said and land somewhere near the truth?"

This draws a huffy laugh. I'll take it. Travis has floppy, messy hair that he pushes aside when he laughs, and I picture him doing it now.

"They hate me, Jo."

"Who hates you?" I push my feet into my Adidas sneakers. "I'll beat them up."

"Mom, for starters."

"I'll beat her up."

Travis laughs again. "She's tiny, but I think she might be scrappy."

"So she bites my ankles, who cares?" I'm probably the last person to ever get in a physical confrontation, but if the idea of it is making a hostile teenager smile, I'll let it roll. "Who else, Travis? Who else should meet the wrong end of my fist?"

"Henri."

"Well..." Henri clocks in upward of six feet tall and twice my weight. "Maybe *I'll* be the one biting *his* ankles."

This time, Travis doesn't laugh. I know it hurts, feeling like your parent doesn't like the person you're growing into. I'll never forget the dirty looks from my mother when I began to question the church's motives and teachings, or the look of disgust on her face after everything happened, the way she cold-shouldered me.

"What happened?" I ask Travis. I'm marveling, in a sick and twisted way, that the same woman could manage to hurt both of us even when she's an entirely different person now.

"Why are you asking? Did that dumb guidance counselor call again?"

I stop what I'm doing and glance down at the phone, like I'm going to be able to see him even though it's a regular call. "Mom emailed," I admit.

"She doesn't even really care," Travis bites out.

I stifle my sigh. "She cares in her own way." God, I'm tired of saying that to him. To myself.

"Mom's a bitch."

"You won't get any argument from me about that." I coax my hair into a ponytail and ask, "So why don't you tell me what happened?"

Travis blows out a noisy breath. "I cut school and she found out."

I'm careful to keep my groan safely tucked away in my throat. "Again? Why?" Now I'm wishing I'd FaceTimed Travis instead of calling him. I needed to get dressed though, and in the interest of not embarrassing myself or him, opted for the call.

"I didn't want to go to school."

I roll my eyes. "Well, yeah. Says every high schooler everywhere. Where did you go?"

"Nowhere."

I swipe my phone from the dresser and take it off speaker. I have ten minutes to get to The Bakery to claim a table and wait for Sawyer Bennett. "Travis, I have something to tell you, and I don't want you to mention it to Mom. I bought an old ranch and I'm fixing it up. When it's finished, you can come live with me again. If you want to, I mean. But," I say sternly when he gets excited. "No bullshit. I want you in school. No skipping class just so you can go *nowhere*."

"How long?" Travis asks. "How long before it's finished?"

"I'm in the process of figuring all that out."

By the time we get off the phone, Travis's voice sounds a

whole lot less like *I hate everybody and everybody hates me*, and a lot more optimistic.

I feel a little bit bad I didn't tell him what the purpose of the ranch will be. But only a little bit. If he knows ahead of time, he'll never come. The last thing Travis wants to be thought of is a delinquent, because he's not. Not really, anyway. He drew the short straw when it came to parentage. As did I.

I look in the mirror, square my shoulders, and head out of the house.

It's time for me to go snag an investor.

LIKE JARED SAID, I KNOW IMMEDIATELY WHO SAWYER Bennett is.

He wears a navy blue suit like it was customized for his body. Underneath is a white shirt, no tie, hipster-cool socks peeking out from his leather tennis shoes. I can't imagine him lasting long in this town of blue-collar workers and ranchers, but stranger things have happened.

"Half a dozen blueberry muffins, please." He orders from Greta, the owner and operator of this place. I can't remember a time when Greta hasn't been behind the counter, either ringing up orders or refilling the displays.

"Could've told you that myself, Mr. Bennett," Greta responds, grabbing a piece of tissue paper from a box on the counter. "How's it going out there? Did you find that retail space you were looking for?"

He nods, and I watch his profile. He's very... pretty. Well-kept. I imagine he's fastidious about his appearance. He smiles at Greta when she hands him the bag. I'm hoping he'll take an open table and sit down, but he strides for the door.

Wiping my slick palms on my thighs, I hustle from the table where I've been conducting my stakeout and catch him on the sidewalk. "Excuse me?" I call.

He turns, searching my face. "Can I help you?"

I take a step closer. "Are you Sawyer Bennett?"

He eyes me. "That depends. Am I going to receive a slap or a medal?"

I smile. "I guess that depends on the answer to my question." Extending a hand, I tell him my name. He shakes my hand. "I'd introduce myself, but that would be redundant. Apparently you already know me?"

"My boyfriend, Jared"—small fib, we're over—"told me he met you recently and mentioned you're looking to move some business here. And I was thinking," I forge ahead, because I'm not sure how much longer I'll have his attention. "I have a business venture that needs an investor."

Sawyer's head tips sideways. "Is that right?"

Here goes nothing. The worst he can say is no. "I bought an abandoned ranch on the outskirts of town with the plan to rebuild it into a ranch for troubled youth. Things happened a little faster than I thought and I'm in over my head and my pockets are empty." I take a breath. "So if you're looking for an investment opportunity, it's literally standing in front of you."

He quirks an eyebrow, but aside from that, remains perfectly still. "Where did you say it was?"

"Southwest of town, an old ranch called the Circle B." His eyebrows shoot up. "I'm renaming it though," I add. "I know it's not the right name for what I'm planning. It'll be called Wildflower."

He nods slowly. "I'm interested. How about I meet you there this afternoon at three? I have a few things to attend to."

"Sounds great," I answer, keeping a lid on my excitement.

"Nice to meet you, and I'll see you soon, Miss Shelton."

I nod, but honestly I can't feel my face right now. There's too much adrenaline pumping through my veins. "See you soon, Mr. Bennett."

He walks away, and I go back inside and order two blueberry muffins to go.

The shred of hope in my heart has brightened up my entire day, eclipsing the streak of sadness I feel when I pass the bank.

There aren't a ton of dating options in this small town, and I just blew through one of them.

But I might save my ass, and Travis's happiness, so all in all, I'm not too upset right now.

18

WYATT

"Why the fuck does he buy these things?" I grumble, fighting to get the bronc into the round pen. You'd think someone had his balls in a vise the way he jumps and flails.

"I think your dad likes fucking with you," Denny says, gritting his teeth as he helps me coax the horse into the pen.

"Keep your nose where it belongs, Denny," Josh barks, glaring at him. Josh is in charge of the cowboys, and he takes his job seriously. Friends or not, Josh wants Denny to keep out of the Hayden family's personal business.

Denny is right, though. My dad loves to buy the meanest bronc he can find, then ask me to tame it. I don't know why. Just because I'm good at it doesn't mean I should be depended on to do it. Like my mom says after every family dinner, '*I might be better at doing the dishes than the rest of you, but that doesn't make me the only person capable of it*'. We all trade off who does the dishes, except for Gramps. That old codger pretends to be asleep. The last time I called him out, he opened his eyes, winked at me, then shut them and pretended to snore when my mom walked into the living room.

Denny and Josh head out to work, and I stay with the new horse. He's beautiful, a light-colored Arabian with a black muzzle. This breed is known for being spirited, and judging from the way he's charging around the ring, I'd say he leans more toward hot-tempered than just plain spirited. He runs and runs like he's so fucking mad at his current situation. I wonder if he would run himself to death, just to spite us.

My dad lumbers up behind me. If I didn't recognize his heavy gait, I'd sense his formidable presence. He comes to stand beside me.

"Hello, Son." His voice is deep, scratching across the inches separating our arms.

Dust dances up from the bronc's hooves and floats into the sunshine. "Hey, Dad."

He sniffs and props a foot on the bottom rung of the wooden fence. "What do you think of this one?" He pushes his chin to indicate the rearing and snorting horse.

I scratch at my chin. "I can't figure out why you bought it."

"Never mind that," he says roughly. "Do you think he's pliable?"

The horse bucks past us. "Do you think he looks like he wants to be trained?"

"Dammit, Wyatt. Answer the question."

The horse's solid muscles ripple in the bright midday sun. Something about all that indignation is... beautiful. Vital. Excess emotion means you're alive enough to feel something.

All horses are trainable. They just have to be broken

first. And the ones that are as damn crazy as this one need to find someone to respect. I pull my ball cap lower on my head and shift my weight to my other foot. "He's trainable. Let him wear himself out. Tired horses behave better."

My dad breathes a chuckle. "We used to run you boys around until you'd drop into bed. Same thing."

I want to smile, but I can't. It feels false, listening to him fondly share a memory of my childhood.

The horse wears himself out, slowing until finally he comes to a stop. I step into the arena. He scuffs at the ground and eyes me, watching me walk to him.

I don't know what it is about me that calms a horse. Considering how much turmoil churns through me on any given day, it doesn't make a whole hell of a lot of sense. I step up to him and look him in his large, dark eyes. I can feel what's inside of him, dormant now but on display a few minutes ago. He's afraid, and he knows only to fight or run. This is when I tell him he need not fear me. Some cowboys use violence to break a horse, but the thought sickens me. Trust and respect, that's all a horse needs. And it starts with a staring contest.

Eventually, he dips his head low, breaking our eye contact. I turn around, heading for the gate. Behind me, I hear his clomping hooves.

I lead the horse to the stable, getting him set up in a stall. My dad's waiting for me outside.

"You name it?" he asks.

"You keeping it?" I counter. Oftentimes he sells the horses I tame.

"If you want it. You need a horse, don't you?"

I nod slowly. Unlike Wes and Warner, who hold tight to Ranger and Titan, I rotate horses. But this one feels special, so I say the first name that comes to my mind. "Amigo."

"Amigo it is."

We head toward the homestead, and I veer off when we get closer. "I need to get going to Jo's. She needs my help." I was too bothered by my run-in with Mrs. Calhoun's grandsons and never got back there yesterday to work on the porch.

My dad hooks two thumbs into his belt loops. "She's been needing a lot of it these days."

I stare at him. "Do you expect me to believe the sheriff got the idea for me to do community service all on his own? I like the guy, but he's not that smart."

"I don't know what you're talking about," my dad answers, but the slightly upturned corner of his mouth says differently.

"The fuck you don't," I say under my breath. I turn toward my truck, but my dad's voice brings me back around.

"What the fuck do you have to be mad about, Wyatt? Hayden's work hard, and I expect the same of you. I've had about enough of you doing whatever the fuck it is you do. This ranch needs a second-in-command, and I'm ashamed you're not stepping up."

The muscles in my upper back coil. "Did you say the same to Warner?"

"He put in his time. He sacrificed, he kept up the Hayden name while Wes was gone. You got the Hayden name by birth, but you damn sure aren't earning it."

I force my lower lip to stop quivering. "I know you're real disappointed my last name is Hayden. You've been disappointed since the day I was born."

"What did you just say?" It's my mother speaking now,

standing on the front porch of the homestead, her arms crossed.

"Ask him." I point a stiff finger at my dad. I pass her on my way into the house. "Ask him why he's hated me since the day he laid eyes on me."

I don't wait around to hear more. I walk through the house, heading toward the door that leads out back. From there, it's a straight shot to my cabin. If it weren't for Dakota standing in the kitchen holding Colt, I'd keep going.

"Hi, Colt." I soften my voice, the pain inside me pushed aside for the moment. They call me the baby and horse whisperer, but they've got it all wrong. It's the babies and horses who whisper to me, soothing the savage beast within.

Dakota turns to look at me, but Colt's head stays fixed in its position. I put a hand on Dakota's shoulder and lean around her into my nephew's field of vision. Once he spots me, he begins to kick his legs. I press a kiss to his temple and tell Dakota I have to run.

There is worry in her eyes, and I assume it's concern about me, so I kiss her forehead too, and keep going out the back door.

I stomp across the brick pavers that make up the back patio and step onto the grass. Once I cross the backyard, I'll hit the trees and be swallowed up by pines. After that, it's a short walk to my cabin.

"You got a bee in your bonnet?" I hear the old, grumbling voice behind me.

A smile tugs at my mouth. I turn around and find Gramps sitting at the outdoor couch, in the direct sunshine. I walk over and stand in front of him, giving him some shade. "Why does it seem like you're always sitting in various places around the homestead?"

"Cause I am. What the fuck else is there for me to do?" He leans over a few inches, half his face bathed in sun again. "Get out of my sun."

I do as he says, but ask, "You want skin cancer?"

"Fuck it," he answers.

I laugh, but it's not an altogether happy feeling. It wasn't too long ago that he was telling us he was old but still had some party left in him. Now it feels like he's losing a bit of that spark, loosening his grip on life. I hate to think of what that means.

He taps a wrinkled finger on his thigh. "You spend a good deal of time stomping around this place, but today it seems like you're a little extra pissed off. What did your dad do now?"

"What makes you think it was my dad?"

"When isn't it your dad?"

I've never talked to him about my father. So Gramps isn't just always sitting in various places around this house, but he's also watching from those seats.

"He doesn't like me, Gramps."

"Is that what you think?"

"Yes."

When he doesn't respond, I say, "This is the part where you tell me I'm wrong."

He makes a noise with his lips, like he's blowing a raspberry. "Your dad's the only one who can do that. My words will bounce right off you."

He's right. He could tell me I'm wrong until the cows come home, but not a damn one of his words would penetrate.

"Sounds to me like you need to talk to your dad."

I lean my elbows on my knees and clasp my hands

between them. "When have you ever known my dad to talk about feelings and shit like that?"

"Never. But that's the point, isn't it?" His left leg twitches and shakes. "He never does and that's made it so that now he needs to."

"I suppose." I rub my eyes. "I need to get going. I have some work to do out on the Circle B." At some point we're going to have to start calling it by its new name. Maybe when Jo gets the sign up.

"I heard about that from your parents. You're doing an awful lot of work out there."

"Jo needs the help."

"Is that right?"

I give him a slow look. "Yes, that's right."

"That all it is? Forgive me, Grandson, but I've never seen you go this far out of your way for someone."

I look down at the ground, studying the way the pavers come together, the corners meeting. "She's special." I like the way she keeps me on my toes, how she calls me on my shit. I like the little mole on her hairline at the back of her neck, and the way she bites the side of her lip when she's working through a problem. Mostly I admire how brave she is, taking on a project like transforming an old ranch and being willing to learn on her feet.

"You should ask her out."

"It's that easy, huh?" I chuckle. "She has a boyfriend."

"Bah." He waves his hand. "Don't let that stop you. Run that roadblock over with your truck. When I first met your grandma there was another boy who was sweet on her."

"What did you do?"

He snickers. "He was a roadblock I ran over with my truck."

"Don't you mean your horse-drawn carriage?"

"Fuck off. How old do you think I am?"

"Do you want me to answer that?"

He cackles. "You always were a mouthy son of a bitch."

I laugh. "Still am."

He's quiet, then he says, "This life is short, Wyatt. If you want Jo, go get her. If you want to tell your dad all the ways he's hurt you, go tell him. There'll come a day when you spend more time thinking back on what you didn't do, and less on what you actually did. Regrets are no fun, Wyatt. I guess the goal in life is to have fewer of them."

I lean back and look at him. He has less hair on his head than he used to, and it seems to have chosen to grow from his ears and nose instead. Rows of wrinkles feather his face, and brown spots speckle his skin. Still, the man is sharp as a tack. He sees what others don't, and it might not be because he has endless hours to watch us all going about our days. Maybe he's just insightful.

"Thanks for the advice, Gramps. You've given me a lot to think about."

He nods. "Get going, Wyatt. You have work to do."

I pat his leg and stand up. "Do you want help getting into the house?"

"You want your ass whooped?"

"Hah." I laugh once, loudly. "Fine. Get up on your own, old man."

"I'll get up when I'm damn well ready to," he counters. Always has to have the last word.

I leave him there where I found him, sunning himself like a rattlesnake, and keep going on my way. His words reverberate through me as I make the walk over to my place and gather my things. I get in my truck and head over to Jo's, trying to sort out my feelings as I go.

I don't recognize the car parked next to Jo's at the Circle B. It's a Mercedes SUV, matte gunmetal gray with powder-coated rims. Definitely not a vehicle that belongs to someone living in Sierra Grande. Probably not a contractor's either, or really anybody working on a jobsite. They tend to drive trucks.

I start with the main house, looking for Jo and this mystery person. When I don't find her inside, I walk around back and hear her talking before I round the corner and see her.

Her back is to me, and she stands beside a man. She's gesturing, and he's nodding. His hands are tucked into the pockets of his suit.

Nobody in this town wears a suit, not even that banker boyfriend of Jo's.

"Hello," I say, coming to a stop a few feet from them. Jo startles and whips around. The man is slower, rotating his shoulders my way with a stoic expression.

The only way to know he recognizes me is the slight widening of his eyes. It's the asshole from the night at the Chute that landed me at the police station, and eventually, here.

"Wyatt, this is Sawyer Bennett. He's a potential investor." She smiles hard at me, like she's saying *don't fuck this up,* but the grin sweetens when she looks at Sawyer. "Mr. Bennett, this is Wyatt Hayden."

I stick out my hand for a handshake and smile like I've never seen him before. There's no fucking way I'm calling him Mr. Bennett. "Sawyer, it's nice to meet you."

"Likewise," he answers, shaking my hand. His eyes are as gray as his G-Wagon.

I believe you can learn a lot about a person by the way they shake hands, and I have to begrudgingly admit Sawyer presents himself well in that department. No limp dick handshake, as Wes would call it.

"Do you work for Jo?" Sawyer asks.

"I do." I nod at the surrounding land. "I'm helping Jo make sense of the ranch and what needs to be done."

Sawyer rocks back on his heels. "Do you have special knowledge in that area?"

His question strikes me as odd, but if he's thinking of sinking money into this place then maybe it makes sense. "I grew up on a cattle ranch." I don't throw around my last name, mostly because in this town everyone already knows, but I never do it when I get the chance. It's obnoxious.

"Gotcha." Sawyer looks at Jo. "I like what I see, Miss Shelton—"

"Jo, please, Mr. Bennett."

Sawyer's lips curve into a polite smile. "If you're Jo, then I'm Sawyer."

Jo nods. Her hands curl into fists at her sides, a sure sign she's excited for his next words.

"Jo, I'm going to talk with my lawyers and we'll get a contract over to your lawyer. Send me their contact info?"

Jo's face falls. "I, uh..."

"We'll get you the info," I assure him.

Jo's worried gaze meets mine and I wink at her. She

walks Sawyer around the side of the house. He looks back and I raise a hand in goodbye, then go into the house.

Jo finds me in the master bath. I'm stretching a tape measure across the floor when she walks in. She's grinning like a fool, like she has just won the lottery. Which, in a way, she has.

"Ohmygosh ohmygosh ohmygosh." Her voice is high-pitched, her hands running through her hair. Her smile falls. "Is this going to work? I don't have a lawyer."

"You do now," I say, stepping on the measuring tape to keep it in place, then stretching it out a little more.

"What are you talking about?" She gathers her hair and moves it to one shoulder. Fidgets with her bracelet. Rubs her lips together. She's too excited to stop moving.

I press my thumb to the extended measuring tape to keep it in line and jot down the measurements. My thumb lifts and the tape snaps back into the holder. I stand and clip the tape to my tool belt. "You can borrow the Hayden family lawyer."

She frowns and leans her lower back against the bathroom counter. "Does it work that way?"

"As long as Chelsea's making three fifty an hour, I don't think she cares what documents she looks at."

Jo's eyes widen. "Three hundred and fifty dollars an hour? I'm in the wrong business."

"Same."

Jo rolls her eyes. "Oh, please. You're from the largest cattle ranch in Arizona. I don't want to hear it."

"That doesn't make me rich."

"It sure doesn't make you poor."

Her comment strikes a nerve. The Hayden name precedes me, always. It creates an image, an expectation, and I've spent so much of my life feeling like I don't fit the mold. The assumption that I'm so much like my family rankles me simply because of how much I feel like I don't fit in with them.

I shove the piece of paper with the measurements into my pocket. "Things aren't always what they seem."

"No shit," Jo murmurs. She taps her fingers on the countertop, her expression thoughtful. "Maybe I should find my own lawyer."

I raise my eyebrows and tip my chin up slightly, waiting for her to explain why.

She looks flustered. Her mouth opens and closes a couple times. She says, "I don't want to be indebted to you."

Indebted? She wouldn't be. And also... why the fuck not? What is it about me she dislikes so much that she can't stand feeling like she owes me something?

My mouth forms a hard line. I look into her eyes, the blue so much like a storm right now. The muscles in her right cheekbone twitch.

"I could make it easy for you." My voice is thick. I'm talking about the lawyer, but... am I really?

"Make what easy?" Her voice shakes.

"The lawyer. If you use mine, you won't have to find another one."

She shakes her head. "Jared—"

"Fuck that guy," I blurt out.

Her eyes widen. "I don't understand your problem with him, but—"

"I don't like the guy, Jo." I'm teetering on the edge now, knowing my next words could forever alter things between us. Here we go. "I especially don't like him for you."

Her lower lip dips in surprise, and her hands slice the air. "What do you expect me to do with that, Wyatt?"

I'm trying to tell her how I feel, but I don't know how to, and I'm afraid she'll laugh if I do. She has safe and stable Jared who will always say the right thing, do the right thing.

But there's something inside me, something that comes from the center of my heart, that tells me not to back down. Jo stares at me, arms crossed in front of her chest, her lips a stern line.

I step toward her, closing the distance so we're less than a foot apart. We were closer when we danced a few days ago, but this feels different. The air is electric, possibility crackling through it. I watch her face carefully as I lift my hand, my knuckles grazing her forearm. Her lips peel apart and her sharp intake of breath says more than words ever could.

I drag my touch up her arm, waiting for her to tell me to knock it off, but no such directive comes. She closes her eyes and swallows hard when my fingers feather over her collarbone.

This feels like a green light, so I come closer, my hand snaking up her throat and around to the nape of her neck. My fingers work into her hair, and I tug gently, tipping her head back. She drags in a thick, shaky breath. Her arms uncross and she leans her backside into the counter, her hands gripping the edge.

Jared fucking who?

A sigh slips from Jo's mouth when my lips ghost her throat. I press the tip of my tongue against her sweet skin and drag it up the length of her delicate neck.

"Jared—"

I growl, something unintelligible and animalistic. I should

be respectful of their relationship, but there isn't a single part of me that wants to. All I want is Jo. It's inconceivable she could be anyone else's. "I've seen you with him, Jo. He doesn't do this to you," I murmur against her flushed skin. "I haven't even kissed you yet, and you're trembling." I press small kisses along her jaw, prolonging the anticipation. She smells like heaven, like honeysuckle and orange peel, and I can't wait any longer. "I can already tell you're going to be the best thing I've ever tasted."

As soon as I say it, I'm hit with that same sense of déjà vu. The words are familiar, but I don't remember saying them.

Jo stiffens. The electric air between us catches fire, and she pushes me away. Her eyes hold fury, but also something like shame, which only confuses me further.

"You're pathetic," she hisses. She straightens a shirt that doesn't need to be straightened, just to have something to do with her hands. I stand in front of her, exposed even though I'm fully dressed.

"Do you think I'm stupid? Do you think I'd fall for this act *again*?" She huffs a derisive laugh while I try to figure out what she means by *again*.

She shakes her head as she watches me scramble to understand.

"What do you mean by 'again'?"

Her cheeks become flames. She crosses her arms, each hand gripping the opposite elbow. She stares at me. "We slept together on that trip we took down to Phoenix. You were too drunk to remember it, apparently." Her gaze falls to the floor.

"No way," I argue automatically. "There's no way I'd forget you, Jo." Her hair falls around her face, strands of pink peeking through. A flush sweeps over her cheeks, and she releases a deep breath.

"But you did, Wyatt." She takes a step, until she's close enough to touch me, one fingertip poking the center of my chest. "You have a small, flat scar on the inside of your upper thigh. I don't know how you got it, because we weren't doing much talking." Her eyes challenge me, daring me to dispute her claim a second time.

I have no words. Right now my brain cannot form an intelligent thought, and my mouth cannot produce a coherent sentence. The best I can do is shake my head slowly back and forth while I try to wade through this information.

Jo mistakes my headshake as me continuing to deny. She nods firmly, the tiny stud earrings she wears glinting in the sun that streams through the bathroom window. "We had sex on every flat surface in your hotel room. There isn't an inch of my body you haven't had your hands on, and... You. Don't. Remember. It." The last part of her sentence slips through clenched teeth.

I turn my hands over and stare at the pads of my fingertips, imagining them running over Jo's lush curves. The underside of her breasts. The warm path between her legs. It is a cruel, cruel punishment to not remember such a thing.

"What can I do to make this better?"

She steps back. "You can't. It's over. I liked you, Wyatt, and you humiliated me." She lifts her palms in the air. "I'm not saying it's all your fault. I'm a big girl, and I made my own choices that night. But I learned a lesson the hard way, and best believe I'm not planning to forget it."

"What lesson is that?"

Her eyes fill with tears. "That you, Wyatt Hayden, aren't worth the heartache." She walks out, her footsteps echoing through the empty house, leaving me alone with her parting words.

Like an arrow, swift and sure, they cut through bone and sinew, piercing my heart. If I've learned anything in the past month since I've come to help Jo, it's that I don't want to spend much time without her. I don't know what she's done to the inside of my chest, but it's irreversible.

To her, I'm not even worth the heartache.

But I used to be. That's what I will have to cling to, holding it out like a beacon of hope. There was a time when Jo thought I was worthy, and that's the place I need to get back to.

I've long since given up trying to convince my dad I'm worthy of the Hayden name. But for Jo, I'd spend forever trying to change her mind.

19
JO

SAWYER'S MONEY IS LIKE AN INJECTION OF EPINEPHRINE INTO the heart of Wildflower. Maybe that's why I've been able to finally start thinking of it by its new name. All of a sudden, it's *alive*.

Construction trucks, a cement mixer, a crew of men directed by Scott, the general contractor Dakota hired to build The Orchard.

After I'd come to my senses and stopped being hardheaded, I'd asked Wyatt for his lawyer's contact info. It's one of the few times we've spoken in the past three weeks. Once the papers were signed and the money transferred, I officially quit working at The Orchard so I could be here full-time.

Wildflower has a pulse now, a heartbeat, and for the first time I'm seeing it as something more than the worst, most impetuous mistake of my life.

Speaking of impetuous mistakes... Wyatt shows up every day, ready to help in any capacity. I keep thinking one day he'll be a no-show, and that will be it. I won't tell the sheriff, he'll go back to doing what Wyatt does, and this will be a blip in time. But, no. Wyatt shows up, takes direction from Scott, and works all day alongside the men who are being paid for their contribution.

I've thought over and over about what happened a few weeks ago, and the only logical conclusion is that Wyatt saw something he can't have, and that made him want it. *Me.*

I'd be lying through my teeth if I said that in that moment, with the bathroom countertop digging into my back and Wyatt's fingers trailing over my heated skin, I didn't want to give in. It was damn near impossible, and I was slip-sliding my way to a replay of that night in Phoenix, until he said those words.

I can already tell you're going to be the best thing I've ever tasted.

The same thing he said to me back then, the words that ensnared me like a rabbit in a trap. And I fell for it, the way I'm assuming other girls have. He'd used the line again because he doesn't remember using it on me once already. It took my embarrassment, threw fury on it, and created a combustible situation.

It's been awkward ever since. My muscles are stiff, my posture rigid when he's nearby. He says very little to me, but his presence looms large.

I watch him in secret when I can, swinging a hammer, smoothing concrete, laying out forms, and try to reconcile this man doing hard manual labor with the Wyatt I thought I knew. He doesn't look at me, not that I know of, anyway. I wonder if he's as affected from learning we slept together as he seemed to be. More than shocked, he appeared broken, as if me telling him had consequences reaching further than I can even guess.

I want to be angry at him. It's safest there, sitting in indignation like I have been for so long. But when he's lost in a task and I get the chance to study his face, the old feelings creep in. A buoyancy settles over me, and my limbs become weightless, making me wonder if I could fly. This is dangerous territory for me to be in.

He's working in the main house today, updating it the way Scott and I have planned. Refinishing the wood floors, new countertops, fresh paint on the walls. The bones of the house are good. It needs only TLC to make it a home.

I step into the house and overhear Scott complimenting Wyatt on the refinished cabinets in the master bath. "Why'd you start with those?" he asks.

"They were the ugliest shade of green. Jo really hated it. I think to her, it represented the project as a whole. I thought if I could make at least one improvement, it'd make her feel better."

I shrink back against the hallway wall, my hand pressed to my chest.

They keep going, moving on to another subject, and I scurry out before they see me.

"Do you want help with that wine order?" I point at the computer sitting open on the bar, and Dakota grins. She walks out from behind the bar at The Orchard and settles herself on the stool beside me.

Dakota wears a sleeping Colt in the baby sling, and she

adjusts herself carefully, being mindful of him. "You don't work here anymore, remember?"

"True." I nod. "But that doesn't mean I forgot everything the second I turned in my keys. I can still help out if you need it. Lord knows you've been helping me enough at Wildflower, and you definitely don't work there."

Dakota pushes away the computer. "Have I told you how much I love that name?"

I think back to the photos of the wildflowers growing in the spring. "It felt right."

"Have you thought about hiring yet?"

Pulling my notebook from my purse, I lay it open on the counter and turn until I find the right page. "Counselors, maybe two at first until there's a need for more. I'll need a professional therapist, for sure. That's the trickier one. How am I going to find someone like that?"

"I think the more important question is how people are going to find out about the place? You can have a brand-new facility and smiling employees, but without campers..." She shrugs. "You're dead in the water."

I wince. "Thanks."

"Sorry," she says. "That was harsh."

"Yet still true." As much as I hate to admit it.

Under the employee list, I make an asterisk and write in all caps, *MARKETING*.

Dakota runs to the kitchen and asks Brandon, the chef, to throw together an early lunch for us. "I don't know about you," she says when she returns. "But I'm starving. Breastfeeding makes me eat like a linebacker."

"I thought pregnancy did that."

She shakes her head, a piece of her strawberry blonde hair escaping from her messy bun. "Everything and anything baby-related makes me eat." She adjusts Colt, who doesn't even stir, and fixes me with a pointed look. "Can we talk about Wyatt? Because you haven't said two words about him and I think it's odd."

I shift, then realize it probably makes me look like I'm uncomfortable talking about Wyatt, so I tuck my hands under my thighs. "Wyatt's fine. Not much to discuss."

Dakota places a warm palm on my arm. Her eyes crinkle with concern. "Wyatt hasn't been himself around the homestead the past couple weeks. I thought maybe something happened."

I take a deep breath and swallow. "He's confusing. The way I feel is confusing. I carried a torch for him for a long time, and then I got over him." Guilt settles into me. "At least I thought I did. Spending time around him has made my anger disappear, and I need that anger so I can keep from liking him."

"Because you're dating Jared?"

I shake my head. "Jared and I broke up."

Dakota's eyes grow big. "You didn't tell me that."

I bite the side of my lower lip and shrug. "I forgot."

She laughs. "Obviously you're so heartbroken."

Remorse pokes through my stomach. "I cared about him. He was safe and stable."

"And *kind*?" Dakota's lip trembles with reined-in laughter.

"Yes," I laugh the word, then grow serious. "He felt like a natural next step in life, like what he was offering was where I was supposed to be heading. But then I started spending time around Wyatt, and I realized how much I don't really feel for Jared. Not that I didn't feel anything for him, only that I didn't feel enough. And I feel bad about that."

Dakota waves off my guilt. "Let's talk about why you think you need to keep from liking Wyatt."

"Because he's Wyatt Hayden. He's a scoundrel."

"Is he, though?"

"He's sleeping with his best friend's wife."

"Why do you think that?"

"The whole town knows it. His truck has been there how many times while Mickey's been gone? And he doesn't deny it."

"Does he confirm it?"

"Why would he?"

Brandon comes from the kitchen and sets down two plates. I offer a small smile and a thank you, which probably isn't good enough because I used to work here and genuinely liked Brandon, but I can't give any more than that right now.

"Jo, I think you need to look a little closer. The story that Wyatt's sleeping with his best friend's wife? That's all it might be. A story."

"What makes you so certain?"

"Wyatt may be a bit... unconventional, but he has a set of steel values, and they don't include what this town has convinced themselves he's capable of."

"Then why won't he defend himself? And Sara? She's taking the brunt of the gossip, too."

Dakota shrugs. "I don't have all the answers. Just the evidence."

Colt stirs, and Dakota gazes down at him, making kissing sounds. His eyes remain locked on her face, his expression unchanged. Dakota makes a big, dramatic face, and I startle. Colt's eyes grow big and his lips turn up into a smile.

And then Dakota starts to cry. Her reaction is so opposing that it takes me a moment to understand she's not happy.

"What's wrong," I ask, rubbing her shoulder. I don't think I've ever seen Dakota cry.

She swipes a finger under each eye and wipes them on her jeans. "I'm worried about Colt."

I'm not an expert by any means, but a cursory glance tells me he isn't displaying any obvious signs of a problem. "What are you worried about?"

She tips her head, her sigh soft and full of sadness. "He doesn't turn toward my voice. He should be doing that by now. He doesn't respond unless my expression changes in a big way."

Oh. That's what she was doing when she turned her kissing sounds into something overly expressive.

"Can you imagine what Wes will say if Colt has a hearing impairment? What if he's completely deaf? Wes's heart is set on passing the HCC down to his son."

For generations, the HCC has gone to the firstborn Hayden son.

"Dakota, I don't think you need to worry about Wes's feelings toward Colt. Wes loves that kid as ferociously as anyone would guess Wes Hayden would love his son. Look at his example. Beau has three sons who are different people, and he loves them the same."

Dakota stops crying and looks at me. "You think Beau loves his boys the same?"

"It seems that way from the outside."

She looks down and strokes Colt's cheek. "Beau loves his sons, nobody can dispute that, but I would never say he loves them the same."

"What do you mean?" I'm not sure if I want to know, but my curiosity doesn't stop me. I've been coexisting with the Hayden family for a long time, and they were always a bit like royalty. Shiny and pretty, something spectacular to look at. Hearing of their dysfunction takes a bit of shine off, and that's not necessarily a bad thing.

"You call Wyatt a scoundrel, but he didn't get to be the man he is all on his own. Just like you didn't get to be so independent and stubborn without some help along the way."

I give her comment a few seconds to sink in, then ignore it. "As far as Colt's hearing is concerned, impairment or not, he can be a cowboy. He can inherit the HCC."

Dakota's gaze drifts down to Colt. "I know. I shouldn't get so worked up, anyway. This is what I get for going on the internet instead of going to the doctor."

"Are you going to make him an appointment?"

She nods, her lips pursed.

"Dakota, I've known the Hayden family for fifteen years. I may not know their insides as well as you do, but I've been seeing their outsides for a long time, and if there's one thing I know, it's that they take care of their own. If Colt needs help, nothing will stop Wes or Beau, or even Warner and Wyatt, from making certain he gets the best of the best."

Dakota nods. "The Hayden men move mountains for those they love."

"Yes, they do."

We finish lunch, and when I drive home, Dakota's words echo through my mind. Is moving mountains the same as coming to Wildflower, working to physical exhaustion, and then doing it again the next day?

If so...

20

WYATT

If I thought it would help my situation, I would've brought flowers. Something tells me if I had, Shelby might have tossed them to the ground and stepped on them.

"She's not here," Shelby says, deadpan, a statue in her front door.

I use my foot to stop the door from closing. Shelby's expression remains locked in place, showing no sign of caring that I've stopped her. "Wyatt, do you want me to arrest you?"

"For what? I haven't done anything wrong."

"Since when? Ten seconds ago? I'm sure I can nab you for something in the past thirty minutes."

I laugh in a very obviously fake way.

Shelby's eyes narrow. "You already know Jo isn't here, so what do you want?"

"I want to talk to you about her."

She crosses her arms and stares at me. "Why?"

Here we go. "Because I have feelings for her and I need

to figure out how to make her see I'm not the guy from two years ago."

Shelby's gaze, previously trained on my face, now drops down the length of my body and back up, like she's checking me for signs of deception. She takes a step back and inclines her head to the rest of the house. "Come in."

I follow her into the living room. She stops me before I sit down, and offers to get us both a beer.

"No, thank you," I answer, and judging by the pleased look on her face, I think I just passed a test.

She disappears and returns with two glasses of water. She sets the water on the coffee table in front of me and takes a seat opposite me on a chair. She draws her feet into her chest, balances her glass of water on her knee, and says, "I'm trying to figure you out, Wyatt."

I lean forward, resting my forearms on my thighs and clasping my hands together. "I know I haven't made things easy. But that weekend in Phoenix, I'd been drinking heavily. Something happened at home, and I looked for comfort in the wrong place."

Shelby's eyes flash, and I realize what I've said.

"The bottle," I clarify, and she cools down. "Believe me, I don't mean Jo. Not remembering being with her is its own type of punishment."

"So what do you want me to do? Because if you're here asking me for an idea for a grand gesture, you're getting zilch."

I lean forward, my elbows on my knees. "I don't want an idea. I want to know if you think I have a shot. Because after what happened a few weeks ago"—I pause to see if Jo has told Shelby about the incident in the bathroom. Her knowing nod is my answer—"I don't want to make her revisit something that upsets her. So...?"

Shelby's eyebrows raise. "Do you have a shot? That's what you're asking?"

"Yes." I hinge forward even more, my entire body waiting alongside the breath in my throat.

Shelby draws out the silence, and I know she's doing it on purpose, making me nauseous with worry. "You do."

I let out my breath and look at the ceiling. "Thank God."

"But," Shelby says, bringing my attention back to her. "Jo prefers action. Your words won't be enough. Damn near anybody can talk. But can you walk?"

"Better believe it," I answer, ducking my chin in a way my mom calls a 'cowboy nod'. "Thank you, Shelby. I appreciate you talking with me."

She follows me out to the front door. "Lucky for you," she says, opening the door and standing back so I can pass through. "You don't have to worry about Jared anymore."

I freeze. "Why is that?"

"They broke up." She says each word slowly.

"When?"

"The night before you put the moves on her in the bathroom." She lifts a flat hand in the air between us. "Hold up. You didn't know they broke up, and you still touched her like that? And came here today?"

I rub my hand over the back of my neck and look down at the braided welcome mat, then back up to where Shelby waits for a response. "The heart wants what it wants."

Shelby lets out a disgusted breath, but I think she's mostly joking. "And here I thought you'd changed."

"I have. Mostly." I shrug. "But I'm still me, and there's no way in hell I'd let that boring ass banker have the best woman I've ever met just because he got there first."

Shelby gives me a look.

I lift my hands in surrender. "Okay, fine, I was there first, but only technically. And it doesn't matter anymore because I'm here now."

Shelby smiles. "Go get your girl, Wyatt."

She closes the door and I climb into my truck. I have one hell of an idea, I only hope I can pull it off.

I'm going to walk, not talk.

THE ONLY REASON THIS IS GOING TO WORK IS BECAUSE THE inspector didn't show up at Wildflower today like he was supposed to. If he had, I'd be left figuring out another way to show Jo I'm someone worthy of giving a shot.

But luck was on my side, and coincidentally, so was Warner.

"Get out of the truck," Warner calls from the tailgate. "I don't have all day."

Tenley is any-day-now pregnant, and Warner doesn't want to be away from her.

I pop a piece of gum in my mouth and pull on my hat on my way to where he is. "Untwist your panties, bro."

Warner grips one end of the bathtub and pulls. "Get the other side," he grunts.

Together, we get the bathtub into the main house. It's porcelain-enameled steel, and I chose it because it's nicer than acrylic and not as heavy as cast iron, which the sales associate told me is a bitch to install.

"Set it down on three," Warner instructs, then counts down. We put down the tub and slide it to where I want it to go. Warner takes a step back and watches as I adjust it a fraction.

"Why did you buy Jo a tub?" he asks, bewildered. He hooks a thumb into each pocket, one booted foot crossing at the ankle. "Isn't that kind of, I don't know, intimate?"

I shrug it off like it's not a big deal, even though I know it is. "She said she likes to take baths, but doesn't get to, and this bathroom was pretty clearly missing a tub."

Warner studies me. I hate when he does this. It leaves me feeling exposed, and even worse, like there's no way he agrees with what he sees. "Thanks for helping me bring this in here," I tell my brother, hoping he'll take the hint.

"Oh, hell no." He shakes his head and smiles. "I will definitely be staying to watch you install this."

I flash him a dirty look. "I thought you didn't have all day."

"I have time for this."

"Be my guest," I mutter, and go out to my truck for the rest of the supplies. When I get back, Warner is sitting on the closed toilet lid, his leg crossed over the other in a figure four.

I get started, first turning off the water and then disconnecting the drain. I already know what I'm doing because I did this last year for Mrs. Calhoun, but I don't tell Warner that. He's expecting me to fumble and curse, then give up. I continue working, and make sure to keep tabs on Warner's expression as it progresses from amusement to respect.

After I've reconnected the water, he asks, "Where did you learn to do that?"

I gather my trash, and without looking at him, say, "Sometimes I help Mrs. Calhoun with jobs around her house."

Warner stands. "Mrs. Calhoun? As in, Dixon Calhoun's grandmother?"

I nod, straightening up to my full height and looking him in the eye. If he's going to give me shit about it, he's going to get a mountain of shit back from me.

"Wyatt, you better be careful. Don't let guilt loosen your lips."

"She needs help, Warner. She's alone." Or she was, anyway, until those shifty grandsons of hers showed up.

"That is not our fault."

I give him a *Come the fuck on* look.

"It's not," he insists. "Her son, and her grandson, made choices, like we all do. Dixon chose to cook meth in the mountains. He knew the risks."

"I'm not going to let an old lady live in a house in need of repair, no matter who she's related to."

Warner scrutinizes me, causing the small scar on his brow bone to crinkle. "Of course not," he says. "I'd never think you'd do something like that."

I'm not sure what to say. I guess I was expecting a shitty remark about how he's surprised I'm not at the bar, or something along those lines.

Warner reaches out, gripping my shoulder and working it back and forth a few times. "So, you and Jo, huh?"

Technically, there isn't a me and Jo, so I shrug it off. "It's nothing. Just a gift."

"Right," he agrees, in a tone that conveys how much he

disagrees. "One more question, and I really hope this doesn't burst your bubble if you're planning on her using this tonight, but does this place have hot water yet?"

I give him a mock salute, fully in the knowledge that if Wes were here he'd school me on the proper way to salute. "Accounted for."

Warner gets up and walks across the bathroom. "Alright, now I'm leaving. I have to go back to the homestead and tell every person I come across that you know how to install a bathtub."

"Nobody will believe you," I counter.

Warner glances back at me as he steps through the bathroom door. "That's where you're wrong, little brother." He keeps going, muttering to himself. I make out the words 'Calhoun' and 'bathtub' before he's too far away for me to hear him.

21

WYATT

It's all set. All I need now is Jo.

I texted her twenty minutes ago, telling her there was a minor problem at Wildflower. I realize that's going to cause her some stress, but hopefully coming upon the scene I've set will make up for it.

I've been sitting here for ten minutes, watching the steam rise.

The lights from her car sweep over the bathroom window, and I quickly light the candle I've placed on a stool beside the tub.

She's walking into the house as I come out from the hallway. Her hair is a mess, tied to the top of her head, and her eyebrows pull together in a worried 'v'.

"What's wrong?" she asks, coming toward me, stress seeping from her pores. I feel bad, knowing she has experienced stress in relation to my text. Even in this disarrayed state, I can't help but drink her in. She is perfect. Why has it taken me so long to really see her?

She fixes me with a no-nonsense stare. "And why are you here this late?"

I look out the wide front window at the final moments of dusk, where the eastern sky is dark but the western horizon still clings to the light, like lover's limbs intertwined.

"I needed a tool for a project I'm working on at home, and I noticed something." I pivot, motioning for her to follow me. Her defeated sigh filters through the air.

"At least this time, I'll have the money to repair it," she murmurs, more to herself than to me, I think.

I stop short of the bathroom and sweep my arm toward the entrance. Jo meets my gaze as she steps past me, her shoulder inches from my chest. My hands press to my sides to keep from taking her in my arms and pressing a kiss to those beautiful lips.

"Wyatt, what is..." She walks in, her steps slowing to a halt. "What is this?" she whispers. Tentatively, she runs one finger along the length of the tub. Steam rises, swirling around her, turning the arid desert into a humid jungle.

I swallow the lump in my throat. "You said you like baths, but you never get to take one."

She turns to face me. Her gaze is tender. Her hands clasp in front of her body, fingers weaving as she searches for what to say. "I don't have a hot water heater yet."

I gulp air that feels like taffy. Thick and sticky. Heavy with steam, but something else, too. Comprehension, maybe, and the slow burn of buried desire. "I found a solution."

She cocks an eyebrow, letting me know she'd like to know how I did it.

In my mind, I see all the burners, the boiling water, the switching of pots. "They left a lot of pots in the kitchen.

Don't worry, I washed them before I used them. And I brought some from home—"

"You boiled the water?"

I nod. "I filled the tub halfway and ran room temperature water until it was full."

Jo swirls her fingers around the surface, her eyes fluttering closed. She's enjoying it even before she's in it. What a beautiful sight.

"Enjoy your bath, Jo." I reach for the door handle, my eyes cast down to give her privacy.

She clears her throat, drawing my attention back to her. She takes a single step from the edge of the bath, her gaze so intense I feel it deep in my chest, a pull, a draw, a magnetic force. She sucks her bottom lip between her teeth and bites down gently, her chest rising and falling with her breath.

Then her fingers find the top button on her shirt. The first one opens, then the second, showing me the swell of each breast held in by black lace. My breath hitches, getting stuck in my throat. She moves down to the third button, somewhere just above her navel, and the room spins.

This need I feel for her, this hunger, is a clear memory. I've felt this before. One other time. For her.

"Jo," I manage, my voice like tires on loose gravel.

She finishes her buttons and drops her shirt to the ground. "Come help me with the rest," she says, her voice low.

I'm there in mere seconds, reaching for her, cupping the back of her head in my hand. Just before our lips meet, I pause, only to drink in this moment with her. I want to make each second a minute, commit every movement to memory, so I relive this for the rest of my life.

And then I kiss her. Slowly, at first, as I learn her shape, the contours of her lips. Jo arches into me, digging her fingers into my shoulders, and my tongue presses against the seam of her lips. She opens up, tasting my mouth, biting down on my lip, drawing from me a sound that is as much a growl as it is a groan.

We become a flurry of activity. Her hands pull my shirt over my head. I unclasp her bra, tossing it aside. Her breasts are full and round, perfect. Jo runs her hands through my hair as I take my time with each, holding her upright when her back arches. "Now, Wyatt," she moans.

It is a small miracle we're both wearing sweats. They slide right off our bodies the way our jeans never would, and we step from them, kicking them aside. I'm naked now, but Jo still has on her underwear. I like that they don't match her bra.

She hooks her thumbs on either side, but I stop her. "I want to do it."

Her hands come away and I kiss her lips. Her chin. Her throat. Her chest, trailing down through the valley of her breasts. On my knees now, I drag my kisses over her stomach.

Down.

Down.

Down.

Until I'm there, breathing a hot breath through the fabric covering her. Above me, Jo lets out a garbled moan. It makes me smile. I don't know how I did something good enough in this life to be with this woman, but God help me, I'm never letting her go.

In one swift, fluid motion I pull down her remaining scrap of clothing and press my mouth to her. I take my time, hooking one of her legs over my shoulder until Jo is shaking and gripping the countertop behind me.

I stand up and watch Jo catch her breath. I can taste her on my lips, and all I want now is to feel her on me. Then I remember her bath, the bath I worked hard for her to be able to enjoy.

"Your bath," I say, and Jo peeks over my shoulder at the water.

"Get in," she instructs.

My thumb traces her collarbone. "It was for you."

She wraps her hand around me, stroking, and it becomes impossible for me to think about anything else. "Now it's for us." She releases me, nodding her head at the water.

The water is almost too warm, but my skin adjusts quickly to the temperature as I settle in. Jo places a hand on the edge, swinging one leg over first, and then the other. She sinks down, straddling me but still partially upright, both hands on either edge, and moans softly.

"This feels so good," she says.

She's talking about the water. I'm not inside her yet.

Jo leans forward, bracing herself with a palm pressed to my chest, and reaches down. She guides us together, and I feel the moment we connect. Eyes locked on mine, Jo sinks down all the way until there isn't a part of me that's not inside her. She has my body, yes, but my heart and soul too.

"I'm in love with you, Jo."

She moves up, then down, a hot breath hissing from clenched teeth. "I know."

My hands run over the dips and curves of her back, holding her upright. "How?"

She smiles, but it's fleeting, replaced by a look of pleasure as she sinks back down on me again.

"You bought a tub for me and filled it with hot water that you boiled yourself. If that's not love..." She trails off, because while she was talking I leaned forward and pulled her nipple into my mouth.

There's no more speaking after that. I grip her hips, helping her move. Water sways around us, wet heat lapping at our skin. Jo begins to tremble, her teeth gently sinking into my shoulder, and she cries out against me.

My back muscles clench, and Jo puts her lips to mine, kissing me so deeply that when I come, my groan fills her mouth.

She presses her forehead against mine, noses tip to tip, and we stay that way while our pulses slow.

I brush my lips across hers, featherlight, and when she says, "I'm in love with you, too," not only do I hear it, but I feel it.

Carefully, she lifts off me and turns around, settling between my legs. Her dry hair tickles my chest, and her wet hair fans out in the water on either side of us.

Her flattened palm skims the surface, and she asks me what I'm thinking.

"Right now, I'm pretty blown away." My fingers follow a path down both her arms. It's like a compulsion, this need to touch her. "It feels like I've been waiting forever for you."

Jo tips her head back and to the side so she can look at me. "I'm the one who has the market cornered on waiting forever."

"Hear me out," I argue, smiling down at her. "I've always felt like there was something more for me. Like a piece of me was missing. I couldn't find it at the HCC, or when I was spending time with my family. I've spent my whole life unsettled. Until you. Until Wildflower. Helping you here, listening to you talk about this ranch and your plan to help people, it makes me feel like I'm finally a part of something bigger. Bigger even than the HCC." All I can reach right now is her forehead, so that's where I plant my kiss. "And that is why it feels like I've been waiting forever for you."

"Fine," she huffs, pretending to be annoyed.

"So," I say, "You've been waiting forever for me, too?"

"Yes," she answers immediately, and I like how quickly the answer comes to her. "The difference is that I knew you were in the room. To you, I was only a bystander. A person on the periphery. An afterthought."

My knuckles run the length of her arms and I watch the water slide off my fingers and run over her. "I knew you were in the room." I always knew she was there. I also knew she was a hundred times too good for me.

She changes positions so she's facing forward again. "You most definitely did not."

I'm transfixed by her pointer finger, cutting a figure eight in the water, my mind busy recalling a very specific moment. "Senior year. Prom. You wore a light pink dress, and Ryan Ellington spilled a soda down your front."

Her head shakes against me. "That proves nothing. Most people in our graduating class remember that."

"Do most people know you bought that dress yourself with the money you earned from working at the Sierra?"

Her finger stills. "How do you know that?"

"I was shopping with my mom that day. I saw you pull cash from your pocket. There were so many small bills, and the cashier was obviously annoyed. She was sighing, like she had something better to do." I see her pinched expression, her judgmental stare. "Bitch," I add.

Jo's finger resumes the path it cuts through the water. "Such a bitch," she agrees.

"We left the store a few minutes after you. I told my mom I forgot something inside and went back in." I chuckle at the memory, causing Jo's head to follow the rise and fall of my chest. "I made sure the cashier was looking at me, then I knocked over a display. And walked out."

Jo looks back at me. "Wyatt!"

I grin at her shock, at how she looks disapproving but also pleased. "I'm not sorry."

A tiny smile tugs at the corner of her mouth. "Why didn't you tell me you'd seen me? Or anybody else?"

I remember Jo clearly from that day, her furtive glance and hunched shoulders. She was embarrassed, but angry too. Resentful. "It felt private. Like something I wasn't supposed to see."

She nods. "Yeah."

It's all she says, and it's confirmation I made the right choice back then. "Your mom—"

Jo sits up suddenly, water sloshing. Her upper half twists so she faces me. "I don't want to talk about my mom. You know what I want?"

My eyebrows lift and I wait for her to finish.

"I want you to take me back to your place and lay me down on your bed, and do everything we just did, but horizontally this time."

She doesn't wait for my reply. She stands up from the tub and climbs out. Goose bumps rise on her skin, and I realize I've forgotten the towels in my truck. I get out too and hand her my shirt. She uses it to dry off, and I do the same. We lock up the house, and then I take her back to my cabin and follow her instructions precisely.

22

JO

It's... him. *Wyatt*. Beside me in his bed.

I'm terrified to make a sound, to even breathe. Any disruption to the current atmosphere might wrinkle the moment. I shut my eyes and exhale so slowly it's uncomfortable.

Last night really happened, right? Wyatt really boiled an ungodly amount of water so I could have a bath? I don't think anybody has ever done anything so kind for me. It's overwhelming.

As soon as I understood what he had done for me, I knew. Wyatt isn't a man who makes empty grand gestures. Wyatt will never do something he doesn't one-hundred-percent want to do.

Wyatt is in love with me. I repeat it two more times in my head, tapping out the rhythm on my chest with one finger. I believe it, but also, I don't. When you've wanted something for so long, getting it doesn't actually make it feel like yours. I can't grab onto it, hold it in my palm, feel its warmth.

Is that what real love is? A measure of faith? Something

you can't see, like heaven, or emotions. You go with your gut, close your eyes, and fall?

It's the scariest thing I've ever experienced.

Beside me, Wyatt shifts. He stretches and groans, protesting the waking world. My breath sticks in my throat. I dare a glance at him.

He blinks twice, those thick, dark eyelashes fluttering and then opening. His tongue darts out, running over the crease in the center of his lower lip. He touches me, fingertips slipping over my shoulder.

"Josephine Shelton, is that really you?"

His words draw a smile from me. "Did you think you imagined last night?" I ask.

"I thought last night was something that could've only happened in my dreams. I figured I must've imagined it."

I push against his chest. "Stop."

He squints. "I'm not kidding, Jo. Last night was important." He looks down and back up. "I know you think I've been sleeping with my best friend's wife. I know you think I drink too much and I don't take enough responsibility on my family's ranch. I know—"

"Stop," I say again. "If all that were true, then I'd be the dumbest woman to let myself end up in your bed again."

His lips purse as I continue. "It might be true that I thought some of that in the past, but that was before. And I'll admit, I still don't understand what is going on with Sara, but everything I've seen from you the past couple months tells me there's something more to the story, and none of us are pausing long enough to understand. Am I right?"

Wyatt's eyes hold relief, and a touch of sadness. He nods. "I can't tell you why I go over there."

Disappointment flashes through me. It's not a lot

though, so I don't press. I am curious about something else though.

I reach for him, curling my fingers over his chest muscles. "I've known you for a long time."

Wyatt smirks. "That probably doesn't work in my favor, does it?"

I laugh lightly. "You've always been wild," I admit. "But you seem different now."

"Good different?" he asks hopefully.

I smile. "Yes. But remember, I liked you when you were a handful, too."

"Why, Jo?"

It's an odd question. I push myself up onto one arm, my chin propped on my hand. "Why did I like you?"

He nods. Vulnerability plays at the edges of his eyes.

"Well." I think back to high school when my massive crush first sprouted. We'd just come from the cult after they asked us to leave, and I was terrified to make a wave. All I wanted to do was blend into the sea of faces, be accepted but not memorable. I kept my head down, my nose in a book, but it was impossible not to notice Wyatt. He was handsome, confident, a Hayden. I'd learned quickly what that meant.

I kept my distance and only made one friend: Shelby. Wyatt was always in the middle of a group. He might have been in the center of everything, but he was quiet. A unique brand of wild. Not boisterous, but he damn sure was going to be the most involved. If there was a prank, he was in on it. If there was a dare, he was up for it. If an outsider showed up and started something with one of his friends, Wyatt would be the one to end it. He was like glue, keeping everyone together, but he himself seemed to float up above it all. He was aloof, but with flashes of brilliance. All of this I knew because I watched and listened, but it made me wonder why he worked so hard to be so... *significant*.

I could tell he was broken. Just like me. Deep, deep down, there were cracks in him. I never knew why, though I'm starting to get the picture.

"I had a pretty big crush on you in high school," I start, sitting up and pulling the covers around me when they slip down. I'm naked, and my level of undress doesn't seem to meet the current mood. "Me and every other girl."

"No way." He rubs my lower back.

"Don't act like you didn't know every girl would've fainted if you'd looked their way."

"I know about everyone else." He smiles. "I just didn't know about you."

I reach behind me, taking his hand from my back and resting it in my lap. I flip his palm over and trace his lifelines. "You seemed sad sometimes." The muscles in his hand strain. "I think that's what drew me to you in the beginning."

"We barely knew each other." His voice is uneasy. "How could you notice that about me?"

"Sadness can be seen from a distance. Sometimes it's an air, or the way you react to something. Sometimes it's the way you *don't* react to something."

Wyatt's hand releases and I resume tracing. "Why did that draw you to me?"

I moisten my lips, thinking about how I should respond. How much should I tell him? "I was sad too, Wyatt."

"Why?"

A flush sweeps over my ears, heating the tips. Shame can be so suffocating. "Before we moved here, we were members of this "church" called God's Redeemers." I put that word in quotes because it was a cult, plain and simple. "And I did something that got us kicked out of the cult. When my mom tried to go back, they refused her. They told her she'd raised a jezebel and couldn't be trusted."

"A jezebel?"

"It means—"

"I know what it means." His hard tone tells me he doesn't like what he's hearing, even if it's all in the past.

"Anyway, we ended up in Sierra Grande, and I stayed behind when she left. She took Travis with her, and when the church refused her return, she went somewhere else to start a new life."

"Why didn't you meet her there? Wherever she went?"

I flip Wyatt's hand over, outlining the shape like there's construction paper below us and my fingertip is a marker. "My mom made it pretty clear what she thought of me. She said I ruined her life. She was right, I suppose."

"What kind of life was it if she was living in those conditions?"

"The kind she was used to, I suppose." I glance back at Wyatt. "Aren't you going to ask me what I did to get us kicked out?"

"Knowing you, it was something incredibly badass, like challenging the institution or exposing wrongdoing."

How I wish that were true. At least I could've left in a blaze of glory, instead of with my chin tucked to my chest.

"Jezebel, remember?" I point back at myself. "The church leader's son took an interest in me. It was the first time a boy ever looked my way. I was flattered, even if I thought he was a bit of a loser. Supposedly we were all sinners and thereby created equal, but there was still a hierarchy, and he was near the top of it. We were allowed supervised dates, very old-school style with meals at his family table and such. One day we found ourselves alone. I'll spare you the details." Wyatt nods encouragingly, having no problem hearing about this part of my past. "He felt so guilty about what we'd done that he confessed to his father, who went ballistic. He'd said the devil had entered me, and I tempted his son the way Eve tempted Adam. He declared me a threat to the entire church, and my mom and I were instructed to leave immediately."

"And you came here?"

This is where the truth gets muddy, and I need it to stay that way. "We bounced around a little, and eventually settled here. Travis was just a baby. My mom was waiting for me to turn eighteen so she could leave me and try to go back. And you know how that ended up."

Wyatt blows out a heavy breath. "I don't know if I've ever heard anything so crazy."

I offer a half smile. "Are you sure? Growing up a Hayden and you don't have any better dirt than that?" I'm trying to lighten the mood, but Wyatt's eyes darken at my question. He has secrets, things he can never tell me.

I do too.

23

WYATT

"I'm having a hard time deciding on the color of the furniture." Jo leans over, offering me a look at her phone. She toggles back and forth between whitewash and teak.

I wrap an arm around her shoulder and pull her in closer for a better look. Her chair scrapes the concrete sidewalk in front of Marigolds. Her shoulder is soft and round, inviting me to place a kiss there. So I do. She smiles at me before looking back down at the choices on the screen.

"I'd stay away from white," I advise. "Think of the dirt and dust, especially from a bunch of kids."

Jo looks up at me, squinting against the bright sun. "They're not toddlers."

I shrug one shoulder. "Teenagers, toddlers, what's the difference?"

She breathes a laugh. I like when she makes that sound.

With one finger, Jo swipes at the screen and the furniture website disappears. "I should stop putting the cart before the horse."

"How so?"

Jo takes her iced coffee from the table and captures the straw between her lips. "The main house isn't even done yet."

"But they're working on it, right?" I don't know why I ask. I'm there all the time, I know what the progress is.

"I guess I'm just being pessimistic. If I assume something will go wrong, I won't be upset when it actually does."

I tip my coffee to my lips, but it's empty, so I take Jo's and try not to grimace. I'm not a fan of caramel. "I think you should let yourself get excited. It's safe. Your pockets are deep these days, you can handle anything that comes at you."

Jo opens her mouth, but across the street someone yells.

"That's not my baby! I want nothing to do with it. I told you we should've used a condom."

My body tenses. Ricky has his cupped hands held to his mouth, and his dopey brother Chris doubles over, laughing. The pregnant woman Ricky yelled at presses a protective hand to her stomach and she is trying like hell to get away from them, but it doesn't look easy. Her stomach is large, her gait awkward, and those motherfuckers howl with laughter like deranged coyotes.

Jo's hands are on me, her urgent voice pressing into me. "Wyatt, don't."

I look down at Jo and realize we're standing. I don't remember getting up from my chair, but it must've made a sound when I did it because the assholes across the street are looking at me. Ricky stares at me, resentful and entitled. It was the exact same look his cousin wore, the very same look Wes couldn't stand. I don't think he understands how lucky he is that it's me who witnessed what he did, and not my oldest brother. Wes would bury both of these people in a shallow grave without a second thought.

I step off the sidewalk and walk over the asphalt street. Behind me, Jo mutters a string of expletives.

This is my town, and I won't have some low-life assholes yelling at women. "Do you boys think her husband would appreciate you yelling at his pregnant wife?"

"Doesn't matter," Chris says, his voice thick and lazy. "He ain't here."

"He will be soon. He owns the gym two blocks over, and I'm damn certain he'll be interested in denting your windpipe so you can't yell at pregnant ladies anymore."

Chris looks at Ricky. Ricky still hasn't lost that contemptuous expression. "You think I'm scared, Hayden?"

"I think if you ever want to order at a drive-thru again, you should probably get the hell out of Sierra Grande."

"You'd like that, wouldn't you?" One side of his face bends into a snarl. Any pretense we had of being civil the first time we met is long gone. "We go away, and you don't have to answer for what you did to Dixon."

"We've had this conversation, but if you're too stupid to remember it, we can have it again."

Ricky leans to the left, peering at something behind me. *Jo.*

He straightens and looks back at me. "Interesting. Hayden has himself a girlfriend. And from what I hear, you also have a little sister." An unhurried smile slides low across his cheeks. "Imagine that. A Hayden princess."

I take a step closer, my hand in a fist, but Jo grabs me from behind. Her touch reminds me we are in broad daylight, in the middle of the busiest street in Sierra Grande, and I don't need to give the sheriff any more reason to dislike me.

Ricky turns, and Chris follows. He doesn't look back. I stand there, watching them go until they reach the end of the street and turn a corner.

"Wyatt," Jo says my name with quiet strength.

I face her. Her hair is pulled half up, and two pieces of hair frame her face. Her head tips to the side, and she studies me, waiting for me to speak.

"They are bad news, and I can't have them coming into my town and acting however they want."

"I agree."

This surprises me. I thought for certain she was upset with me. "You do?"

She nods and reaches for my arm. "I like watching you jump into action, even if it scared me a little bit."

I pull her into my chest and kiss the top of her head.

"You should be a police officer. This town needs you."

It makes me think of Dan, and what the hell he was doing with Ricky and Chris. To Jo, I say, "I prefer to break the law, not enforce it."

Jo pulls back so she can be certain I see her eye roll. I take advantage and lean down to capture her lips. She steps back, ending the kiss far too soon.

"I have a meeting," she reminds me. "Sawyer and I are going over the budget."

I frown. I'd forgotten.

"Stop," Jo instructs, giving me a look. "He's nice."

My frown deepens. I'm not sure about the guy, but if he's the person who's making it possible for my girl's dream to come true, I'll allow some measure of distrust without acting on it.

Jo kisses me goodbye, reminding me that she's coming to dinner at the homestead tonight, and walks away. I go back to our table across the street, throw away our cups, and take off down the street.

There's someone I want to visit.

THERE HE IS. SHOULDERS HUNCHED, FINGERS TAP-TAPPING away on his keyboard. I approach him from behind and notice he has a large mole on his hairline. I wonder if a barber has ever nicked it during a haircut.

"Hey there, Dan." He jumps when I clap my hand on his upper back. I pat twice more, softer this time. Just so he gets my friendly vibe. Because that's what I am. Friendly.

So friendly.

Friendly Wyatt.

Dan whips around, his metal chair squeaking as it rolls with his sudden movement. "Christ, Hayden. What the fuck?"

I lean on the small desk behind me, crossing one ankle over the other. "Jumpy, aren't you? Everything all right?"

Dan glares at me. He has beady eyes and a jaw that extends beyond the line of his forehead, making his head look slightly inverted. "In trouble again, Wyatt? I can only assume that's why you're here."

I cross my arms. "You know what they say about assuming..."

"Cut the shit. What do you want?"

"Ricky and Chris Marks. What do you know about them?"

He pinches the bridge of his nose and sighs. "Who?"

I'm willing him to look at me, but he doesn't. He removes his glasses from his desk, followed by cleaning solution and a cloth.

"So you don't know them?" I ask.

He looks me straight in the eyes and lies.

Sheriff Monroe comes through the front door of the station, boots stomping on the ground.

"Wyatt," he says, stopping when he sees me. "To what do I owe the pleasure?"

I smirk. Pleasure is a bit of a stretch.

I grip Dan's shoulder and squeeze. He shifts, but I hold on. "Just dropping by to see an old friend."

I could press the issue, maybe even ask the sheriff to look in on the Marks brothers. He would if he knew who they were related to. Dixon Calhoun was a menace to this town, and the sheriff knows apples don't fall far.

But I have a feeling whatever Dan is up to with them is bad news, and I'd like to give him enough rope to hang himself.

The sheriff gives Dan a stern look. "Socialize on your own time."

"I didn't—" The words die on Dan's lips. The sheriff literally waved him off.

He starts for his office, and says, "Come with me, Wyatt."

I turn back. "Bye Dan. Nice visiting with you."

He gives me a hate-filled glare. I smile and wink, then follow the sheriff into his office.

"What can I do for you, Sheriff?" I ask, folding myself

into the same chair I sat in when he doled out my community service.

He stops behind his desk and grips the back of his chair. "How long have you been out at Jo Shelton's ranch?"

"Two months."

"How many hours?"

I shrug. "I haven't been keeping track."

"Would you say one hundred hours?" His eyebrows raise and his chin drifts like he's leading me to an answer.

I nod slowly. "That sounds about right."

"Good, good." He pulls out his chair and sits. "I hereby declare you finished with community service."

"So formal."

Sheriff grunts a laugh. "Don't get mouthy with me, boy."

I stand. "Am I good to go? Do I need to sign anything?"

"Just don't attempt to drive after you've been drinking ever again."

I duck my chin. "Yes, sir." I move for the door, but his voice stops me.

"I don't know what you have planned for yourself now that you don't have community service, but I was out at the HCC this morning, and Wes could use some help." He sorts through papers as he says it, avoiding eye contact.

"They don't need me out there until my dad brings home one of those damned horses that don't want to be contained."

Sheriff lets go of the papers and looks up. He scrutinizes me for a long second, then says, "Family dynamics are a bitch."

"Sure are." I open the door. "See you around, Sheriff."

I'm walking out the front door when Shelby comes

walking up from the parking lot. She eyes me warily. "What did you do this time?"

"Very funny," I reply, holding the door open for her.

She steps through and pauses. "Everything okay?"

"Everything is just fine."

"Jo's happy."

"So am I."

Her cheeks twitch like she wants to smile, but she keeps it in. "I'll kick your ass if you hurt her."

"I'm aware."

"Bye, Wyatt." She backs into the building and the door closes behind her.

I hop into my truck and pull the list my mom gave me this morning from my pocket. Time to start on her errands.

24

JO

The front door to the homestead is as intimidating as the Hayden family. Maybe it's by design. The thick, solid wood door is nearly twice my height, and in the center is a copper door knocker in the shape of the letter H. I knock with a fist instead, assuming the knocker is for show.

I wince. It's not for show. That felt like punching a tree.

Wyatt's little sister answers.

"Jo, hi." She has a wide grin ready, and she draws out her greeting so it sounds like *hiiiiii*. I don't know Jessie very well because she's so much younger than me, but I've seen her around town enough.

She steps back from the door and throws open an arm, welcoming me in. "Here, let me take that." She reaches for the bruschetta I made this afternoon. "Everyone's in the family room," she says, pushing the door closed with her foot. "Go on in."

I wish I weren't so nervous. I wipe my hands on the front of my dress and smile at Jessie. She's beautiful, her face plump and youthful. Her honey-blonde hair matches her mother's, the total opposite of the Hayden men. Still, it's unmistakable that she's a Hayden. Strong cheekbones, full lips, and the swagger they all carry.

I find Wyatt in the gigantic, open family room. He sits beside Tenley, his hand on her stomach. She guides his hand to a spot, and an astonished smile tears across his face.

"That is the coolest thing," he says before he spots me. "Jo," he says, getting up and striding to me. His eyes light up when he sees me.

"Thank God you arrived, Jo," Warner says. He sounds irritated. "I was getting tired of watching Wyatt fondle my wife's stomach."

"Get used to it," Wes says from where he sits in the oversized armchair. Dakota sits across his lap, her legs dangling off the side. "He did that during my wife's entire pregnancy too."

Wyatt rolls his eyes. "There's a person living inside another person. It's magic, guys."

Wes and Warner shake their heads and laugh, sharing a look.

I follow Wyatt to the couch and take the seat he vacated, next to Tenley. Wyatt takes the seat on the other side of me.

Tenley says something to Dakota, Warner says something to Wes, and it's just me and Wyatt now. His gaze holds mine, so intent. I love how he looks at me that way, like he's memorizing me, swallowing me whole, absorbing my every detail.

"What did you do this afternoon?" he asks. I get the feeling there are other things he'd like to say, but he's keeping it basic for the sake of our audience.

"I met with Sawyer. We had to go to the bank." It was awkward being there with Jared. He'd acted petulant, like a small child who'd been picked over at kickball. It was embarrassing, especially with Sawyer standing there seeing it all.

"Did you see him?" Wyatt asks.

"Sawyer? Yes, of course." I know what he's asking, but I like to tease him. He always rises to the occasion.

Wyatt pushes his lips out and narrows his gaze. His head dips toward me, his voice low. "Try again."

I nod.

"And?" Wyatt feathers his fingers over the back of my neck, and down to my collarbone. A boulder forms in my throat and I swallow against it.

"What are you even asking? There's no comparison, and you know it." Wyatt is a myth of a man, and he still needs reassurance. Are all men that way, or is it him?

"You didn't feel anything for him? Nothing residual?" His fingers slide up my throat, fluttering over my jawbone.

I do my best to give him a withering look, but it's hard when his touch is causing other parts of me to awaken. "No," I answer. "Unless you count irritation. He—"

"Um, excuse me?" Tenley leans forward, head sideways, eyes darting from Wyatt to me. "We're going to need to know why Wyatt is fondling your face. Pretty sure there's not a baby in there."

My gaze flickers to Wyatt, then out to the four people staring at us expectantly. Everyone looks shocked, except for Dakota. She's beaming.

I open my mouth to respond, but I'm stopped by Wyatt's mouth coming down on mine. Dakota squeals, and I think it's Tenley who gasps.

Wyatt lets me go. "We're together," he says, looking out at his family. "Surprise."

Dakota thrusts a fist into the air. "Yes," she hisses, looking back down at Wes. Amusement tugs the corners of his lips.

"I always thought there was a vibe between you two," Tenley says, adjusting her dress so it covers her knees.

Wyatt rubs his shoulder against mine and mouths the word *vibe*.

"It was the bathtub, wasn't it?" Warner asks, nodding confidently.

A blush crawls across my face. "I... uh... um..."

"Don't worry, he would have got me with a bathtub delivery like that, too." He laughs at his joke. "I have one question though. How did you take a bath without a hot water heater?"

I look at Wyatt and think of walking into the house that night, and the hope in his eyes. I remember packing up all the pots he took from the homestead to make it happen. "Wyatt boiled water."

The smiles drop from everyone's faces. It's silent. Tenley is the first to speak.

"He boiled your bathwater?" Her voice is disbelieving, incredulous, and so damn happy. "That's the most romantic thing I've ever heard. Don't be surprised if it makes its way into a movie. I'm definitely going to tell some scriptwriters I know."

"Did you hear that, Wes?" Dakota pokes Wes's chest.

Wes tips his head to the side and looks at her. "I did something kind of big for you once upon a time, too."

Dakota knows instantly what he's talking about, though I don't have a clue. She leans down and kisses him, and doesn't say anything else.

"Dinner," Jessie calls, her voice reaching us before she does. When she appears, she holds Colt in her arms.

We all get up, and Wyatt takes Colt from Jessie.

Wes says to Wyatt, "I can't believe you boiled water."

"Don't be upset, Wes. You can come to me anytime you need tips on how to romance your wife." Wyatt winks.

Wes lifts his fists like he's going to box, and Wyatt nods down at Colt. "Sorry, can't fight you right now. I'm holding your kid."

Wes takes Colt, shouldering into Wyatt as he leaves the room.

"Boys," Dakota says, rolling her eyes, but there's so much affection on her face.

This dynamic is foreign to me. Siblings fighting and loving, teasing and talking. It makes me resent my mom even more than I already do.

WE'RE SITTING OUT BACK, WATCHING WES AND WARNER PLAY horseshoes. Warner's oldest kids, Peyton and Charlie, roast marshmallows at the fire pit, the flames licking the air. The warm daytime temperature has given way to a cooler night, and I snuggle deeper into the blanket Wyatt brought outside for me.

Beau sips whiskey from a tumbler, Juliette beside him. Beau was quiet throughout dinner, not that it was any different from how he usually acts. He is a man of so few words, it gives greater weight to the words he does speak.

That's why I feel my body shift when he opens his mouth. I sit up straighter, leaning forward slightly in anticipation.

"Did Wes tell you about the grass?" Beau stares into the fire, the shadows from the flames flickering over his wrinkled, tanned skin. I'm not sure who he's talking to. I look to Juliette, but she stares into the flames too.

Beside me, Wyatt doesn't move from his relaxed position, one leg crossed over his knee, his arm slung around my back, but I feel his muscles tense.

"What about the grass?" Wyatt asks. His tone is low, something that sounds like dread running through it.

"It's dying," Beau growls. Juliette pushes against him with her shoulder, and he frowns. "It is," he adds, digging in his heels.

"Where?" Wyatt asks, looking around at the lawn. It's too dark to see far, but what the outdoor lights show is lush, green grass, all the way until the tree line.

"Not here," Beau says. "The back pastures. They border that land that switched hands a couple years ago. Something is sucking them dry, but I can't see without going out there and it's private property."

Wyatt dips his head. "That's frustrating."

Beau's gaze snaps to me. *To Wyatt*. "Is that it? It's *frustrating*?"

Juliette places a hand on Beau's arm, but he ignores her.

"What do you want me to say, Dad?"

Somewhere on the periphery of this conversation, it strikes me that the sounds of horseshoes hitting the metal stakes has ceased.

"I want you to give a shit, Wyatt. That's what I want."

"Beau." Juliette's voice is sharp.

"Wes needs help with this place, and it's not the cowboys' job to pull extra weight like they have been." Beau stabs a finger toward the ground as he talks. "This is the Hayden ranch, and I want it run by Hayden men."

Wes intervenes. "Dad, come on. We can do this tomorrow. Tonight's about family time."

"You telling me this isn't weighing heavily on your mind? You need to move the cattle soon, and where are you planning to move them to? An imaginary green pasture? Hayden beef is pasture-raised, Wes. Not corn, and not whatever that dry shit is out there." He waves a hand in the direction of what I'm guessing is the dry grass.

Wes drags a hand over the back of his neck. "No, Dad, I'm thinking about it. But this isn't going to solve the problem."

"What will?" Beau's not really asking a question. He's challenging Wes.

"Not this," Wes says sharply. Dakota's eyes widen, and I get the feeling Wes doesn't use that tone with his father very often.

Beau stands. He reaches a hand down to Juliette and when she takes it, he pulls her up alongside him. "Are you ready to call it a night? I am."

Beau looks down at Wyatt as he passes, and suddenly it all makes sense. Wyatt's need to be in the middle of everything in town, his desire to be important, to run across the street and confront the men yelling at the pregnant lady. When you don't feel significant to the people you love, you look for it elsewhere.

"Don't listen to him, Wyatt." Wes's voice is gruff. He picks up a stick and pushes aside the logs on the fire. "He's stressed and in a bad mood."

"For my whole life, you mean?"

Warner speaks up for the first time. "Knock it off, Wyatt. Don't act like you got the short end of the stick around here. We were raised by the same parents."

Wyatt stares into the fire, his lips pursed. He gets up suddenly, striding off across the yard and into the trees.

I stand too, smiling apologetically at Tenley and Dakota, and start after Wyatt.

"He's going to his house," Warner calls, and I stop. "Take your car. If you go after him now, you'll likely get lost. He knows his way in the dark."

I murmur my thanks and make my way back to the homestead. Beau and Juliette must have already gone to their room, because there's nobody in sight. I retrieve my purse and walk out front. I take two steps when Jessie says my name.

I turn and see her dark figure off to the right. She's balanced on the porch rail, one foot crossed over the other, her back pressed against a stone column.

"Jessie, hi. I can't talk right now, I'm trying to—"

"Go after Wyatt?"

I blink. She wasn't outside just now, so how does she know what happened?

"I was coming around the side of the house when my dad started up," Jessie explains. "I'm sorry you had to see that."

"Yeah," I say, coming closer. "Does that happen often?"

"Does my dad act disappointed in Wyatt often?" She chuckles, the sound holding no mirth. "Too frequently, for sure. I know Warner thinks they were all raised the same, but that's just not true." Her head shakes slowly back and forth. "I didn't see it until a few years ago. I wasn't grown up enough to see the big picture like that."

"Why do you think your dad sees Wyatt differently?"

She shrugs. "I think it's because he's different from Wes and Warner. They are cut from the same cloth as my dad, but Wyatt is... softer, somehow." A grimace twists her lips. "That's not the right word, but I can't think of a better one."

I'm not sure what else to say, so I thank her and continue down the porch stairs. I'm almost to my car when she yells after me.

"Sensitive."

I look up at her. She's backlit by the light shining through the front window, her face in near darkness. "He's sensitive," she continues. "And that trait's not only under-appreciated out here, it's also seen as a weakness."

My heart folds in on itself. This is the brokenness I saw the first time I laid eyes on Wyatt, all those years ago.

I nod at her and wave, then drive to Wyatt's cabin.

I FIND HIM ON HIS SMALL BACK PATIO. HE'S SITTING ON ONE OF two chairs. A bottle of amber liquid sits on the bistro-sized table set between them.

I take the second seat. He hasn't turned on a light, but the moon is full and bright, peeking over the canopy of trees. Just enough light slides across the land, giving me a general sense of Wyatt's emotions.

He's well on his way to being drunk.

His eyes flicker over to me when I sit down, then back out to the darkness. There's nothing to be seen out there, but maybe Wyatt's seeing something that's only visible to him.

The quiet is loud. The cicadas have long since stopped their keening.

"I'm sorry you had to see that." His voice is heavy, tinged with shame and another emotion I can't identify.

I long to touch him, to reach over the bottle he has just pulled away from his lips and run the tips of my fingers over the planes of his face. "Every family has their shit, Wyatt."

He nods slowly, his lips pushing out. "Did you know my dad had a brother?"

Wyatt looks at me, and I shake my head. *Had*. Past tense.

"He died when they were teenagers. Hung himself in the living room."

The living room we sat in earlier, teasing and laughing? My lungs drag in much-needed oxygen, and it isn't until this happens that I realize I was holding my breath.

Wyatt traces the label of the bottle in his lap. "As soon as my dad took over the HCC, he demolished the home he grew up in and rebuilt it into what you see today. He couldn't stand being in the same place where his brother took his own life. He hated what his brother did." Wyatt sips from the bottle again, and I reach out my hand, silently asking for it. I'd like to take it away, save him from himself, but I don't dare.

He hands it over, and I take a drink of the fiery liquid. *If you can't beat them, join them.*

Wyatt brushes a hand over his jeans, but I'm almost positive there isn't anything there to dust off. "He thinks I'm like him," Wyatt says, his tone soft but his voice hard. "His brother."

"No, Wyatt—"

"Yes, Jo. This is fact, not speculation."

Our gazes connect, and in his eyes I see anguish. I want to reach inside him, gather the emotion in my hands, and take it away. A single tear slips down his cheek and he jerks his head away. He coughs. "Would you mind going inside and getting us some water?" He's working so hard to push away his emotion, it might as well be a physical act.

I do as he asks, opening up cupboards in his kitchen until I find the glasses. He keeps a pitcher of filtered water in his fridge, and I'm pouring it when I hear the back door open.

When he grips my hip bone, I set down the pitcher.

When he gathers my hair over one shoulder and drags his lips across the back of my neck, I close my eyes.

He turns me around so I'm facing him. His lips meet mine, his tongue pushing into my mouth urgently, and I taste the sting of whiskey. His hands are on either side of my face, holding me in place.

I recognize this.

Two years ago, he kissed me this way. In that hallway outside the shop, this same kiss is what started it all.

One hand drifts away from my face. A rush of air meets my thighs as his hand dips under my dress. He pushes the fabric until it gathers around my hips. I exhale sharply into his mouth when he lifts me up and sets me down on the counter.

He presses kisses to my neck, my collarbone, the top swell of my breasts. I push the straps of the dress off my shoulders, giving the dress enough slack so Wyatt can pull down the front. He flips the cups of my bra and lowers his mouth to me.

I work at his jeans, unbuttoning them and pushing them down, first with my hands and then with my feet, until he can step from them himself. He wraps an arm around my waist and hauls me roughly to the edge of the counter. He slides my underwear down my legs and I lean back on my palms, steadying myself. His eyes are on mine, hooded and dark, as he drags himself along me.

"You are so beautiful, Jo," he says, taking his time when all I want is for him to slip inside me.

I tip my head to the ceiling and take a deep breath. "You're just saying that because you want to get laid."

He laughs and fills me at the same time. His laughter dies quickly, replaced by primal need, a pleasured exhale, the sound of two bodies coming together.

The back of my head hits the cabinet behind me, and he slips his hand between me and the cabinet so that I bump him instead. His other hand stays locked on my hip, and his gaze doesn't stray from mine.

What I see in his eyes rips me from the moment. Soft sadness, reluctant acceptance, and enduring hurt. I have to look harder to see these things, past the desire he so clearly feels for me.

I've seen this exact look before. I recognized the way he kissed me, and I recognize the way he fucks me.

And like that night, I allow it. I want to be the person Wyatt seeks refuge in. He's asking for me to soothe him now.

He was asking me to soothe him then, I just didn't know it.

I was there tonight. I saw how he ended up here. Which

begs the question: What happened two years ago that wounded him so?

Wyatt's hand leaves my hip, reaches between my legs, and he presses his lips to mine so that when I come he can swallow my moans. He finishes just after me, shaking and then stilling. He presses a kiss to the corner of my mouth. "I love you," he murmurs against me.

We're still connected, so I sit up taller, wrapping my arms around him in a hug. "I love you too, Wyatt."

25

WYATT

Two Years Ago

"I don't want to rest, Juliette."

Stubborn as a damn mule. That's what my dad is. He's been giving my mom a hard time since he got home from the hospital.

The heart attack he had at the annual cowboy barbecue scared us all, but I think it scared him a lot more than he's letting on. To make up for that, he's doubling down on how much recovery time he thinks he needs. Which is to say, *very little*.

"I don't give two shits what you do or don't want to do, Beau Hayden."

I smile. My mom is the only person I've ever heard go toe to toe with my dad and win.

"This ranch needs me out there," he growls, but now it sounds more like he's arguing for the sake of arguing instead of arguing to win.

"Too bad. Your family needs you to be healthy, so you have to follow the doctor's orders. Which means you need to rest."

"Bullshit," he mutters.

"Honestly," my mom says, her tone holding more affection than it did a moment ago, "if you weren't putting up this much of a fuss, I'd think maybe they'd transplanted your personality at the same time they performed your bypass."

"Very funny, Juliette."

"Try to calm down. It's not good for you to get worked up."

"Calm down? My life's work is currently without a leader. A ship needs a captain."

"You know Wes is taking care of things. He's perfectly capable of it."

"In the short term. But what about the long term?"

Mom sighs deeply. "I don't know. I have no idea if this thing between Wes and Dakota is going to work out."

"And if it doesn't?"

Neither of them speak, but I can picture my mom lifting her palms in the air.

Dad continues. "Warner's personal life is in shambles, and I doubt he'll be married much longer anyway. She's already taken off, all he needs now is a real divorce."

My muscles constrict. This is it. He's going to start in on me.

"I don't understand how I managed to have three sons, and nobody to take over the HCC."

Wow. He actually left my name out of his tirade. Unbelievable, considering—

"Wyatt's become someone I don't even know. Hand to God, I'm not certain I even raised that boy. He's someone my brother would've raised, if he'd lived long enough to have kids. Sometimes I think he's just like him."

"Hush," my mother says, her tone sharp. "You might be his father, but that's my kid you're talking about."

I should be grateful she's defending me, but I can't summon the feeling. The bone-crushing sadness weighs more.

My dad has never been shy about how he felt about his brother. He thought he wasn't strong enough, or tough enough. He wasn't mentally hardy enough to live on a cattle ranch, a place where weakness is despised and hard decisions must be made. He was too emotional, I remember my dad saying once, and his tone of voice conveyed everything we needed to know. Emotions were to be dealt with swiftly, with the confidence of a surgeon and the detachment of a firing squad.

And here he thinks I'm like him. That we are so similar, I could've been raised by him.

I am a man. A grown adult. So how is it I feel like a child again? I'm too old for this. Too old to give space to the hurt that never really leaves, the hurt I work tirelessly to keep buried deep inside.

I get in my truck and call Kyle. "You still going down to Phoenix this weekend?" When he says yes, I tell him I'm coming too. Then I call the resort, book a room, and go to my house to pack a bag.

I'm getting the fuck out of Sierra Grande, and I'm not going to tell a damn soul where I'm going.

26

JO

Sometimes I think people, me included, keep their heads down and their eyes focused on what's in their direct field of vision. Then something makes them lift their gaze, maybe a problem or an idea, and they are amazed by what they see when they widen their lens.

This is me right now.

Clutching my pencil and trusty notebook, I've been walking from room to room in the big house, noting everything that needs to be repaired but doesn't really fall under the job of a contractor. The list is titled *Handyman*. And it is lo-ong.

Standing in the middle of the living room, now open to the dining room thanks to Wyatt and his sledgehammer, I lift my eyes from my list. My sigh sticks in my throat when my gaze settles on the view outside the large window.

Wide open space. The outbuildings framed, like a skeleton awaiting muscle and skin. No workers here today, it's Sunday. Quiet. The view from Wildflower, from this window, steals my breath.

It's mine.

And the bank's.

And Sawyer Bennett's.

But also, *mine.*

I've been looking down for so long during this entire process, my gaze focused on plans and worries and money and problems. Until now, I haven't taken the time to look up and see what I've accomplished here.

I hope it helps people. I hope it heals and repairs families. I hope it takes a bad feeling and makes it good.

My phone rings when I'm tucking the notebook into my purse. My stomach sinks when I look at the name of the caller. *Mom.*

"Hello?" I answer, not making even the smallest effort to hide my reluctance.

"We need to talk about Travis."

Shit. No greeting. No easing into the conversation with a perfunctory and meaningless *How are you?*.

I toss my purse on the floor and sink down onto the same overturned crate I sat on the night of the storm when Wyatt and I danced. "What happened?"

"Your brother happened." I picture her hands, fisted on her hips, vein on her forehead popping.

"I think you mean your son," I remind her tightly. "What happened?"

"Travis threw a party when I stayed at Henri's farm last weekend." Mom sighs into the phone. "My house is trashed. This is the thanks I get for all I've done for him." Her voice increases in volume, until it sounds more like a screech. "I gave him a phone. I gave him freedom. He comes and goes as he pleases. Is he thankful? Nope. This isn't the boy I raised. I don't know who this ungrateful child is, but he's not mine."

My blood simmers with the anger that has begun pulsing through me. I remember when she said words like this to me, standing over me in that ankle-length skirt and high-necked shirt, her long hair plaited and wound into a bun. She called me a whore, and told me I ruined her good standing in the community. When I told her it was her fault for not explaining to me what sex is, she slapped me across the face. If I think about it long enough, I can still feel the sting of her hand.

"You need to calm down, Mom. Take a deep breath and—"

"I'm sending him to military school."

The air whooshes out of me, as if her words are a punch to my stomach. "What? No."

"He needs to be straightened out."

"Military school?" I ask in amazement and horror. "No, Mom."

"I can't take care of him anymore." She doesn't even sound sad. Just matter of fact.

"I'm coming to get him." The words are out of my mouth before I have a chance to really consider them.

She is quiet, the seconds pass, then she asks one question. "When?"

The single word is enough to ignite sheer hatred. I *hate* her. I hate that she arranges her life around men. That's how we ended up at God's Redeemers, because she had fallen in love with a man who was a member. She changed her entire life to be with him, and he sided with the church when push came to shove. Now she's with the pot farmer, and instead of investing in her son, instead of spending time with him, she's handing him a phone and freedom and acting shocked when he acts out. I can do better than her.

"Now," I bark. "Have him ready for me."

My hand is shaking so badly I can barely press the button to end the call. What did I just do? How will this work?

Travis can sleep on the couch at Shelby's house until the main house is ready. It's summer, so we don't have to worry about school.

My fingers shake as I send a text to Jerry, the one and only handyman I know. He's also apparently the only handyman most people know, and he isn't available for three weeks.

I search the internet for handyman services, and come upon one in the nearby town of Brighton.

"Vale Handyman Services." A pleasant sounding woman answers the phone.

I tell her what I need and where I live, and she tells me she can fit me in three days from now.

"Perfect," I answer, picking my purse up from off the floor and going toward my car.

"My son Connor will be there at eight a.m. on Wednesday," she confirms. We hang up and I get on the road.

I stop only for gas and something quick from the convenience store. It's a five-hour drive to my mom's house, two down to Phoenix and three more on the I-10.

I call Shelby when I get on the road and explain what's going on. Her only response is to tell me she'll wash the extra set of sheets because they haven't been used in so long. I wish I could hug her, and when I tell her that she says she'll remind me later when I return with Travis.

I call Wyatt as I'm passing Black Canyon City. The name

is a misnomer. It is not a city, not by a long shot. It does, however, have a little restaurant right off the highway that's famous for its pies.

Wyatt doesn't answer, so I leave him a message. I tell him only that I'm headed to a town outside Phoenix to get something and I'll be back later today. I don't feel like launching into the story on voice mail.

By the time I pull up to my mom's small house, I'm sick of driving. I park in the short driveway and get out. The citrus trees in the front yard burst with fragrant blooms, and from those blooms grow colorful fruit that won't be ready until winter. I drove down to visit last Christmas, and my mom complained about all the fruit the trees were dropping onto her lawn. I thought about picking a rotting orange off the ground and tossing it at her.

Today, if there was rotting fruit on the ground, I'd definitely make good on that thought.

The front door opens before I can knock. Henri stands there, one hand curled around the doorframe. He is handsome in that classic French way, his salt and pepper hair wavy and tucked behind his ears, his face displaying a permanently vague look of bemusement. He is tall and thin, and he wears clothes expensive enough that they fit well. He looks nothing like a pot farmer should look, though I'm willing to admit I'm typecasting the career choice. My mother once told me Henri recognized a lucrative business opportunity and took it, but he doesn't partake in what he grows.

Henri nods his greeting. He dropped the compulsion to kiss cheeks quickly after he came to the States twenty years ago and had his fair share of awkward introductions.

I step inside at the same time my mom comes around

the corner. She still wears long skirts, but this time it's her choice, and instead of being made of sturdy, stiff fabrics, they are chiffon and jersey. Her hair is shoulder-length, the same color as mine. I look like her, but that's where our similarities end. Thank God.

"You look nice," my mom says, eyeing the pink tips but keeping quiet. She knows better than to criticize me. She's dating a pot farmer.

"Thank you." I smile politely. The conversation stalls after that. I have nothing to say to this woman. Or, at least, nothing to say to her that would serve any real purpose, other than airing all my grievances, and what's the point of that right now? I'm here to collect Travis.

"Do you need money?" my mom asks.

I shake my head. I wouldn't take her money even if I did. I don't have a lot, but Sawyer's investment in Wildflower allowed me to stop using my personal funds on the ranch, and I have enough to support me and Travis until it turns a profit.

"Travis and I will be fine, but thank you for offering."

Henri slips an arm around her lower back, and she leans into him, just slightly. In a low voice, she says, "Are you sure you're ready for this?" The care and concern in her eyes serves only to anger me.

"Yes," I grit out.

She lifts her palms so they face me. "Okay, okay. I remember you at fifteen, and it's not a walk in the park. Adolescence is difficult."

I swallow. "I spent the first half of my adolescence in a cult."

"Church," she corrects me quickly. She refuses to admit it

went far beyond the confines of an everyday religious institution.

I huff a contentious chuckle, letting that be my argument. She says nothing.

"Travis," Henri calls. He's probably had enough of our bickering.

"Coming," Travis calls back. In the silence that follows I hear the thump of shoes hitting the ground, the sliding of zippers and shuffling of fabric.

We all look when Travis steps from his room. He's taller than the last time I saw him. His legs look too long for his body, his arms more like sticks protruding from his black T-shirt. He wears a blank stare. God forbid he show an ounce of emotion right now. A flash of fear streaks through me. My mom knows I'm not ready for this. I know I'm not ready for this. It doesn't mean I won't do it though.

Travis stops at the end of the hallway. Henri clears his throat. My mom breaks into action, stepping through the little circle we've formed and walking past me to the front door. She opens it and smiles. It's a fake smile, but she's trying.

"Have fun with your sister, Travis. Call me if you need anything, okay?"

I take one of his bags. "Come on," I urge, nodding outside.

He walks ahead of me, stopping to hug my mom. She pats his shoulder, and in a high-pitched voice says, "I'll see you soon, Travis." She's acting like it's a visit. Like he's going to summer camp and she'll send him a care package so his name will get called when they hand out mail.

"Bye, Mom."

She pulls me in for a hug too, and I'm not expecting it.

My chin hits her shoulder, and she pats my back the same way. "Good luck," she whispers.

I try to smile at her when I pull away, but even I can feel how wrong it looks on my face.

Travis and I wave at Henri, and he returns the gesture. I think he feels bad. It's hard to tell though.

We deposit a suitcase and two duffel bags in the trunk. Travis climbs in, and with a small wave toward the house, we're off.

"WHY DID YOU ORDER SO MUCH PIE?" TRAVIS STICKS A FORK IN the first slice the waitress sets down in front of us. Seven more slices follow, each one sliding across the old, chipped tabletop. I smile my thanks at the woman, and she winks and disappears.

"Well," I say, choosing a slice at random and sinking my fork into it. "Why not?"

"It's weird." Travis looks around. Every seat in this place is occupied, mostly by families who are probably traveling to or from Phoenix and stopped off the interstate for a bite and a clean restroom.

"Nobody cares that we ordered eight slices of pie, Travis." As I say it, I realize what he's thinking. I remember it vividly, how doing something 'weird' or 'different' was the kiss of death to any and every teenager.

"I promise not to bring eight slices of pie to school when you go back in the fall."

Travis gives me a small smile and tries a different slice.

"See?" I tap his fork with mine. "You can have a single bite of each slice and it adds up to having one, but you get something new each time."

"Maybe it's not so weird," he offers.

I drink from my water. "So, you threw a party? It had to have been pretty major, because"—I look around the room and then pointedly back at him—"we're here. And we're about to be in Sierra Grande."

As if he's a balloon and my question is a pin, he deflates. His shoulders slump and he leans back in his seat.

"I didn't mean to," he starts, shaking his head. "I didn't mean for it to get so out of hand. It was only supposed to be a few people. But they called people. And then *they* called people. It was like... like..."

"Compound interest?"

"I'm not sure what that is, but it sounds right."

"Basically, it means something grows and grows, like it feeds on itself."

He nods.

"Were you drunk?" I ask. I have no idea if Travis drinks, and fifteen seems young, but what the hell do I know anymore?

"No," he answers, but there's guilt in his eyes. It's fleeting, but it's there.

"Were you high?" I ask what I think is a natural follow-up question.

He nods quickly, like he's miming a bobblehead. I try not to faint.

"It was my first time." He's watching me closely, evaluating my reaction to his candor. "I don't think I could've kicked people out if I wanted to. I was seeing shapes in the air."

I don't know what to say. "I've been high once," I admit. "But it made me really paranoid, and I hated it."

Travis huffs a laugh. "I can't picture you high."

I lick a swipe of cherry off the tip of my fork. "Me neither."

We end up eating too much pie. So much for taking a single bite of everything. Travis groans as he's fastening his seat belt.

"Trav?" I ask, not looking at him as I merge my car back onto the I-17. "No parties, okay? No getting high, no drinking."

"Sure, Jo."

I can't tell if he's lying. I'm not even sure if I can ask such things of him. He's a teenager. It feels like setting him up for failure.

By the time we get home, I've had to stop once more for food. Travis eats like a horse, not shockingly. I round the car and open the trunk, handing the suitcase to Travis and shouldering the duffels.

"I hope you like couches," I tell him. He follows me inside.

"Couches are great," he answers.

Shelby grilled hamburgers, and even though we ate not too long ago and it's late, Travis eats again.

When it's time for bed, he helps me spread the sheets over the couch and tuck them into the cracks. He uses my bathroom, and when he comes out, I see a much younger Travis. I don't know if it's his pajamas, which are really just basketball shorts and a T-shirt, or the fact that his hair is messy, but my heart lurches. He's been through so much already, and he's only fifteen. Almost the same age I was when he was born.

He settles on the couch and rifles through one of his bags. Playfully I jostle his hair on my way out of the room. I'm almost gone when I hear a soft, "Thank you, Jo."

A lump forms in my throat. "Anytime, Trav."

When I'm nestled under the covers, I dial Wyatt. He's called three times since I left him a message earlier, and I haven't had a chance to call him back until now.

"Hey there," he says, his deep voice crackling over the line.

My phone beeps and it's him, asking for me to FaceTime. I hit the button and his gorgeous face comes on the screen.

"You make for pretty good eye candy," I tell him, my chest feeling a little lighter at the first glimpse of him.

He frowns. "Why are you in bed?"

"Because I'm tired." Mentioning my exhaustion conjures a yawn, and I cover my mouth.

"What I mean is, why are you not in *my* bed?"

I tell him about Travis and my drive to Phoenix. And about the pie.

"I'm going to make sure the main house is livable as soon as possible," Wyatt promises. He's in his kitchen, heating up leftovers Juliette brought over from the dinner he missed, and I can hear the beeping of the microwave.

"Why did you miss dinner?" My voice is getting thick, my eyes heavy.

Wyatt takes so long to answer that it draws me from my tiredness. I force my eyes all the way open. He looks conflicted.

"Sara needed help at her house. There was some damage to a wall and I helped her patch and paint over it."

My lips press together. I nod, but all it manages to do is

mess up my hair. I want to understand why Wyatt runs to help Sara, but he is so guarded about it.

"I'd be lying if I said I'm not uncomfortable about you racing to help her. Or why she calls you instead of her brother, or her dad." She has both, and they don't live that far away.

"I know." Wyatt looks contrite. "I'm sorry. I really need you to trust me on this one."

"I'm choosing to."

"Thank you."

I smile my acceptance. Sleep is coming back, and quick.

"My dad asked me to run an errand with him in the morning, but I'll come by Wildflower after." He winks. "Put me to work."

"Only if you wear that tool belt." The words sound like they're swimming through fudge.

"I only wore that in the very beginning. Are you telling me you liked it way back then?"

"So?"

"You were someone else's girlfriend, remember?"

"Maybe I have a little outlaw in me too."

Wyatt laughs. "Go to sleep."

"Good night." I make a kissing sound.

"Love you, baby."

His words are a poor excuse compared to the feel of his arms wrapped around me, but they'll suffice for now. "Love you too."

I fall asleep before I say goodbye.

27

WYATT

I can't remember the last time I found myself alone in a truck with my dad.

He asked me to go with him to the feed store, and even though we're on the outs, my dad isn't a person who does well with being told no.

So, here I am, bumping along in his truck and wondering why the hell he decided to go the back way.

We haven't had words since, well, probably as long as we've been alone in a truck together. We dance along the edges of an argument, tossing around passive-aggressive comments but neither of us engaging. Until a few nights ago, and only because he's worried about whatever drought is happening on the back end of our property. He wants me to care about the HCC enough to help Wes run it. I want to know why the hell I should.

Wes has cared about the ranch since the day he was born. The soil is in his blood. Warner served his time out of a sense of obligation, and a much lesser love of our land.

And me? I love our land. I think that's what my dad's

missing out of all this. He fears I don't appreciate what's been handed down to me by way of last name. He doesn't understand that I can pick up a handful of her soil and feel the hooves of the horses that have pressed their weight upon her. My soul is attached to the HCC the way anyone else's is. Mine just doesn't wear the same costume, and therefore, to him, we're not performing in the same play.

Love out loud, and love internal, is still love. It's strength, no less fierce. It's voice, no less heard.

"How are things with Jo?"

I flinch at the suddenness of his question. Idle chatter is not something he normally partakes in.

"Things are good, Dad." I prop an elbow on the car door and scratch an itch near my temple. "Really good, actually."

Dad nods. "I like her, for what it's worth. She's quiet, but she has a backbone."

"She doesn't let anybody give her shit, that's for sure."

"Least of all you."

I bristle. My fingers flex. "What's that supposed to mean?"

Dad side-eyes me, then looks back at the road. We're coming off the back road now and onto paved asphalt.

"You can be a handful, Wyatt."

"Christ," I mutter, rubbing an open palm over the stubble that rings my lips. "Why do you say shit like that?"

"Why do you get your feelings so damn hurt?"

I hate this. I hate feeling berated for having feelings. I go silent. What else is there to say, in this enclosed space that suddenly feels warm despite the air conditioning blasting from the vents.

"I don't want you to fuck it up with Jo," my dad says, his

tone gruff. "She's probably the best thing that's ever happened to you."

I blow out a noisy, angry breath. "And knowing me, I'm likely to fuck it up, right?"

My dad pulls into an open parking spot at the feed store. "Cut the shit, Wyatt. I know why you missed dinner last night. Does Jo?"

"I told her where I was."

"Did you tell her the truth about why you were there?"

Of course not, because I can't. Because nobody knows the damn truth, including the man who's sitting beside me casting judgment.

I don't want to talk to him anymore. I don't want to plead my case or tell him it's not what it looks like. I want him to back me, to assume I'm doing right even when it looks like I'm doing wrong. The way he would for Wes or Warner.

"Let's go." I get out of the truck, walking around to the front and waiting for him. Trey, the feed store owner, has everything we need all ready to go. We've been placing and picking up the same order for longer than I've known how to tie my shoes.

We're silent as he rings us up, but I can feel his curious gaze. Usually I joke or make conversation with Trey, but not today.

Warner calls as we're leaving. "What's up?" I say into the phone as I press the speaker button.

"Tenley's in labor. We're at the hospital." Excitement trickles through his voice. "They say it's progressing quickly."

"We're stopping for gas, and then we'll get your mother and Gramps and make our way over," my dad says, leaning over to talk into the phone.

Warner gives us instructions for what room they're in and we wish them luck and hang up.

"I'll be damned," my dad says, a smile on his face. "Another grandbaby."

I wish I'd recorded that. Nobody would ever believe those words came from the mouth of Beau Hayden.

Dad pulls off for gas on the way home. There are only two pumps, and one of them is out of service. We have to wait in a short line, and both of us are antsy.

When it's our turn, my dad shifts the truck into drive and inches forward. I'm starving, and thirsty, and I'd better rectify that before I go sit in a hospital and wait. As soon as we're at the pump I'm going to run inside the convenience store and grab—

"What the fuck?" my dad growls, his fingers tightening on the steering wheel. A small, shiny sports car has cut the line and slipped in front of us, lining himself up with the gas pump. The owner gets out and walks around the back of his tiny car, refusing to look our way.

The passenger door opens at the same time my dad rolls down his window. "Hey, asshole. You think you're too good to wait in line like everyone else?"

The driver grabs the pump and turns, fixing my dad with a contemptuous stare. It's the same look as the Marks brothers, but on a person with far more money. I guess entitlement can develop independent of wealth.

"You snooze you lose, old man." The guy inserts the nozzle into the car and releases it.

The passenger climbs reluctantly from the car. *No fucking way*. Sawyer Bennett.

He has the decency to look embarrassed. He murmurs

something to his friend, who glances at the side of our truck where the HCC logo is affixed, and shrugs.

Sawyer walks into the convenience store, and his friend gives us an obnoxious and poor attempt at a salute before following him inside. Wes would throat punch him for that.

I start to open my car door but my dad stops me. "Don't, Son."

I don't give a fuck anymore. Contracts are signed, Sawyer can't pull his funding from Jo, which means he gets to answer for the company he keeps. "I'm not going to do anything crazy, but they don't get to show up in my town and act like—"

My dad lets off the brake. The truck rolls forward.

"Dad, what the hell are you doing?"

"Teaching a lesson those fancy pricks won't soon forget."

The truck inches forward, and when the front bumper kisses the car's back bumper, there's barely anything to indicate it has occurred. A small tap on the gas is all it takes for the car to move. Dad keeps going, giving it enough gas to move the car out of the way. The hose from the gas pump grows taut, and Dad stops before it disconnects from the line above. I climb out, pull the pump from the Audi TT, and insert it in our truck. Someone in line honks, and I look over. A man has his hand out the window, and he yells, "Show them how it's done, Hayden!"

"This is going to be all over the town in no time," I say to my dad through the open window.

He shrugs. "Add it to everything else people say about us. At least it'll be true."

I open my mouth to comment but there's a shriek behind me.

"You... you..." The entitled dickhead can't get more than

that one word out. He stares at his car. In one hand is a soda, in the other a candy bar. Sawyer is behind him, and though he's shocked too, he's far more composed. He might actually think it's funny if the upward curve of one corner of his mouth is any indication.

"You moved my car." His voice has an edge now, and he comes toward me. I stride forward to meet him, but Sawyer pulls him back, so I slow.

"Don't come into my town and act disrespectful," I bark at him. Behind me, the gas pump clicks, signaling the tank is full. Sawyer steers his friend around me and all the way to their car.

I finish up at the pump, then climb back in. My dad pulls around the Audi, still sitting in its spot. The guy is circling the car, looking for damage. I doubt there's any.

He looks up at me as we pass, a sneer curling his lip. I offer him a one-fingered wave.

"Who was that?" my dad asks as we pull back onto the road.

"No idea. I've never seen that car before."

"The passenger."

"Huh?"

"Who was the passenger?"

My dad's curiosity confuses me. Why does he care?

"Sawyer Bennett. He's the silent investor in Jo's ranch."

"Bennett," my dad repeats quietly. He runs his tongue along the inside of his cheeks, and hand to God I can see the man's wheels turning. "I'll be damned," he says under his breath.

"Why?"

Slowly, he shakes his head. "No reason."

He's lying.

Not bullshitting. Lying.

Tenley has a girl and names her Lyla. She is tiny, with a shock of dark Hayden hair. We each take turns holding her, though admittedly I take the most time. I earn my name of baby hog. After a while, Warner kicks us out. Tenley needs to rest.

I start my drive over to Wildflower, but after the situation at the gas station this morning I change my mind. I have an important and impromptu stop to make.

"Farley," I say when he opens the door.

The short, stocky, sixteen-year-old boy walks away, leaving the front door of his apartment wide open. "Why can't you call me by my first name like everyone else?" he says over his shoulder. He's wearing plaid pajama pants and a Guns N' Roses T-shirt.

I step into the apartment. It smells like Hot Pockets. "Because your first name is worse than your last name. Farley is the lesser of two evils. Unless you want me to shorten Eldridge to El. That I can do."

He stops in the doorway of his small room. "I like El. El Capitan."

"Farley it is."

He gives me a dirty look and sits down at his desk. His room is filthy and I don't even want to name what it smells like.

"I need your help."

"I told you last time was the last time."

"Do you want me to tell Tenley how I came to be the one to return her underwear?" I give Farley a warning look, and he shrinks.

"No," he sighs. Farley has a huge crush on Tenley, especially since he met her in town a few months ago. Before that, his crush was less innocent and a lot more perverted. He'd let himself into the house where she was staying when she first came to town, and stole her underwear. He'd put them up for sale on the internet, and didn't realize the sign visible through a window in the background of one of his pictures was recognizable to anybody who'd grown up in Sierra Grande. Farley and his mother live within a stone's throw of the Merc, and clear as day was the Merc's sign with the bright green light-up Saguaro beside the M. From there I'd asked around, listened in on some teenage conversations at the diner, and when I learned who this kid was, I posed as an interested buyer and watched him respond to me from where he sat at the diner, slurping his strawberry milkshake. He about peed himself when I walked up and tapped his shoulder. He begged me not to tell Tenley, and since then I've been milking his hacking skills.

"What do you need?" Farley asks, picking up four Skittles from the pile lying on top of his desk.

"I need to know what Sawyer Bennett's connection is to this town." I frown as I think of my dad's reaction. "And to the Circle B."

"You mean Wildflower?"

I stare at the side of Farley's head until he looks at me. "The new sign isn't up yet. How do you know it's called Wildflower?"

"I can't tell you all my secrets."

A muscle in my jaw tics and Farley relents. "Fine. You're

so intense." He looks back at his computer. "I overheard Jo and Dakota talking, and I was curious so I looked it up and saw the articles of incorporation had recently been approved."

"Hmph." I walk away and stop at the door. "Tell me when you have info on Sawyer Bennett."

"Aye, aye, captain," he says sarcastically.

I keep going into the short hallway. "And stay the fuck out of Jo Shelton's business."

"You're an asshole," he yells after me.

"At least I'm not a virgin," I yell back.

He's saying something else but I don't hear it, because the front door is closing behind me.

28

JO

"So, this is the place?" Travis peers out the windshield as we take the turnoff for Wildflower. He sounds skeptical.

I nudge him. "Give it a chance. Pretty soon those buildings will have walls, and there will be horses in the pen, and the main house will have more outward character. Right now all the charm is on the inside."

"And a sign?" He thumbs behind him. "Because that old dirty sign said Circle B."

I ruffle his hair and he tamps it back down. "The new sign comes this week."

I picked it out a couple weeks ago, from a metal workshop in the next town. It looks like plain metal, until the sun shines on it, and the whole sign lights up in color. Just like a field of wildflowers.

We pull up and get out. I almost can't believe it's ready. Livable. Our new home. Travis eyes the main house in front of us.

"Not bad," he says, looking around.

I point to the step he's standing on. "A few months ago

you couldn't have stood there without falling in. Wyatt Hayden fixed it."

"Wyatt Hayden? Peyton Hayden's uncle?"

I nod, realizing I never think of him that way. "I'm surprised you remember him."

"I remember all the Hayden's. They'd be hard to forget. I remember thinking that they were all real cowboys. The whole family."

I chuckle. "Yeah. I guess they are."

"Why was he out here? Doesn't he work on his family's ranch?"

"He does. But he's been helping me get the main house ready."

"Why?"

I'm definitely not telling him the whole story, so instead I opt for a sprinkle of truth. "He and I are seeing each other."

Is that what we're doing? Last night was the first time we've spent a night apart since the day he hauled in a bathtub and filled it with hot water. *Seeing each other* sounds anticlimactic when I consider how I feel about Wyatt.

He nods once. "That's cool."

Travis tells me he's going to explore the property. I wait out front for the handyman, who arrives a few minutes later. His truck has a Vale Handyman Services decal on the side, and the driver hops out and strides forward.

"Jo?" he asks, sticking out a hand. "I'm Connor."

We make small talk and I tell him about Wildflower. He thinks it's a great idea, and asks me to show him what needs to be done. As I'm walking him around, he mentions he has a one-year-old son and a wife. When I jokingly mention I'm still figuring out how to market Wildflower, he tells me his wife has a knack for sending the right message to the right people.

"She's like this bright light and people gravitate to her." I wonder if he knows he smiles when he talks about her. "She could sell ice to an Alaskan in the dead of winter."

I ask for her number and he texts it to me. I text her immediately, explaining who I am and what I need. *Carpe diem*, right?

Wyatt shows up about halfway through my walk through with Connor. They shake hands, and Connor says he wrote a report about the Hayden Cattle Company in high school. Wyatt does his closest approximation to blushing, and Connor asks if any of the rumors are true.

"Probably most of them," Wyatt responds, and Connor laughs.

Before Connor leaves, we agree on a time when he can start. He takes off with a wave, and I thank him for putting me in touch with his wife.

Wyatt wraps his arms around my waist and kisses me on the mouth. It sends shivers from the top of my head to the tips of my toes and reminds me that we missed out on being together last night.

He pulls my hips into him, pressing his length against my stomach, and a garbled moan swims up my throat.

"Jo?" Travis calls for me from inside the house. I take a step away from Wyatt, my expression one of longing and apology, and a few seconds later Travis walks from the house.

I know Travis knows who Wyatt is, but he doesn't come forward, so I make the introduction. Travis acts a tad awestruck. I get it. I spent years feeling that way when I looked at Wyatt.

Wyatt asks Travis questions about school, about his interests, about sports teams. Travis wants to know about cattle ranching and lights up when Wyatt tells him he has more to do with the horses than the cattle.

The furniture delivery guy gets lost and calls me, and I guide him to Wildflower. He pulls in with his large truck, and Wyatt starts helping the two men carry in the furniture.

"Travis, help us out," he calls, nodding Travis over.

I watch Travis join in, as tall as the full-grown men but not nearly filled out. He laughs when one of the delivery guys makes a joke, and I'm struck by how much older he looks right now. He helps with every piece of furniture, and when everything is in, he asks Wyatt if there's any more work to be done. Wyatt tells him he could use a hand on the property, starting tomorrow.

"It's unpaid," Wyatt warns. "But the experience has value."

"Sign me up," Travis replies. I wonder if he would be so enthusiastic if it were me asking him to help. Probably not.

Wyatt runs into town to grab takeout, and Travis and I put sheets on our new beds.

"I like him," Travis says, pulling the fitted sheet over the corner of the mattress, while I do the other side.

"You don't say," I tease.

"He seems like a real man. Henri is nice, but he's"—Travis lifts a limp hand in the air and swings it around—"kinda girly."

I laugh. "I don't think you're allowed to describe things as girly anymore, but I get your point. And I don't disagree." Wyatt is a hundred times more manly than Henri could ever hope to be.

Wyatt returns, and we eat dinner. I joke about how much

food he's brought, but it's like he has seen the future and he knows Travis will eat enough for two adult men.

"My mom used to complain about how much we ate, especially when she had three teenage boys in the house at the same time."

I stab a piece of chicken before Travis can. I've already learned to be quick and stake my claim on food, or I'll go hungry. "I can't imagine how much food she made to keep you three fed."

"She tripled recipes. I helped her in the kitchen sometimes. It wasn't my favorite thing to do, but she liked it. And Wes and Warner definitely weren't up for it. Warner didn't cook at all until Anna left and he was forced to learn so he could feed his kids. I'm not sure when Wes learned. The military, maybe."

Travis hangs on Wyatt's every word. "I wish I had siblings."

I clear my throat in an obvious way. Travis rolls his eyes. "You know what I mean. Someone near me in age. Someone I can fight with and grow up with."

I know exactly how he feels. I used to feel that way too.

When dinner is finished we sit on the new couch in the living room and play Heads Up! on Wyatt's phone. Wyatt and I are awful, but Travis gets almost every clue.

I stay up after Travis goes to bed and Wyatt helps me tidy the kitchen. I look around at the living areas, thinking of what needs to go where. There's so much to do, so many purchases to make so this house feels more like a home, but I'm getting there.

"Are you ready for bed in your new home?" Wyatt's lips graze the skin just below my ear. I melt into him, my toes curling in anticipation.

We lock up, and he follows me to the bedroom, with a new bed and fresh sheets. Everything feels like a fresh start, and my heart soars.

We're quiet and slow, savoring. I love how Wyatt can be tough and rugged, but sensitive and sweet. The kind of man who can be a good example for a young, impressionable teenager.

Who'd have ever thought I'd say that about Wyatt Hayden?

I fall asleep with a smile on my lips and Wyatt's arms wrapped around me.

I have Wyatt, and I have Travis. I've never been so happy.

THE INSISTENT TRILL OF THE PHONE WAKES ME. I REACH MY hand to the nightstand, where I flip my phone over and see it's not my phone ringing. I blink against the brightness of the screen. The clock reads 1:24.

"Wyatt," I mutter as the ringing continues. "Someone's calling you."

We'd left the bathroom light on and the door ajar, just because it was impossible to see anything when we were going to sleep. In the soft light, I watch Wyatt blink awake, confused, and then throw off the covers and look around. Naked, he hurries to the jeans on the floor and pulls the phone from his front pocket.

"What's wrong?" he asks, not bothering with a greeting.

I scramble onto my knees and watch him, trying to pick up any hint about who in his family is calling.

Could it be about Beau? Another heart attack? My stomach turns to lead. *Gramps.*

Wyatt cradles the phone between his shoulder and his head and shoves his legs into his jeans. "I'm on my way. Lock yourself and the kids in the bathroom." He hangs up.

What the fuck?

"What's going on?" I ask as I watch him dart around, shoving his wallet and keys into his pockets and pulling a shirt over his head.

"Where're my shoes?" he asks, looking around in the dim light.

"By the front door, but—"

He rushes from the room, and I climb off the bed and follow.

"Wyatt," I whisper-hiss, glancing down the hall at Travis's closed door as I go. "Tell me what's going on. I'm scared."

He looks up at me as he pushes his feet into his boots. "Mickey showed up unexpectedly, and he's drunk. He hurts Sara when he's been drinking, and he said he heard around town that she's been stepping out on him while he's away." He lets out a short breath and shakes his head. "This is my fault. I should've found a better way of helping them."

"You can't go there, Wyatt. What if Mickey gets violent with you?"

"That's why I go. So that he'll have someone else to fight."

It hits me that this isn't new to Wyatt. Sara calls him for help. And it explains all the times I've seen Wyatt with bruises and assumed he was getting in drunken bar fights.

"You need to call the police, Wyatt."

Wyatt shakes his head. "Absolutely not. Mickey won't ever come back from it if the police are called."

He rushes from the house and jumps in his truck. Leaning out, he yells. "Don't call the police, Jo."

I nod.

"Promise me," he says.

"I promise." Even as I say it, I know I won't keep it.

He hits the gas, and just like that, he's gone.

Wyatt thinks he will burst into the situation and calm it, like some kind of human salve. If Mickey heard Sara is cheating on him, it's likely he also heard the rest of the rumor. And Wyatt is walking right into it, using that signature confidence that might get him in a lot of trouble. It's a risk I'm not willing to take.

I run to the bedroom, grab my phone and dial.

"Do you know what time it is?" Shelby asks, voice thick with sleep.

"Schultz's house," I pant, pulling on a sweatshirt. "The police need to get there. I don't know the address, but I know you do. Go there. Send someone there. Now, Shelby. Now."

"What's the problem, Jo? I need more to go on." All sleepiness is gone from her tone.

I wipe tears I don't remember crying. "Domestic dispute. Wyatt's on his way. Sara called and he told her to hide in the bathroom with the kids."

Shelby hangs up on me. If it weren't for Travis, I'd be headed there now.

I know I promised him, but I couldn't sit back and blindly follow his instructions. I'm capable of thinking for myself, and I made the choice I thought was best. I hope he sees that.

I climb onto the bed, press my back to the headboard, and wait.

29

WYATT

I was too late.

By the time I got there, Mickey was on his knees in the front yard. Handcuffed. He met my eyes as they led him to the squad car. His gaze hardened, his jaw flexed. I reminded myself that he thinks I'm sleeping with his wife. He wouldn't look at me so hatefully if he knew the truth.

Sara sobs in the front yard as she talks to an officer. She holds the baby, while Shelby distracts the three-year-old.

"Wyatt," Sara cries when she sees me. Shelby and I share a look in the light from the front porch.

Sara drifts away from the police officer, coming toward me.

"What happened?" I ask, taking the baby from her. With her arms empty, she shudders and grips her arms in front of herself.

"He walked in the front door and scared all of us. I was giving Bryce a bath and the baby was asleep. He was drunk and carrying on about how he'd heard what a whore I'd been. He said he bet Eliana isn't even his."

I look down at the baby girl in my arms. "I'm sorry, Sara. I tried to get here."

Tears roll down her cheeks. "What am I going to do? I don't have a job. We have no money saved. None. We're two months behind on our mortgage."

"You'll get a job, Sara. You have a degree."

She makes a disbelieving sound. "I can't imagine the demand for a psychologist is very strong. This town doesn't produce the kind of men who would use my services."

"Then you'll have an all-female clientele."

"Yeah, and I'll become public enemy number one because all the wives are enlightened and in touch with their feelings." Her laugh is hollow as she wipes her face and looks down at the surrounding houses. Every single house has a light on, and people outside. "I can't imagine what they're going to say about me now. This'll be the juiciest gossip to ever be whispered."

"I wonder which one of them called," I murmur, my gaze running over each home.

Sara sniffles and shakes her head. "That's what I can't figure out. There wasn't any yelling. Any arguing. I was terrified because I knew it was coming, and I called you."

Immediately I know it was Jo.

"Can I see Mickey Schultz?"

The front desk sergeant is bleary-eyed, steam rises from a fresh cup of coffee on his desk. Maybe in a big city he'd tell me no, but this is a small town, and the rules are sometimes pliable.

He leads me back to the holding cells. There are three, and Mickey is in the last one. He sits on a metal bench, his elbows on his thighs and his head in his hands. He doesn't look up at the sound of our approach.

"You have fifteen minutes," the officer grunts, glancing at Mickey before he leaves.

Mickey raised his head as soon as the officer spoke, and now he watches him leave. When he's out of earshot, Mickey says two words. "Fuck you."

He leans back against the painted brick and crosses his arms in front of his chest. "Fuck you," he says again, this time with more of an edge to his voice.

"It isn't true. What you've heard is wrong."

Mickey leans forward suddenly. "You're not fucking my wife while I'm gone earning the money that pays for our home and puts food on the table?" He stands as he talks, walking closer to the bars.

I stand still and look him in his eyes. "No."

"Then why did I hear your truck is leaving marks in my yard when I'm not there?"

"People don't know shit in this town, Mickey. They see my truck at your house and make an assumption, because they'd never think I'm there to intercept you or clean up after you."

"What the fuck's that supposed to mean?"

"Do you ever look in the mirror and see what you've become? Do you really see yourself?"

Right now he looks like shit. Red, swollen eyes, his hair sticking up in places. An angry scratch stretches jaggedly down the side of his neck. But these physical characteristics aren't what I'm referring to. I want to know if he sees his heart, his soul.

"I'm a man trying to keep his family together. And now that's ruined. The police are going to press charges, and my family is fucked."

"I'm waiting for you to show some remorse, but it doesn't seem like I should hold my breath. You were hurting Sara. Your *wife*. What the fuck is wrong with you?"

"It was only a few times, and they were more like accidents. I didn't mean it. I'd had too much to drink, and—"

"Bullshit. That's weak. You know how liquor makes you act, and you drank it anyway. Over and over and over. You came home hammered, and you hurt your wife. Scared your kids. You created this situation." I gesture around the place. "This is your doing. And I'm to blame too. I enabled you. Every time I showed up and let you use me as a punching bag instead of your wife. Every time I came over and distracted you until you sobered up. All because Sara thought you'd change back to the guy she first married. Because I felt like I owed you. You saved my life once, and I thought I was saving yours. But now I see there's some shit you can't come back from. You did this. You put yourself here. This"—I swirl my finger above my head—"is on you."

I turn to leave, but his voice calls me back. "You'd be dead if it wasn't for me."

"That doesn't mean I have to clean up your mess every time you make one."

I walk away, and leave him standing there.

Without even thinking about it, I drive straight out to Wildflower. Jo's sitting out front, her knees pulled into her chest. She stands when I park, but stays at the top of the stairs, leaning against the porch railing.

"I know you're probably mad at me," she starts, trailing off, waiting for me to confirm.

I sigh and look up at the sky. It's the darkest part of the night. Fitting, since this also feels like one of the darkest moments of my life. I pride myself on caring for the people I love, even if that means using nontraditional ways, and I failed Mickey and Sara. Whether it was my responsibility or not, I wanted to help them figure out a way out of their mess. I don't know how I thought it all would end up, but I'd prayed this wouldn't be it.

I level my gaze on Jo. Her hair is tied in a messy knot on top of her head, her sweats are as ratty as her shirt. My heart squeezes, and I think about what I'd do if someone hurt her the way Mickey hurt Sara. They'd never get the chance to hurt anybody again, that's for damn sure, and nobody would ever find the body.

"I'm not mad at you, Jo." I'm at odds with my dad. My friendship with Mickey is very likely over. The last thing I want is to have conflict with the woman I love.

I reach for her, and she starts down the steps, placing her hand in mine. I pull her into me, wrapping my arms around her. The world around us is still, even the insects are asleep. She feels like an anchor, a tether, keeping me attached when everything feels off-kilter.

"Just to let you know," Jo says into my chest, "I take promises seriously. But I'll break them when I think safety is threatened."

I kiss the top of her head. "I wish I'd done the same."

"How so?"

"Sara made me promise not to tell anybody what was happening with Mickey, or call the police. That's a promise I should've broken." The weight of it all pushes down on my shoulders. Now that the problem has grown wings and expanded beyond the four walls of the Schultz home, I see how stupid it was to keep such a thing contained.

Jo palms my cheek, reaching on tiptoe to lightly kiss me. "Don't be so hard on yourself. You like to take care of people. In your own Wyatt way."

I look down at her. "Wyatt way?"

"Outlaw logic," she whispers.

I rub her lower back. "Can I call you Lady Outlaw?"

She laughs. "Hardly. I'm a rule girl."

"I bet you'd break some rules if you had to."

"Let's hope I'm not forced to."

"Can I force you back to bed for some sleep?"

She nods, a yawn widening her mouth at the mention of sleep, and I follow her inside. At the sight of the closed door at the end of the hall, I ask, "Did Travis wake up?"

Jo shakes her head as she pulls back the comforter. "He's a heavy sleeper." We are exhausted, physically and emotionally, but she needs the same thing I do right now. We slip under the covers, and Jo pulls at me until I'm on top of her. She presses her face to my neck and tells me how scared she was. I push inside of her, and admit how relieved I am it's no longer my burden to carry. I tell her I love her, and she says it back.

Later, when she's asleep with her head on my chest, I find I can't quite calm my mind down. I keep seeing Mickey, the metal bars casting shadows on his face.

I'd been in shadow too, on that day when he found me.

30

WYATT

Seventeen years old

Hunting.

A ritual. A rite of passage.

A Hayden tradition. I remember when Wes went. I remember waving goodbye to Warner when he went. I dreaded knowing I would be next, but I wouldn't be seventeen for two more years, and two years may as well have been ten as far as I was concerned.

Except two years really passed like two months, and today is the day. It's deer season. I want nothing to do with hunting deer. I want everything to do with making my dad happy.

My mom knocks on my door twice before she pushes in. She hands me a bag. "It's a new jacket," she explains unnecessarily as I pull out the thick, tan fabric. "It'll be cold at night."

I finger the stiff fabric. The inside is softer. "Thanks, Mom."

"Sure." She twists the gold bracelet on her wrist. I think she has more to say, but she's holding back. "Are you looking forward to it?"

I give her a look.

She smiles lopsidedly. "Stupid question, huh?"

"I don't want to go, Mom."

She purses her lips, making a noise when she releases them. "You're very lucky you were drawn. Not everyone gets a tag."

I give her another look. "Was it just luck that Wes and Warner were drawn their first time entering too?"

Her only response is a long, hard stare. I sound ungrateful. Maybe I *am* ungrateful. How many of my friends wanted to get drawn for a deer tag? How many whispered behind my back that the only reason I got one is my last name?

"Never mind," I mutter. "I'm sure it'll be fine."

My mom touches my shoulder. "Your dad's been looking forward to this for a long time. And don't tell him I told you this"—she pretends to look for him around my room—"but I think he's sad. You're his last son. Which means this is his last father-son hunting trip."

"He and Warner go hunting all the time."

"You know what I mean. The last of the tradition. I think it's hitting him hard."

"He can take Jessie in twelve years."

"Quit arguing with me."

"I'm seventeen. I'm supposed to argue."

She smiles affectionately. I know she has a soft spot for me, mostly because Wes and Warner don't let me forget it.

"Wyatt," my dad calls from somewhere beyond my bedroom. "Load up, Son."

I shoot my mom a look. She nods encouragingly. "Go have fun. Make some memories." Her hand drifts through my hair. "Before long, you'll be grown."

She's feeling nostalgic. Wes ships out in a few weeks. Warner is always with his girlfriend. Jessie and I are all she has left. Then again, our business is run by family, and it's not like any of us, with the exception of Wes going into the military, are going to go very far.

Despite this, she's doing her mom thing. Soft-focus gaze, misty eyes. It's in conflict with the way she is the rest of the time.

"I'm already grown, Mom." I stand six inches taller than her.

She laughs once, a single sound. "Oh, Wyatt. You're still young enough to not know all the things you don't know."

"That sounds like a riddle."

Dad calls my name again, and she urges me on with a palm to my back. "You'll figure it out one day."

We walk out to the living room, and there's my dad, wearing brown pants and a camouflage long-sleeved shirt. He tosses a matching shirt in my direction.

"Can't wear red to go hunting," he says, bending over to rifle through his pack.

No shit. I know better than to say it out loud. "I brought a shirt to change into."

"Change into the shirt I gave you."

I do as he says, pulling off my T-shirt right there. My mom grabs it from me, sending me a wink.

"You boys have fun." She kisses my cheek, then pecks my dad on the lips. "Bring back my son in one piece."

My eyes protest as the binoculars press into the skin around my eyes. We've been glassing all day, and my limbs are stiff from sitting in one place for so long.

This is day two of the hunt, and I'm not looking forward to repeating all this tomorrow. The entire experience isn't the worst, there are parts of it that are actually enjoyable. I like the smell of the campfire. The quiet, and solitude. I don't mind sleeping in a tent, especially when I can see through the flap at the top and stare at the stars. I wish my dad was more of a talker, but it's not like his tendency to keep his thoughts to himself is a big surprise.

I don't even mind it when—

"There, there," my dad whispers with quiet urgency. He points out in the distance, and I train my binos in that direction.

"Buck, a hundred yards out," he whispers excitedly. "Ten-pointer."

The animal is huge, beautiful, a deep, tawny brown with lighter-colored ears. It nibbles at something on the ground, unsuspecting.

"Get your rifle, Wyatt." His voice is low, his tone holds irritation that I didn't automatically grab for my gun.

I do as he says, setting up the gun and training my scope on the animal, even as my stomach sinks with a lead feeling.

"He's quartering," my dad says, squatting beside me. "Aim for the shoulder you can see."

The shot is lined up. Everything is in place. The cold

steel trigger feels more like a flame against the pad of my finger.

My breath sticks in my throat, my heartbeat thunders against my ribs.

"Go on, Son. Now."

This is the moment I show my dad a third son wasn't the worst thing, that I can be worthy too. But the longer I look through that scope, the deer in my sight, the more I know I can't sacrifice its life.

The deer lifts its head, spooked by something unseen to me, and darts up, skirting the hillside and disappearing from view.

"Damn it," my dad shouts, the need to care about noise long gone. "What the hell, Wyatt?"

His hands are in the air, and his eyes hold that old familiar look. *Disappointment.*

I'm not sure what to say next, but it doesn't matter, because he has plenty to say.

"Wes and Warner both bagged good-sized bucks on this hunt, and neither of them had the opportunity you just choked on."

"I—"

He steps closer, near enough I can smell the burned black coffee he's been sipping on all day. "Don't tell me you didn't have a clear mark. He was close range and you have the best shot of any of your brothers."

I gnash my teeth together, thoughts and words flying through me, turning to grit on my tongue until finally I let them out. "I don't want to shoot an animal."

He laughs, a disbelieving sound. "The cattle rancher's son doesn't want to kill an animal. How ironic."

"At least not that animal," I explain, in an attempt to

salvage something out of this. "It was unaware. Eating something. Innocent."

"Is that your criteria? It must be aware of your presence, hungry, and guilty of something?"

My jaw aches from how tightly my muscles clench. "Maybe that last one." It strikes a chord with me, the idea of something bad happening only when you've done something bad. Some might call it karma, but I think of it as some other type of justice. Vigilante, maybe, or outlaw.

My dad stares at me for a long time, and I pretend for a brief second that he is going to drop the macho act and open his arms, tell me he accepts me for who I am, and doesn't need a third son who behaves like the other two.

My daydream is snatched away when he breaks the silence by asking, "Do you know what you just gave up?"

I look into his eyes that match mine, a face that I will likely resemble more and more as I age, and answer, "Yeah. I do."

We walk back to camp. We pack up, disassemble our tent, and make sure all our trash is picked up. Neither of us speak, and we don't say anything the entire two-hour drive home.

My mom told my dad to bring me home in one piece, but now I see she didn't mean physically.

Mentally.

Emotionally.

I am fucking shattered.

The Outlaw

THERE'S A CANYON EIGHT MILES OUTSIDE OF TOWN. DEVIL'S Canyon, it's called, I think because it's hot as hell at the height of summer. I've always considered the name to be incorrect, seeing as how heat rises, but maybe it gets its name from the people who dare to rappel it. Sometimes water flows through, courtesy of the Colorado River. Other times it's dry, and there's nothing but jagged pain at the bottom.

It's the perfect place to end a life. A life that never should have been, if you ask my dad.

I don't want to die. Not really. But I do want to stop hurting.

I love my brothers. I love my mom and my sister. Gramps. I love my dad too, in that way that a dog loves its owner even when the owner abuses it.

But wouldn't it be nice if none of it had to happen anymore?

I kick my leg out, let it bounce against the canyon wall. I'm sitting at the top, gathering small rocks and tossing them in. By the time they reach the bottom, I can hardly see them land.

It would be quick. I think.

A plane flies overhead, a passenger jet, and I think of the two hundred or so people on board, none of them aware of what they flew over. For a split second, I shared the same sliver of earth with those strangers, and now they are miles away.

In the distance, I hear a rumbling, but it's not another plane. It's clearly an engine, and from what I can tell, not very well maintained. I look back, watching it approach.

Closer and closer it comes, until I know it's my best friend, Mickey Schultz. I didn't tell him I was coming out here, only that the trip was a failure and my dad now hates me more than before.

Mickey climbs out of his dad's old truck and comes my way. He's a few inches shorter than me, and stockier, which makes him a damn good football player.

He nods at me when he gets close. His eyes are weary and worried. "This isn't your usual scene."

I nod.

"But I thought maybe you were going off the grid. I tried the lookout first. When you weren't there, I figured what the hell, and tried this place."

"Bingo," I deadpan.

Mickey comes closer, kicking up dirt with each slow step.

"Don't," I say sharply, my hand stuck out. "It's dangerous." I know this is ironic, considering I'm the one sitting on the edge with my legs dangling over.

Mickey ignores me. He sits on the ground a few feet away, scooting forward until he's sitting like I am. His brown-blond curls hang low on his forehead and he squints in the dying early evening light that shines in his face. "What now?" he asks.

"I came out here to think," I explain, even though he didn't ask. It's a lie. Maybe. I'm not sure yet. How certain is anybody when they make the decision?

Mickey folds his hands in his lap and stares down at them. Quietly, he says, "If you jump, I jump."

"That's not why—"

He repeats himself. "If you jump, I jump." This time he says it with his face turned toward me.

I shake my head. I don't want to be seen as a person who

might do what I'd been considering. "You've got it wrong, man. I—"

"If you jump, I jump." Rougher, louder, more insistent, and he inches across the canyon edge, closing the distance between us until we're less than a foot away. "Fuck your dad, Wyatt. Fuck him. Fuck him for hurting you. Fuck him for acting like your brothers are more important. They're not. It's that simple. They. Are. Not. I love you, okay?" He holds out a palm like a handshake, but that's not what he's asking for. "Don't make me say all that shit again. Because I will."

Somewhere between the bleakness in my heart and the utter despair that coats my chest, a tiny flicker rises, like the flame from a lighter.

I place my grip in Mickey's, and he uses his other hand to steady himself on the ground and push himself away from the edge, watching hawklike to make sure I do the same. He does this until we're fifteen-feet back, as though he's afraid to let me go, fearful I may take that leap after all.

Mickey gets to his feet and pulls me to standing. He hugs me once, quickly, a strong clap on my back. He drives behind me all the way to the ranch, turning around after I make the right under the massive Hayden Cattle Company sign. He waves at me from his open window and disappears from sight.

31

JO

I'm so relieved Wyatt isn't angry with me, I'm nearly floating. He's still sleeping, and I have no plans to wake him. He carries such heavy burdens on those wide shoulders of his. He deserves to rest.

I'm the only one awake right now, so I take my coffee and make my way out front. I knew when I was ordering furniture I'd have to include chairs and a table for the porch, and I'm so glad I did. I think this is going to be my favorite spot in the whole house. Except the bathtub.

The morning sun is strong enough to warm my skin, and a slight breeze pushes through the overgrown grass. I raise my coffee to my lips, and through the steam spot a flash of red.

The male cardinal dashes across the open sky, settling in a tree. It's always amazed me how incongruous the red feathers are with the desert landscape. As if, upon creation, God asked the bird if he'd like to blend into his environment the way most birds do, and the cardinal refused.

I watch the male chase a female, this one colored a

grayish-brown. She hops from branch to branch, making his pursuit a little more exciting, and then they both fly away. I'm assuming his advances were accepted. Lucky guy.

"Hey you," Wyatt rasps, stepping from the front door. His hair sticks up in the most perfectly adorable tufts, and as if he's read my mind he reaches up and runs his hands through his hair. With one eye open, he trudges toward me and settles in the chair beside me. I hand him my nearly empty coffee and he takes the final sip.

"More," he groans.

"I'll bet you need it," I answer. "We both do. Come on."

He gets up and follows me in, but not without kissing me first. The look in his eyes is captivating. He looks lighter, like overnight he let go of a weight he'd been carrying. And in a way, he did.

I pour us each a fresh cup of coffee. Wyatt reminds me we don't have food yet, not anything substantial we can make for Travis.

Travis.

I can't believe he's really here. With me. Living in my house.

It takes him another hour to wake up, and I use the time to go out to the future camper's building and measure rooms so I can get the beds ordered.

Travis finds me in one of the rooms, sitting on the floor and pouring over different beds on a website. "So this place is going to be a camp, huh?"

I look up. "Yeah."

"It's a little small for a summer camp."

"It's going to be a special type of camp."

"Like what?"

I tuck the phone in my back pocket. "A wilderness therapy camp."

"Therapy? Like physical therapy?"

"More like emotional therapy."

Travis crosses his arms and leans back against the wall beside the open door. He wears a nondescript white shirt and black jeans. "A camp for bad kids."

"No."

"That's what it sounds like."

"That's not what I said." I climb to my feet and dust my hands on the seat of my jeans, waiting for him to say more.

"Did you buy this place and build all this because you think I'm a bad kid who needs your camp?" He says it like he's completely devoid of emotion, but I see all of it swimming in his eyes. How badly he needs to hear that he's not my reason for all this.

"No, because you're not a bad kid. But I am really happy that you're here, because I think you could be pretty useful around this place."

He tips his head. "Yeah?"

"Mm-hmm. I do. So does Wyatt. He can teach you a lot, too. I've already learned a lot from him."

"How does he know how to do stuff around here?"

I palm his shoulder, guiding him away from the wall and out the door. We reach the door at the end of the hall that leads to the outside. "I have absolutely no idea, Trav. He's just a person who knows stuff."

Travis nods, and I watch my words sink in like butter on warm toast. My mom tried to tell me adolescents are difficult, and maybe she's right and the difficulty is on its way, but she failed to mention how rewarding it is to watch them grow.

Travis tries to order a chocolate milkshake to go with his breakfast. It's where I have to draw the line.

"I'm cool, but I'm not *that* cool," I say, laughing with our server, Cherilyn, as she gathers our plastic menus.

"I know you don't remember me," Cherilyn says to Travis, "but your big sister used to bring you in here on Fridays after school let out. You ordered a sundae with strawberry topping, and half of it always ended up on your face and your shirt."

Travis smiles shyly. "It's nice to see you again."

Cherilyn gives him a hearty wink before she walks away.

"I definitely don't remember her," Travis murmurs and makes a funny face.

"Don't worry about it," Wyatt says, pulling his straw from his drink and placing it on his napkin. "Wes grew up in this town and when he came back from the Army he didn't remember her either."

I frown playfully at him. "I think it had more to do with him never coming to town after he got back as opposed to a faulty memory."

"Thank God for Dakota," Wyatt says, and adds, "And Tenley, too. Both my brothers are a hell of a lot nicer with those women in their lives." Wyatt discreetly rubs his hand over my thigh. "I'm told I am too."

I lean my shoulder into his. "Is that right?"

"Every cowboy on the ranch has made a comment to me over the past month. And every member of my family, because of course they can't keep their noses out of my business."

"Even your dad?" As soon as I say it I wish I hadn't.

Wyatt's face falls a fraction. "Not my dad. He doesn't count when I say stuff like that."

He changes the subject after that, asking Travis when his birthday is. When Travis answers, Wyatt looks at me with wide eyes. "That's only two months away."

"So?" I ask, uncertain of where Wyatt's going with this.

Wyatt directs his attention across the Formica tabletop at Travis. "Do you have your learner's permit?"

"For driving?" Travis asks.

"No, for walking." Wyatt grins at Travis to let him know he's joking, and Travis laughs. "Yes, for driving."

Travis shakes his head. "My mom never got around to it when the time came a few months ago."

Wyatt smacks his palm on the table, and I jump. "Well, what do you say, Travis? Do you want to learn to drive a car?"

My stomach tenses. Travis... drive a car? Isn't that meant for people older than him? My head is stuck on a different time when he was younger, when every tumble drew tears and required kisses. But of course, he's not a baby anymore. One glance across the table tells me that.

Travis doesn't even look at me before answering excitedly. "Yes. When? Whose car?"

"My truck," Wyatt answers, leaning back against the booth and putting his arm around my shoulders.

"I don't know," I say, biting the side of my lower lip. "Shouldn't he learn on something smaller, like my car?"

"Sure, if you want him to," Wyatt responds, shrugging. He grins at Travis. "Or, you can learn on an HCC truck.

Warner has the nicest truck right now, don't even get me started on that, but you can learn on mine."

Travis's lower lip dips in astonishment. "I can learn to drive using an HCC truck?"

Wyatt nods, nearly as excited as Travis. "Sure."

"I remember when your brother used to pick up Peyton from school in a massive truck. It was lifted and had huge tires, and I think it was a Power Stroke, and it had..." He keeps going, and I'm lost almost immediately. I'd completely forgotten Travis's old obsession with cars, the way he would study car magazines and memorize facts, pointing out vehicles and chattering endlessly every time we went anywhere.

"If you like cars, wait until you see Tenley's old Bronco. Fully restored, it's gorgeous. She named her Pearl and it has—" Wyatt cuts off, his attention grabbed by the TV in the upper corner of the wall closest to us. "Jo," he says, pointing at the screen.

Across the bottom are the words **BREAKING NEWS** followed by a man with too-perfect hair holding a microphone and gesturing with his free hand. In smaller writing that's harder to see, below the headline, **Four Dead in Shooting at Teen Therapy Camp.**

My heart sinks at the same time my stomach lurches, and they meet in a way neither ever should. I feel sick but also empty.

My first thought is of the people who died, closely followed by a far less charitable thought.

What does this mean for me?

My teeth dig into my knuckles as I watch the man continue to speak. Without sound, I can only guess he's reporting details of the shooting.

Ugh. The shooting. Such awful words.

Wyatt has already pulled his phone out, and now he pushes it over to me. The image used in the article is a split screen. One half is an aerial picture of woods and a lake and several small buildings. The second image is of first responders surrounding a stretcher, a white sheet covering the person lying on it.

I whimper at the sight, and Wyatt quickly reaches over, scrolling down to the details. I skim them quickly, unable to absorb too much right now.

"It was a camper," I whisper. I cup my hand over my mouth to stifle my urge to sob. "In Tucson. He shot another camper and two staff members."

"Jo?" Travis's hands snake across the booth. "It's going to be okay. This isn't going to happen to you. To Wildflower."

I try to smile at him. To accept his comfort. "Thanks, Trav."

Cherilyn arrives with steaming plates. "These are hot," she warns, sliding the plates in front of us.

"Thank you," I murmur, glancing up at the screen.

"Damn shame, isn't it?" Cherilyn says, tucking her oven mitt into the front pocket of her apron. "So young. Took his own life, too." She shakes her head and looks over the table. "I'll be right back with that green chile sauce you love, Wyatt."

"Thank you, ma'am." Wyatt nods at Cherilyn when she comes back. She leaves again, and the sounds of forks scraping plates are the only interruption to our quiet little corner.

"You need to eat," Wyatt reminds me gently when my food remains untouched. Nothing smells good. Not the bacon, the eggs, or even the gooey cinnamon roll Travis ordered.

"People are dead. At a teen therapy camp. Because of a camper." My head shakes slowly as my brain tries to make sense of a senseless situation. "What if it were my camp?"

"It's not," Wyatt says, grabbing the fork from my hand and preparing a bite for me. He hands it to me and I take it, mechanically placing the food in my mouth.

"Right, but—"

Wyatt shakes his head and points at my plate. "Take care of yourself, Jo. Eat. Everything else can happen second."

He's right. I do what he suggests, forcing myself to eat food I barely taste when normally I love it. Travis isn't sure what to say or do, so he stays quiet.

We pay, and I overhear Cherilyn tell Wyatt how thrilled she is to see him so content. She even goes so far as to tell him that she's been waiting a long time to see him this happy and that he deserves it as much as his big brothers.

We stop at the grocery store, then spend the rest of the day at Wildflower. I wander around the main house, cleaning and putting things away in places that will inevitably change once everything is up and running and I refine my processes. I do my best not to pay too much attention to the buildings where the campers will eventually sleep.

Wyatt spends the entire afternoon teaching Travis how to drive. He even grabs two big empty cardboard boxes and sets them up to teach him how to parallel park, which is a feat because I don't think I could parallel park that beast of a truck.

Travis is thrilled at the chance to spend time with Wyatt, and even more excited that he feels like he knows how to drive. "You'll have to study the manual and learn all the rules, and then you can take your test to get your permit."

On his way back to his bedroom, Travis says, "I don't know how you guys met, but I'm glad you did."

I'm still waiting for Travis to morph into this awful teenager my mom spoke of.

I know she's a lot of things, but now I'm starting to think maybe my mom is a liar, too.

32

WYATT

When my phone rings, I'm holding a mortar-covered trowel in my hand. I've been expecting this call though, so I stop what I'm doing and answer.

"Farley, what do you have for me?" Using one finger, I swipe across the edge of the trowel to gather the excess mortar and apply it to the blade, then spread it across the bare wall in the kitchen.

"Get ready, Hayden. It's good."

It's been two weeks since I visited Farley, and I'm more than ready to hear this news. Balancing the phone between my ear and my shoulder, I say, "Go."

"You sure this Bennett guy doesn't already ring a bell?"

I don't like that he's giving me a lead, like he's throwing a treat in front of me and watching to see if I pounce. I set down the trowel and pick up the next sheet of subway tile Jo chose. Pushing it into the mortar, I huff, "I wouldn't have come to you if he did."

"God, you take all the fun out of everything," Farley complains.

"Talk, Farley."

"Bennett starts with 'B', right?"

I sigh and pick up another tile sheet, fitting it into the previous one on the wall. I'm going to maim this kid if he doesn't come out with it. "Farley, would you like Tenley's autograph?"

He stumbles over his next sentence. "Well, yeah, I... uh..."

"Say what you have to say."

"The 'B' in Circle B is Bennett. The ranch was owned by Cynthia and Kenneth Bennett before the title was transferred into"—he pauses—"Tower Properties. Looks like a real estate investment trust."

"Shit," I say in a low voice, looking around. Nobody notices me, or my expletive. I get why the family would transfer the property into a REIT, where all their properties could be together, but why choose Jo out of all those buyers with much deeper pockets? It doesn't feel sinister, just odd.

I wipe off the excess grout between the tiles. I'm doing a shitty job. I need to tell Jo, of course, but what will telling her do? I don't know anything. And she has everything hung on this ranch. Her hopes, her dreams, it's like her entire life depends on Wildflower opening. On Travis coming to live with her.

"I have something else for you," Farley says, his voice dripping with excitement. "I heard about Mrs. Calhoun's grandsons showing up in town to visit with her. I saw them acting like assholes at the Merc one day, so I decided to dig a little deeper. Turns out they're ex-cons—"

"I'm aware." Honestly, all it took to figure that out was a basic internet search.

"Are you aware Mrs. Calhoun is mother to only one

child? And that one child fathered one child? Making the Marks brothers—"

"Fuck," I hiss. I drop the trowel in the empty bucket I've been using to mix the grout. "Those motherfuckers aren't her grandsons."

"Sure aren't. But they did know Dixon. Turns out, they did some work with him before they served time."

Work. What an interesting word to describe cooking meth.

I wash my hands quickly, splashing water all over the counter and drying my hands on the front of my jeans. "You're a genius, Farley."

"I'll make sure to remind you of that the next time you call me a name."

"Hang on," I instruct, holding my phone at my side.

I pass Jo on my way to the front door. She's talking with Scott. She looks at me, bewildered when she takes in my state. "What's wrong?" she asks, eyes crinkling with concern.

"All good," I respond, nodding at Scott and kissing Jo quickly on the mouth. I see her suspicion, but I don't have time to stop and explain. She'd want to come with me, and there's no way I'd allow that, plus she's knee-deep in what's going on at Wildflower. The additions and updates are so close to the finish line, I can't distract her now.

"Scott, can you get someone to grout that tile?" I thumb behind myself toward the kitchen. "I have to take off."

Scott doesn't look nearly as concerned or confused as Jo. "Yeah, sure."

"I'll call you later," I say to Jo, kissing her temple.

When I get outside, I press my phone back to my ear. Farley's still there.

"Are you on your way over there?" he asks.

"Yeah," I grunt as I throw myself in my truck and shift into reverse, navigating the sea of trucks.

"I have a bad feeling about these guys, Wyatt."

"Don't go soft on me now."

"For real. Can you call your brothers or something?"

"You don't want me to swing by and pick you up?" Adrenaline allows me to make jokes right now. I love this feeling, this sharp euphoria. Wes gets all the credit when it comes to protecting those he loves, but it's the way I operate too. Our methods aren't even that different, it's just that what he does is straightforward and visible. I operate more subtly, a torpedo moving undetected in the depths.

Farley snorts. "Not unless you want a partner who runs screaming into the woods at the first sign of danger."

I tap the side of my thumb on my steering wheel in rapid succession. "You sound like a liability."

"I would be. What are you going to do about Bennett?"

I pinch the skin at the bridge of my nose. "Not much, for now. Seems there are bigger threats to handle first."

Someone calls for Farley. His mom, I think. Sometimes I forget he's a teenage kid.

"I gotta go," he says. "Call your brothers, okay?"

"Will do."

I hang up, considering my phone for a moment. Do I really need to call Wes or Warner? I don't want to need them. Ideally, I'd save the day and they'd find out later, and begrudgingly respect me. I want them to stop seeing me as the wayward little brother, the guy who comes and goes as he pleases.

I toss my phone into the cup holder.

I can do this on my own.

NOBODY IS HOME.

I can't think of a time when Mrs. Calhoun wasn't here, but that's because I always show up at a previously agreed upon time. Showing up out of the blue like this means I should've expected to be met with an empty house.

I knock once more, even though her car is missing from its spot under the covered carport. I go down the stairs and walk around the side of the house. Hands cupped against the windows, I squint and try to peek in. The midday sun makes it difficult to see anything through the dark sunshades on the windows.

I don't know what I'm looking for anyway. Just... something. A sign of what the Marks brothers are really doing here. I know what they've got going on up on that mountain, in Dixon's old spot. But what are they doing here, with his grandma?

I try one more time to see into the house, blocking the sun from different angles around my head, and give up. I'm backing away from the window when it happens.

A blunt force, something like a fist, lands in my side. "Oof," I grunt, air hurtling from my throat. I spin, fists raised, and lash out before I see my attacker's face.

Just as I connect, my brain processes who it is, and it comes as no shock. *Ricky*.

He stumbles back, at the same time Chris's meaty body bull-rushes me. Together we fly into the house, my back taking the brunt of the contact. I use the heel of my hand to jam against his nose in an upward motion. He screams and stumbles back, both hands on his face. Blood is already pouring down, bright red drops squeezing around the cracks in his fingers.

I don't have a second to recover, because Ricky's coming at me now. His fists are flying, and I duck. He makes contact with the house instead of my face. I'm not so lucky a moment later, when his next punch lands. The pain ricochets through me, and I blink against it. He uses the seconds I'm taking to absorb the pain to his advantage, hitting me two more times. My back is still pressed against the house, I don't have the ability to move much, but I do the best I can. One benefit to having been in my fair share of fights is that I have experience getting myself out of the losing end.

Instead of protecting my face or throwing a punch at his face, I go for a cheap shot, driving my knee into his crotch as hard as I can. When he's bent over and gasping, I bring my elbow down in the middle of his back. He yells and falls over, writhing on the ground. I kick him in the stomach, not as hard as I can, but enough.

"You pathetic piece of shit," I mutter, stumbling away from him. "Next time you want me, come at me from the front, like a fucking man."

"Fuck you," he spits, rolling over and struggling to sit up.

"Fuck you," I answer, standing over him. "What the fuck are you doing here? You're not a Calhoun."

He pushes up off the ground, getting to his knees. I'd love to deliver a foot to his chest and knock him back on his ass, but I want answers.

He manages to get on his feet. "You did something to Dixon. I know it. I talked to him before he died, and he told me about you and your family. Fuckin' royalty," he sneers.

"Dixon put himself in a grave when he started cooking out there. Nothing good comes from the life he was leading. You of all people know that."

Ricky wipes the back of his hand across his lips and nose. "You act like you're better than us, but you're not. There's a thin line between villains and heroes, and your last name allows you to be either one."

"Anybody can be either one. It's a choice."

Ricky's gaze skirts me, and I follow. Chris is coming our way, his shirt stained red, holding a small revolver. It's not trained on me, but held to his side, barrel pointing down. When he gets closer, he points it at me.

"I'll do it," he says to Ricky. His hand and his voice tremble.

I give Ricky my longest, hardest stare. "I called my brothers on my way out here. Go ahead and shoot me, but they'll find you. And whatever you do to me, they'll do ten times worse to you. Thin line between villains and heroes, right?"

Ricky slides his tongue between his lower lip and his teeth. "I'll make a deal with you. You let us keep minding our own business up there, and make sure no one else pays us any mind, and we'll keep our hands off the women in your life. Would be a real shame if Mrs. Calhoun died in her sleep one night. Or that pretty little sister of yours tried a little of what we're selling." He grins wickedly. "The things she would do for a hit..." He palms his crotch and I lunge at him.

My forehead meets cold metal, and it's all that stops me from wrapping my hands around his throat. Ricky laughs, so brave and bold now that he has his dopey brother to point a weapon at me.

"We got ourselves a deal?" Ricky asks. Chris pushes the gun against my skin.

I'd love nothing more than to end these sons of bitches right now, but I have to think of my endgame.

"Deal," I grit.

Chris grins stupidly at Ricky. "Between this guy and that cop, we're—"

Ricky cuts him off with a glare and Chris shuts up. Ricky moves to sidestep me. At the last moment, he leans in and punches me in the stomach. "Just to make sure you remember our deal," he says. "Now get out of here."

I stand up as much as I can, my stomach throbbing, and walk slowly toward my truck. The brothers follow ten feet behind me. They watch me climb in and pull away.

I don't bother to look at myself in the mirror. I've seen myself bloody and broken before.

It's time to make some plans.

Fuck being a hero.

Fuck being a villain.

I'm an outlaw.

33

WYATT

My truck lurches heavily when the asphalt makes the abrupt change to dirt road, and I grunt against the round of pain it releases in my body.

For being a skinny, pockmarked piece of shit, Ricky can throw a punch.

The homestead looms in the distance. It's big and beautiful, the keeper of secrets and the protector of Haydens. That house brings me as much comfort as it does pain. As does this land I'm driving over. It's amazing how a person can feel love and pain simultaneously, from the very same source.

I don't know who's going to greet me when I walk in right now, but I'm expecting that old familiar look, the one that so clearly tells me how the beginnings of a new bruise on my face aren't a surprise anymore.

My steps on the front porch stairs are heavy, my footfalls thunderous. I let myself in the unlocked front door, then think about how maybe it's time we start locking it. We live in the middle of nowhere, people are always coming and going, but Ricky's words tumble around my mind. *The things she would do for a hit.*

Jessie steps from the hallway as if my thoughts have conjured her. The sight of her twists my heart in two. She is young, innocent, and naïve, no matter how much we joke about her being chaos on two feet. Her features contort into horror when she sees me, and she rushes to my side.

"Wyatt, what happened to you?" She wraps an arm around the middle of my back, supporting me as if I can't walk, which I'm capable of even if it hurts.

"A bad situation," I answer, gritting my teeth as she guides me to the bathroom off her bedroom. She lowers me to sit on the closed toilet and bends down, pushing my hair out of my eyes with tenderness. Her charm bracelet is cold on my skin and her eyes hold tears. "Who did this to you?"

"It doesn't matter." The less she knows, the better.

Anger rips through her gaze. "Such bullshit," she says through clenched teeth. "I fucking hate how you all try to shelter me. I'm not a child."

She stands up and moves to the medicine cabinet, searching through it and choosing various things. Bandages, antibiotic ointment, arnica cream. She wets a washcloth.

"I think you'll always be a baby to us, Calamity. Sorry about your luck." I hiss as she presses the washcloth to my temple. I hadn't realized I was hit there, but judging by the pain, I'd say it was a good one. "Just accept your station in life. I have."

The tenderness is back on her face. One side of her mouth pulls up as she keeps the cloth pressed to me. "Dad loves you, Wyatt."

"I didn't say he doesn't."

"You don't seem to think it."

"He loves me because I'm his kid."

She removes the compress, her eyes circling my face as she surveys the damage. I lift my shirt, showing her where the first punch landed from behind. Damn coward.

She bites her lip and reaches for the arnica cream. She squeezes some onto her fingers and, as gently as possible, rubs it across the blossoming bruise.

"He loves you because you're you." Her gaze remains trained on the bruise, as if her life depends on thoroughly covering the skin that will soon be dark, betraying the telltale signs of an injury. "You should ice that."

To my face, she applies antibiotic ointment. When I look in the mirror, I see why. Scrapes, mostly superficial, swipe my jaw and cheek like a painter's brush.

I look at my little sister through the mirror. I know I said we see her as a baby, but it's not entirely true. She's a woman now, as hard as that is to admit. She has my mom's feminine features, but the Hayden personality. One day, she will be a force to be reckoned with.

"Stay out of town for a while," I instruct, my voice grave. When she starts to argue, because it's in her nature to question everything, I repeat my instruction. "I mean it. There are people in town who are bad news. I can't be worried about you right now on top of everything else."

She crosses her arms and levels me with an even stare. "If you don't tell me what the danger is, I'm going to get in the first truck I find, even if it's yours, and I'm going to take my ass into town."

I brace my hands on the counter and take a deep breath. "Why do you have to be so damn difficult?"

"Right back at you," she counters, giving me a little extra headshake, like she's writing an *S* with her whole head.

The extent of Jessie's knowledge about Dixon and his meth house is the same as the public's knowledge. Publicly, he blew himself up. Off the books, someone may have made certain his place exploded. Nothing has ever been made clear to me either, and I've accepted the half-truth I've been privy to. Telling Jessie now feels like a delicate dance.

"Do you remember when that meth house exploded?" I point in the general direction of the mountain where it happened.

She nods. "It was all over the news."

"There are some guys in town who were... friends of Dixon's. Associates, whatever. They've got trouble on their minds, and they mentioned you specifically."

Her eyes widen, and I rush to say, "Only because of your last name. Your relation to me. To the Haydens. They think we had something to do with the explosion."

She leans on the doorjamb. "Is that right?"

I stare at her through the mirror. Her calm response to this information might be the most concerning thing that has happened today. "Yes," I answer, my tone hard. "So stay home."

"Okay." She nods.

Down the hall, we hear the sounds of boots on the wood floor. Jessie cranes her neck to look toward the sound. "Hi, Dad," she says, shooting me a wide-eyed look before she bounds away.

I turn, leaning my lower half against the vanity. My dad appears in the doorway. He takes in my face, his eyes roaming over the rest of my body. I know he can't see through my clothes, but at this moment I think it's possible his eyes are capable of such things.

"What the fuck happened to you?" he asks.

"Like you fucking care," I mutter, walking past him and down the hall. I've kept my filter in place for so long, and I'm just about done.

"Don't walk away from me, boy. Not in my own damn house."

That, I can give him. I'd never let someone walk away from me in my house either.

I stop, pivoting slowly. A hard, harsh look twists my dad's lips, and he adjusts his stance. I feel it bubbling to the surface, the years of discontent with one another, the hurt feelings that morphed into anger and resentment.

How fitting that we're finally having this standoff right in the heart of the homestead.

"You ever going to say what stays stuck up there in that head of yours, or do we all get to watch you stomp around and guess at why you distance yourself from this family?"

Laughter, short, derisive, and disbelieving, trickles from my throat. A sound that so clearly indicates how incorrect I believe his interpretation to be. "For a man who prides himself on taking responsibility in life, you sure do pick and choose what it is you're responsible for."

"Speak your mind, Son. I don't have all damn day to do this dance with you. Either say your piece or get the fuck over whatever it is."

I'm the same size as my dad, but his presence is commanding, even overbearing, making him seem bigger. My first instinct is to cower, to skulk away and cover my wounds the way I have for years. But then I picture Jo, and think of the man I'm trying to become, and suddenly I almost feel bad for him. "It must be hell not to like your own child."

The only movement in his face is the tightening of the skin around his eyes. "What the hell are you talking about?"

I shake my head. "You don't need an explanation, Dad. You've been living this life with me for thirty-two years. You know damn well what I'm talking about."

Now he becomes animated, a statue coming to life. His head shakes, and his fists ball at his sides. His lips press into a stern line. Before he can say more, I keep going. "You hate that I'm not more like Wes and Warner. I know what you think of me. I'm emotional. I'm *soft*." I put emphasis on the word, making it sound like it's so terrible to be described as such. "You don't value heart."

"Your brothers have plenty of heart, and—"

"Right. For the things you have heart for. But what about me? Remember what happened when you took me hunting?"

His nod is barely perceptible.

"You and mom wanted a girl, you wanted one so badly that you kept trying after Wes. Three attempts, all boys, and I can only imagine how disappointed you felt. You kept trying. How many miscarriages did Mom have after me? Three? Four?" My forearms shake, my eyes fill with hot tears, and I wish it weren't happening. I want to be impassive and detached, like the cowboy in front of me, but it's not how I operate. "I've always felt your disappointment in me, but that day, when I couldn't make myself kill that deer, I saw it in your eyes. What a bitter pill it must've been, to have to continue on being a dad to a child you didn't like. To someone you *still* don't like."

"You've got it wrong, Wyatt." His head shakes back and forth slowly. He lifts a hand like he wants to touch me, comfort me, but the simple fact is that he doesn't know how to.

"I heard you, two years ago after your heart attack. You told Mom I'm like your brother. You despised him."

His head drops, his chin to his chest. "I don't know what to say, Wyatt."

"There's nothing you can say, Dad. Sometimes, there are circumstances that can't be fixed. Hurts that can't be healed." I gesture between our chests. "This is one of them."

My phone rings, and it's Jo. I answer, and all I can hear is hysterical crying.

"Take a breath, Jo," I instruct, trying to break into her heaving and gasping. "I can't understand you."

"Tra-Travis," she stutters. She draws in a shaky breath. "He was playing with firecrackers. I don't know where he got them. But... but a field caught fire."

"Shit," I hiss, running a hand through my hair. "What now?"

"He's in trouble. I don't know how much. But it gets worse, Wyatt. People are saying my ranch is going to bring trouble to the town. They're having an emergency town meeting in the morning."

"To do what?"

Jo chokes on a sob. "To talk about shutting the project down."

"How can they do that?" For some reason I look at my dad, who's still standing there waiting, as if he can make this all better. Vestiges from childhood, from a time when a parent was a panacea.

"I don't know," Jo wails.

"Try to stay calm, Jo. Where are you?"

She tells me she's at Wildflower, and I tell her I'll be right there.

"What's wrong?" my dad asks as soon as I hang up.

"Jo's little brother accidentally lit a field on fire with firecrackers and now the town's holding an emergency meeting. Apparently people are starting to think her ranch will bring trouble to the town."

He nods. "People have been talking. That shooting down in—"

"That shooting didn't happen here," I cut him off. "Someone probably got mugged in a big city yesterday on their way to get coffee. Didn't stop everybody in the country from getting coffee this morning. This is bullshit."

He considers me for a long moment, then steps aside. "You better get going to her then. She sounded pretty upset."

I move past him, forgetting our entire conversation. For the moment, I'm putting aside the Marks brothers, too. As long as they can keep going toward what they're trying to accomplish, they won't bother anybody. As much as I despise it, I'll have to let them continue on with their plans for a little while, until I can form a plan of my own.

Jo is my focus right now.

WORKERS ARE STILL HERE, FINISHING UP INSTALLATION OF THE barn doors leading into the laundry room. I nod my hello and cut across the house, to Jo's bedroom. I knock twice and let myself in. She's sitting cross-legged on top of her made bed, hands folded in her lap and staring out her window.

"Hey," I say softly, rounding the bed. I settle beside her, but she doesn't look up. She looks so... sad. Her eyelashes are wet, evidence of recent tears.

"I've come so far," she whispers. Her lips quiver. "How can it all disappear now?"

"It won't," I insist, though I don't know what I'm talking about. I have no idea if a town can stop a project. Especially one as far along as this. The outbuildings are finished. The main house is livable. All that's left are the finishing touches.

"Maybe I can switch the focus. Make it more of a traditional camp. Maybe—"

"Is that what you want?"

"No."

"Then fuck that," I say. "Don't settle. You're going to attend that meeting, and you're going to walk in there like you're not scared, even if you're terrified. You're going to tell them what this camp is about and what you stand for. Nobody is going to tell you what you can and can't do."

Using the pointer finger on her right hand, she drags her fingertip up and down each finger on her left hand. "What if they're right? What if I can't take care of these kids?"

"They're not right, Jo. Nobody gets to tell you whether or not you are capable of this."

Finally, she looks at me, her cheeks flushed with her distress, arcs of sunlight streaming through the window and illuminating her. Her eyes widen, a look of horror on her face. "What the hell happened to your face?"

For a brief second, I'm confused, and then I remember. So much has happened since this morning that I'd already pushed the Marks brothers from my mind. In an effort to avoid adding to Jo's worry, I tell her I had words with Mrs.

Calhoun's grandsons but leave out the fact they're not actually her grandsons.

Jo feathers a caress over my hairline, taking care not to touch my wounds. "What did you argue about?"

"It doesn't matter." I shake my head, and it makes my face throb. I need a cold compress, but I highly doubt Jo has those stocked in her freezer. "Tell me what happened with Travis. How did he get his hands on fireworks?"

"We went into town for some supplies. He wanted to wander around, so I told him he could meet me at the park in an hour. I was at the Merc when I saw smoke. Maia and I ran outside, at the same time Travis was running toward me with two police officers chasing him. They grabbed him and pushed him against the wall, and I kept shouting, 'He's a child'."

She starts crying again. "They took him to the station, and I followed. Sheriff Monroe said they couldn't release him to me because I'm not his parent. So I raced back here, grabbed a document, and took it to the police station. And they released him to me."

"What document?"

Jo reaches over to her nightstand, where a trifold piece of paper lies. She opens it, her eyes roaming the page, and passes it to me. Suddenly it feels like all the air is gone from the room.

Travis's birth certificate.

Father's name left blank.

Mother's name. *Josephine Shelton.*

34

JO

FIFTEEN YEARS OLD

MY FIFTEENTH BIRTHDAY WAS YESTERDAY.

And I'm pregnant. Happy birthday to me.

I don't understand how any of this is actually happening. Or how it's all my fault, like they've said.

Ezra told me what we were doing wasn't a big deal. He said if he only put it in a little bit, we were still technically virgins.

I assumed he knew what he was talking about, because I definitely didn't. My mom never breathed a word to me about sex. I asked her a question once, and she told me not to be a foul girl. It was the first and last time I would ever ask her about it. Everything I learned was gleaned by whispers from other kids.

How was I to know I could get pregnant my first time? My only time?

And then Ezra, so bold when he pushed up my skirt and

pulled down his pants, cried to his father the very next day. He said I'd shown him my breasts, and tempted him.

What really happened was that he lifted my shirt and lost his mind, touching me frantically. Nothing he did felt good. I was just happy to feel wanted.

His father came to our little house, his face red. Two other men stood on either side of him, like I posed a threat. As if my feminine wiles were so powerful I could take down any man with a simple look. Or perhaps they thought I would remove my top, my breasts entrancing them like a snake charmer. They must've believed there was power in numbers.

They ordered my mom and me to leave. They gave us three weeks to find a new place to live, somewhere far away from God's Redeemers.

I found out I was pregnant last week, and my mom forced me to tell Ezra and his father. I hadn't wanted to, but she said I didn't need to add to my sins by hiding a child from its father.

Ezra cowered behind his dad while I took the verbal lashing. According to our distinguished church leader, I was a whore and carried the spawn of Satan in my stomach. The child growing in my abdomen did not belong to Ezra, because Ezra had been taken over by the devil, therefore the child was not his.

I'd laughed. A real, honest to goodness laugh. My mother smacked me.

It was the last time I saw Ezra.

The Outlaw

WE FOUND WORK ABOUT AN HOUR AWAY, CLEANING A MOTEL. The owner, an older woman named Taffy ("Like Laffy," she'd joked), took a great deal of pity on us. She let us live in one of the rooms for almost nothing. We didn't tell her right away that I was pregnant, and it wasn't obvious for a few more months.

When it became clear, she sat my mom and I down and asked us if we had medical insurance. We told her we did not, which I'm sure she expected. She said her sister was a retired labor and delivery nurse, and when my time came she would come help me.

I was making a bed when the first pain ripped through me. By then I'd been to the library and read everything I could about what to expect. But nothing could've prepared me for it in real life. The pain seared me, splitting me in two, and I hobbled back to our room and called Taffy at the front desk.

Donna, Taffy's sister, arrived shortly. She explained to me what was going to happen, and she felt for the baby. The pain was constant by then, and she told me to push. My mother sat nearby, as stoic as ever. I think she wanted to be happy, to supersede all her other emotions about my pregnancy, and revel in new life. Maybe she did it on the inside.

Travis was born at 2:08 in the afternoon on a Wednesday. His hair was blond, and his eyes were blue, just like mine. He didn't look a bit like his father.

After three months at the hotel, my mom decided it was

time to move on. Taffy was sad to see us go. She gave me a blanket she'd knitted for Travis, and a little bottle of nail polish that still had the one-dollar sticker on the side. "Every girl deserves to feel pretty," she'd said.

We settle in Sierra Grande, Arizona, a place where my mom had been once and said it was the most beautiful place she could remember visiting. I didn't agree with her assessment, at least not at first. It was mostly desert, until the higher elevation started and it turned into pine trees and cottonwoods. The people were so nice, so welcoming, that the whole place started to become beautiful, and I understood what she meant.

My mom goes to school at night, earning her licensed practical nurse degree after being inspired by Taffy's sister. She works weekends, all day Saturday and Sunday, at a restaurant in the next town over. I go to school during the day and spend the rest of my time taking care of Travis.

My mom tells people Travis is her son, and I don't argue. She's ashamed of me, and I'm ashamed of myself. By the time Travis turns one, I've given written consent of legal authority over him to my mother. I want to give Travis the very best, and this feels like the only way. And, selfishly, I want a life too. I want the chance to be like my peers at school. I want to laugh and talk with my friends, buy food from the cafeteria instead of unwrapping a sad-looking cheese sandwich while hiding in the girls' bathroom every day.

I love Travis fiercely, but he terrifies me too. When my mom decides she is going to rejoin the church, I argue against it. But I know, deep down, that Travis will be better off there. If she leaves and I insist on keeping Travis with me, his quality of life will be worse. I cannot keep him here with me, trying to make ends meet while I juggle school and a job. By the time I pay a sitter, I'll have nothing to feed him and clothe him and pay rent. I have to admit that my child's best option doesn't include me. My heart feels ripped to shreds.

My mom leaves, taking Travis with her. When she returns a year later after being refused by the cult, we continue the farce. I do not correct people when they assume Travis is her son and my younger brother. She has told me enough times what people will think of me, how they will look at me, how I will never get another date in my life, if people know the truth.

It's incredible how one simple lie can become a mountain, and how that mountain can become insurmountable.

35

BEAU

Wyatt's not entirely wrong.

I had a brother who I thought was a coward, more lily-livered than what's sustainable on a working ranch like the HCC. He whined, he lied to get out of work, and he couldn't take it if anyone criticized a damn thing he did or failed to do.

I said Wyatt is like him, and it's unfortunate he overheard me. Especially because he didn't hear what I said later, once Juliette and I had gone to our bedroom. The conversation continued that night, after she kept giving me grief for not taking it easy enough after my heart attack.

She'd stood at the sink, brushing her teeth, while I showered. I told her the rest of my thoughts, finally getting out the words I found elusive earlier. "My brother wasn't all bad. Before all those qualities I hated got real bad, they started out good when they were in moderation. He liked to talk his way out of situations. He was creative, and he had a knack for seeing someone's character. More than half the damn time he'd use that insight to get people to do what he wanted." Juliette handed me a towel as I turned off the water.

"Wyatt does all that shit. But the real difference between them is that my brother lacked an ability to see beyond himself. He was as selfish as he was creative, and the ranch is a place where everyone depends on everyone else. We're all moving parts, and when one of us doesn't do our job, it has downstream effects. Wyatt might come and go as he pleases, and he damn sure doesn't put in the same amount of work as his brothers, but he does the jobs he knows he's supposed to do. That kid has never left me high and dry. Never." I finish toweling off and pull on my pajamas. "I wish he'd be up to the task of taking over the HCC, because I think he'd be damn good at it."

Juliette rubbed the last of her moisturizer across her forehead and touched my shoulder. "Look at it this way. You should be grateful our three boys aren't land grabbing this place, or they'd be fighting to the death in our front yard."

Juliette was right that night, and Wyatt is wrong now. He stood in front of me a few minutes ago, just before he flew out of here like his tail was going up in flames.

I make my way to the bar cart next to the dining room table and pour a finger of whiskey. Behind me, I hear the sounds of my dad coming down the hall. The guy never could sneak up on anybody, he's louder than a damn ox.

"Why are you crying in your whiskey?" he asks, peering at me when he gets close enough to actually see me.

"Family problems," I mutter, swirling the burnt amber liquid before taking a sip.

"What, I'm not family?" He points at a second rocks glass on the cart, telling me to make him one. This ought to be fun. He has very little tolerance for alcohol.

With a glass in each hand, I take a seat at the table and slide his whiskey across the wood. He settles into his seat and looks at me expectantly.

"Wyatt and I had it out."

"Finally."

I lean back in my seat and glare at my dad. "What do you mean 'finally'?"

"It's a damn good thing you're a rancher and not an English professor like Warner. The word 'finally' means—"

"Cut the shit, Dad."

He laughs, his face crinkling like balled up tissue paper. "Wyatt's feelings have been hurt for a long time. You're the only person in this house who doesn't see it. Well, you and Wes, though he's not as blind as you."

I feel like a shit parent right now. "I always thought he was spoiled. He was the baby of the family, before Jessie, and he was treated as such. I never imagined he thought—" My words fall away and I picture my son's face, eyes filling with tears, as he bared his soul. That took the kind of bravery most men don't possess, to be willing to honestly confront what has hurt you. God knows I never have, and I'll never get the chance either, because the person who hurt me is dead and can't listen to me tell him how I think what he did was bullshit.

"Thought what?" My dad cocks his head to the side, listening intently.

"He thinks I'm disappointed in him."

"Aren't you?"

"No," I say, too loudly. "No," I repeat, softer this time. "He thinks we've been disappointed in him since the day he was born. It's true we wanted a girl, but"—I shake my head and frown, feeling my own wrinkles deepen—"the first time you see your kid, it doesn't matter if they're your first or your tenth. You love them with the strength of your entire herd. Including every one of those hardheaded bulls." I motion outside to my land. "Wyatt might not understand until he has kids of his own. How can I tell him how much I love him when he's been receiving a different message his whole life?"

"Is that the message you've been sending?"

"Not on purpose."

"You ever think your feelings about your brother have clouded the way you've parented Wyatt?"

"Christ, Dad," I murmur, draining the last of my whiskey. "Good to know you're not worried about hurting my feelings."

He grumbles. "I don't have time to worry about nonsense like that. I could die in my sleep tonight."

"So could any of us."

"Well, then, you'd better get to saying to Wyatt what you need to say."

He's right. Except, the time for talking is long gone, and I'm not much of a talker anyway.

Real men take action.

36

JO

He hugged me after I showed him the birth certificate. Wyatt gathered me in his arms without needing to hear any more of my story. He kissed my head and said, "I love you."

It wasn't the reaction I was expecting, and I wasn't entirely certain I could trust it. He was being too nice. Too accommodating. Wasn't he supposed to run away, boots smacking the ground in his haste? That's what my mother always told me would happen. I'm grown up enough now to know her words no longer hold weight, but it's amazing how heavy a parent's mistakes can be.

I told Wyatt everything. Every last detail. His arms tightened, muscles coiling, when I repeated what Ezra's father said about me. It made me smile. Wyatt, my defender.

"I understand if you look at me differently now," I tell him, fingering the edge of the bedspread. How could he not?

Wyatt squints one eye and cocks his head to the side, pretending to study me. "Nah, sorry. You're the same person you've always been, with one exception."

My hand stills. "And what would that be?"

"You're not as perfect as I always thought you were. It's a relief."

My mouth opens in surprise. I don't know what I thought he'd say, but that wasn't it. "Um, thanks?"

He smiles. "I'm seven shades of fucked up. It's nice knowing you're at least one shade."

I allow a little laugh until I remember what Travis looked like when he saw me holding his birth certificate up to the sheriff's face. Everything inside me falls an inch. "Travis knows."

"What did he say?"

"He won't talk to me. He went into his room when we got here and I haven't seen him since." I'm not sure what I'm supposed to do now. He's never been mad at me. That honor always went to the woman he thought was his mother.

Wyatt rubs the small of my back. "Would you mind if I talked to him?"

I tuck one leg into my body and rest my chin on my knee. "That depends. Are you going to teach him the best way to shoplift?"

His hand stills on my back, trembling with his rumbling chuckle. "Only if you want me to."

One corner of my mouth lifts into a smile. I search his face. The slight stubble, the olive of his skin, his eyes so brown with flecks of topaz. Even now, in the saddest of states, he makes my heart feel as though it could fly. "Maybe you can teach him that another time."

Wyatt nods once, winking. He stands up from the bed, but instead of walking away like I expect him to, he pivots and leans down, placing a hand on either side of me. His face is inches from my own. Eyes trained on mine, he says, "I love everything it took to make you who you are." Then he kisses me, swiftly but so sweetly, and his lips taste like a promise.

He pulls away, but before he can get too far, I cup his cheek. "Same, Wyatt. I don't like that you've been hurt, but I can't deny how much I love the person it forced you to become."

He turns his face into my palm, holding my hand in place and pressing his lips to my skin. "Now I officially know I'm an outlaw."

"Why's that?"

"Josephine Shelton, I do believe I've stolen your heart."

I make a noisy, amused sound with my nose. "Corny."

Wyatt grins. "So corny. But you love it."

My heart flutters. "There's no denying that."

Wyatt releases my hand, and I let go of his cheek. "I'm going to talk to Travis."

Some of that fluttery feeling simmers down. "Please make sure he knows how much I love him." A sob sticks in my throat, and I force my next words out around it. "I thought I was making the best choice for him back then. And I've been half alive since."

"I'll talk some sense into him, Jo. I promise." He looks around the room. "You should get out of here. Go for a walk and clear your mind. I hate to think of you sitting in here and being sad."

I nod in agreement. "I'll go start on the list the new marketing person sent me. She wants pictures of the ranch." I watch Wyatt walk out of my bedroom. When he first started his community service here, I'd assumed he was inherently good at fixing things. Never did I imagine he'd be applying his skills to my relationship with my son.

37

WYATT

Isn't it some shit that I happen to know exactly how Travis is feeling right now?

Feeling unwanted by a parent? *Check.*

Feeling there must be a flaw that rendered you unlovable? *Check.*

I'm making some assumptions here, but I think they're a safe bet. I'm also guessing Travis feels shocked that the two most important women in his life have been lying to him since the day he was born. In that feeling, he is alone. I cannot empathize.

My knuckles hit the solid wood door twice, and I say, "It's Wyatt."

A few seconds later, the door swings open. Travis is already retreating to his bed, but it's as much of an invitation as I should expect to get right now.

"Hey, bud," I start, closing the door behind me. I grab the chair from the desk and pull it over, turning it around and sitting on it backward. "How's it going?"

Travis stares at me. "What happened to you?"

Shit. Right. "Sometimes standing up for someone gets messy."

He nods, micro-movements joined by a contemplative expression. I think he likes the idea of standing up for someone. It doesn't surprise me, given what Jo is attempting to do with this ranch.

Travis adjusts himself on his bed, trying to cross his legs, but they're long and gangly and he gives up. He ends up scooting himself across the bed and leaning his back against the wall. "Did Jo send you in here?"

"Sort of," I admit. "I volunteered to come in here. And she seemed grateful."

"She's my mom."

"Yeah." My mind is blown away by that too, but I have to push that down for now. This kid needs me.

He's quiet, tugging at a loose thread on the bottom hem of his shirt. "I always thought it was weird how old my mom was. So much older than my friends' moms." He huffs out a sound that is equal parts disbelief and disgust. "Turns out she's my grandma." He shakes his head.

"Sometimes, the people who love you do some shitty things." I run my thumbnail across an itch on my chin. "The best I can tell you is that some of those shitty things come from good intentions. Jo was fifteen when you were born. That's the same age you are now."

"That's what I keep thinking about. She must've been so scared. She must've hated me." He rubs the heels of his hands across his eyes, trying to get rid of the moisture.

"She didn't. She loved you."

His lower lip trembles. "Then why did she let my mo—"

Travis squeezes his eyes closed, then reopens them. "Why did she let my *grandma* take me?"

"You were right when you said she was scared. She'd also just come from a really bad situation and she had some trauma from that." I don't know how much Travis knows about the church and all the drama that happened there, so I leave that part out. "You have every right to be pissed, Travis. Really. But maybe in time, you'll start to see that Jo made a hard choice in a nearly impossible situation. She broke her own heart when she let your grandma have guardianship. Personal cost meant nothing to her when it came to what was best for you."

Travis looks away. He's a fifteen-year-old boy, how much of this can he be expected to understand? I can tell he's a sensitive kid, but he's still a teenager. Raging hormones, confusion, and selfishness reign supreme. I remember pretty clearly.

A memory slams into me. My dad, during the time when the Bennett family was undercutting the entire Arizona beef industry pricing, and things weren't looking good for the HCC. He sold his collection of antique nickel-plated, pearl-handled Colt revolvers to keep our family afloat. His grandfather willed them to him, and on his deathbed wheezed a final wish for him to keep them in the hands of a Hayden. I never thought of it back then, but he sold his most prized possessions to make sure his family didn't go without.

The memory doesn't erase all the hurt, but it's cause for thought. Sacrifices a parent makes for their child, the ways they'll willingly break their own hearts, like taking on water just to keep their kid dry.

I've felt unwanted and unloved by my dad for most of my

life, but how much of it was me internalizing his mistakes? I picked them up and put them on, sheathing myself in the hurt he caused, and used it to feed the angry fire within.

Until Jo.

She's the reason I sat up and began to take stock of what I've been doing. Being forced to help her here at Wildflower is the best thing that has ever happened to me. I wasn't waxing poetic when I told her I love everything it took to make her who she is. I'd never utter a word I don't mean when it comes to Jo. Wild ways and desperado-like behavior aside, Jo gets the best of me.

Travis shifts, tipping his head so the back of it touches the wall. "I don't know how to look at her now."

I sniff, thinking. "I'd say it's like anything hard. It's only new the first time you do it, and it gets easier from there."

"It makes sense the longer I think about it. She's always been really protective of me. She visited a lot, she took me shopping when she came. She'd ask if I needed anything and my"—he gulps—"grandma acted annoyed. I thought she was just an awesome big sister. Makes more sense to me now." Travis sighs deeply. "What happens from here? Is she my mom now?"

"You'll have to talk with her about that."

"Who has custody?" He makes a face. "And why does anybody need to have custody of me? I'm fifteen. I'm not a baby. In a few years, I'll be an adult."

I'm not about to argue with a kid who craves the same independence I did. "Legally, you need a guardian, even though you're pretty close to being an adult." Three years is a long way off, but I get the feeling Travis needs a little boost, and far be it for me to be the one who denies him. "Maybe you should go find Jo and talk to her."

Travis leans over closer to the end of his bed, looking out the window. "Do you know where she is?"

"Somewhere on the property. She's taking pictures for the woman she hired to do the marketing."

Travis glides over the comforter, placing his feet on the ground. He starts to stand but pauses. "Did she buy this place for me?"

Technically, the answer is *yes*, but I don't know that a kid needs to have that knowledge, and the pressure that might accompany it, so I shrug. "This ranch has been a dream of hers for a long time. I'm sure having you here with her is a part of it."

He gets up and goes for the door. I realize I haven't found out where he got those firecrackers, so I ask.

"A couple guys in town. They said they bought too many and didn't need them. I didn't know they were illegal, I swear. If I'd known what they could do, I would have thrown them away."

I know the answer to my next question already, but I ask it anyway. "Was one taller than the other? Looked kind of alike? A little worse for the wear?"

"I guess? I didn't notice a whole lot about them. They seemed nice enough. The taller one told me his name was Ricky, and he shook my hand and told me to make sure I remembered him."

Fuck. Just like Dixon, picking their way through town, trying to find the loner, being friendly to a kid they think they can eventually turn into a client. Fresh meat.

I nod. "Thanks, Travis."

He continues out of his room, and I put the chair back where it belongs.

I think I did okay, as far as heart to hearts go. It's a scary thing, holding a kid's feelings in your palm. Makes me look at my parents differently. Especially my dad.

It also gives me a renewed sense of purpose. Those assholes aren't going to fuck with my family, and as far as I'm concerned, that includes Travis.

I'm going to end them.

38

JESSIE

Some people learn lessons the hard way, and I'm one of them.

When Wyatt told me to stay out of town for a little while, it only piqued my interest.

I wanted to know who beat up my brother. And it didn't take long to find them, either. I put on a sundress, sat my ass on a bench on the busiest street in Sierra Grande, and like a moth to a damn flame, those assholes showed up.

Now I'm wishing my curiosity had stayed put. These men are terrible people. And they don't accept the polite brush-off. I'm honestly scared to use my impolite direct communication.

The taller one, Ricky, has teeth browning on the outer edges. He sits too close to me, his knee pressed to mine. The other one, I don't remember his name, keeps space between us, clearly deferring to Ricky.

"I wish you'd tell us your name, sweetheart." Ricky's finger runs along my forearm, his jagged fingernail scraping my skin. A shudder snakes through me.

"Yes, well, I guess I like to make men work a little harder for me." I start to stand, but Ricky grips my arm, discreetly holding me down. Unless I want to make a big deal out of this, which I'm tempted to, I need to stay put.

"I need to go. I'm meeting a friend." I brave a look into his face. My stomach turns at his sour breath.

"You look scared," he says, adopting a patronizing tone. "Don't worry, I already know who you are. I make it a point to know all the family members of the people who come up against me. Brothers, sisters, grandpas. Nephews and nieces." He leans in even closer and I taste bile at the base of my throat. "Every last one of them." He releases me suddenly and stands. The other one does, too, and both look down at me.

"We'll be seeing you around, *Jessie*," he winks at me, and they walk away.

I wait for them to get far enough away, then head for my car, phone in hand. Once I'm safely tucked away in the drivers' seat, I hit the lock button and dial.

"Jessie?" He sounds surprised. I don't call him often.

"Wyatt was beat up earlier today, and—"

"By who?" Wes roars.

I tell him the name I caught, and everything else that was said to me. "We have a problem, Wes. A very real problem."

"Not for long we don't. Come straight to my place. I'm calling Warner."

I hang up and point my car toward my oldest brother's house. I have no idea what's about to happen, but I'm in.

39

WYATT

Jo sleeps soundly beside me. I'd love to lie here beside her and be here when she wakes, watching those blue eyes blink and join the waking world, but I've got shit to do. Lives to ruin.

I leave her a note, promising I'll be back in time to drive her to the town meeting this morning, and slip from the bed. On my way into town I stop for coffee and a breakfast burrito, then continue on to my destination.

The sports store opens early to accommodate all the early risers and their various activities. Fishing, camping, hiking. *Rappelling.*

On my way out of Mrs. Calhoun's house yesterday, I took notice of the length of thick rope in the back of Ricky's truck, along with the harnesses and slings, all still in their packaging.

I'd never have guessed either of those dipshits to be outdoor enthusiasts of any kind, but you won't catch me looking a gift horse in the mouth. And this discovery is as good as being handed a present tied up with a big red bow.

All I need is a little information, and I know exactly how to get it.

"Drew Dunbar," I say, my voice booming into the empty store. It opened approximately four minutes ago, and I'm the first customer.

Drew, the manager and a Sierra Grande native, comes out from the aisle. He's holding a box of meal replacement bars that probably taste like ass, and an expression that screams how unhappy he is to see me. In high school he was a weasel, always saying dumb shit to girls and seeing what he could get away with. He went too far once and I put a stop to it. He never got over it.

Drew loads the bars onto the shelf. "Out early today, aren't you, Wyatt? Or have you not been to sleep yet?"

"You're funny." I sip my coffee. "Know what else is funny? I saw two pairs of shoes in the stall of the men's room a few months ago at the Chute. I was taking a piss and listening to the sounds of people who were having themselves a grand time. I found myself a little curious, so after I left the bathroom I kept a watch on the door to see who would come out. Pretty little redhead walked out a few minutes later, and you snuck out a few minutes after that. Funny thing is, I remember your wife being a brunette."

"You didn't see shit," Drew snarls, throwing the rest of the bars down on the shelf.

I take a bite of my burrito and chew. "Grace, is it? Your wife's name? It's Grace, right?"

His jaw clenches and he throws the box on the ground. "What the fuck do you want?"

"I want to know who sold some of your rappelling gear recently."

"How the fuck should I know? I have multiple employees."

I take another bite, using the pad of my thumb to brush crumbs from the corner of my mouth. "Grace works at the bank, right? I thought I recognized her the last time I went in there."

"You're a fucking asshole," Drew hisses.

I crumple the paper my breakfast came wrapped in and toss it into the box at his feet. "That may be. Doesn't change a thing though. Who sold that rappelling gear?"

Drew walks behind the checkout counter and picks up the phone, pressing two buttons. He glances at me, eyes flickering away when he meets my gaze.

"Come out here," he barks into the phone.

The door at the back of the store swings open, and a heavyset older man walks out. Worry wrinkles his face. He looks at Drew, who waves his hand at me.

"This guy wants to know who bought rappelling gear recently."

I smile at the employee. He returns the gesture, his lips wavering. The poor guy thinks he's done something wrong, all because Drew is mad I know his secret.

"Sir," I say, offering my hand. He shakes it. "I already know who bought the gear. Can you tell me about their plans to use it?"

He looks at Drew, who mutters, "Just tell him."

I have to stop myself from rolling my eyes. They're acting like they're handling sensitive information. "I need to know because I can't reach them and I don't know where they went," I explain.

"They said they were going to try Devil's Canyon today. I told them it was better suited for more advanced climbers, and they told me they knew what they were doing. I warned them there was a lot of rain in the high country and to expect the canyon to start filling up as soon as the rainwater went downstream. I don't know if they took me seriously." He looks at me with concern. "Are they friends of yours?"

"Something like that." I shake his hand again. "Thanks for the info." I turn to leave, lifting a parting hand in the air and saying over my shoulder, "Say hi to Grace for me."

Behind me is the sound of a box being kicked. I get in my truck and drive back out to Wildflower, as promised. As soon as the town meeting is over, I'll be paying a visit to a certain canyon.

40

JO

It's awkward with Travis this morning, even after our talk yesterday.

When he'd come to find me, I was taking pictures of the campers' lodge. I'd heard the sound of approaching footsteps, expecting it to be Wyatt. I was shocked when I saw my son coming toward me.

My son. Now that he knows, I want to grab a megaphone and scream it from the street corner. I know better, though. I have to tread lightly. A tremendous betrayal, at the hands of me and my mom. The two people he trusts the most.

Travis asked me one question. *Are you my mom now?*

I wanted to answer by saying *I never stopped being your mom*, but the truth is that I did. I gave up my chance to walk him into his first day of kindergarten, to kiss his bumps and bruises, to sign him up for Little League.

I had my reasons, and they were good, too. His safety and security came first, and I couldn't have made it on my own. I explained it all to him. He stayed quiet, but he listened. And I'm grateful for that.

I didn't try to hug him, even though I'm dying for one. He'll have to come to me on his own time, and I'll be here waiting for when that happens.

He's sitting at the kitchen table now, eating a bowl of cereal. When he walked into the kitchen and saw me, he said, "Hi, Jo," and faltered on my name. My guess is that it's only the beginning of the awkwardness.

The town meeting is in an hour. My nerves are already shot, leaving me little room to make myself even sicker over the meeting. I'm only drinking coffee this morning, for fear of whatever I eat making a return on the floor of town hall.

Wyatt walks in the front door. As promised, he is back in time. He strides in, the supple leather of his boots shining in the sunlight pouring in from the windows. He wears a pressed white button-up, clean jeans, and a real cowboy hat.

He comes into the kitchen. He doesn't kiss me though, glancing over at Travis like he is unsure how to greet me. Travis asks Wyatt why he's dressed up. I haven't told him about the meeting. There was too much happening at once, and I don't want him to feel bad.

"Uh," Wyatt starts, looking at me. "There's a, uh…"

"A meeting," I say, half smiling at Wyatt. "A town meeting this morning."

"Why?" Travis's eyebrows pull together suspiciously, his loaded spoon suspended midair.

My hands tighten around my coffee cup. My first inclination is to dumb it down, protect him from the truth. But I have the feeling that's the last thing he needs right now. It's more important that I'm honest with him.

"After the firecracker incident, there are some people who aren't sure if my ranch will benefit the town after all. So they're holding a meeting to discuss it."

The milk and cereal fall back into the bowl. "Can they hurt your ranch?" he asks. "Hurt your dreams, I mean?"

"They could take a vote. Declare it unsafe. Figure out a way to stop it. Tell me my buildings aren't safe. The inspector comes this week to sign off on the property. And even if they can't make it legal, do I really want to bring a business into Sierra Grande when everyone hates it?"

"Hell yes," Wyatt says, at the same time Travis says, "Yes, you do."

"It's not about what everyone else thinks, Jo. It's about what you want." Wyatt steps closer, brushing hair from my face. "This time, *you* get what *you* want. Not what you think is best for someone else." He dips his head, eying me meaningfully.

"Right," I whisper, knowing Travis is at the table listening.

"I'm coming with you," Travis declares. He gets up and puts his bowl in the sink.

"Travis, I don't know. You might not—"

Travis shakes his head. "You wouldn't be in this mess if it weren't for me. I knew those firecrackers weren't a good idea, but I didn't care. And I'm really sorry, Jo." He stumbles over my name.

"I know. It's okay, Trav. Everyone makes poor choices." Don't I know it.

"We'd better get going." Wyatt glances at his phone. "I'm all for ignoring the rules of polite society, but this might not be a meeting you should be fashionably late for."

Wyatt drives us in his truck. I focus on taking deep, even breaths, and try not to cry as I watch Wildflower growing smaller in my side mirror.

THE MEETING IS BEING HELD IN THE ROOM ON THE RIGHT. IT'S a basic room, nondescript. White folding chairs have been set up in neat rows. People stand talking, and when we walk in the conversation dulls to a murmur. At the front of the room stands Mayor Cruz, his salt and pepper hair smoothed back. He talks with his administrative assistant, Adam, motioning rapidly with his hands, while Adam's fingers fly across his phone screen like he's taking notes in time with the mayor's words.

Wyatt places a steadying hand on the small of my back. I'm uncomfortable in my slacks and blouse. I haven't worn these clothes since my last shift at The Orchard.

Wyatt leads me and Travis to the chairs at the back of the room. "This way you can keep an eye on the room," he says under his breath. "You get to know who's doing what."

I look up at him and feel an overwhelming urge to throw my arms around him. It's not the time or place for that, so I settle for a grateful smile and a squeeze of his hand. Wyatt must understand, because he sends me a look swollen with affection.

Mayor Cruz steps to the center at the front of the room, where a podium has been placed. He turns off the microphone, and I'm happy about that. His voice booming through this small space would have made all this a little more difficult.

"Good morning, folks. Thank you for coming out." He claps his hands together, then spreads them apart in a welcoming gesture. "There's been some concern around the town recently, and we're here to talk it out."

My stomach rolls. A few glances dart my way.

The mayor continues. "The intention of a town hall meeting is to provide an open space for discourse. Our opinions may differ, but please remember that, above all, we are neighbors. Friends. Disrespect of any kind will not be tolerated." He pauses to give a parental look around the room. "Who would like to start us off?"

In the front row, Waylon Guthrie stands, his eighty-odd years of life making it a slow process. "I'll go first."

Mayor Cruz extends a hand. "The floor is yours, Waylon."

Waylon turns to look at the crowd. "There aren't a lot of you who are as old as me in here, so you might not remember the Circle B the way I do. But let me assure you, it was never meant to house delinquents. That used to be a respectable ranch, and it's a shame to see it being turned into an asylum."

"Give me a break, Waylon," Wyatt shouts. "You can't—"

The mayor cuts him off. "The floor isn't yours, Wyatt."

"The floor doesn't belong to that lunatic," Wyatt counters, not as loudly as before but with enough volume for the people around us to hear. He earns a few scowls and scattered laughter.

Waylon sends a dirty look our way, but chances are fair that he can't see us very well, and he most definitely didn't hear Wyatt.

"Are we going to talk about the field that burned yesterday?" A fifty-something woman in the third row stands. Waylon takes his seat. The woman is a newcomer to town, one of the many people who've come this way escaping sprawling Phoenix for the slow pace of small-town life. And I'm not saying she can't have an opinion, but... it doesn't hold water for me.

"I think that's where the discussion should be focused." Her forehead wrinkles and her lips purse. "We don't need to imagine future problems when we had one presented to us yesterday." She's wearing a white visor, the kind someone would wear when they're playing tennis. It annoys me more than it should.

"Down at my country club in Phoenix, we had a group of boys sneaking onto the golf course at night with golf clubs and making divots in the course. Those boys were caught and punished, and I think the same should be done with that troublemaker who started a fire yesterday. I heard he's in town to attend that ranch, and who knows what he'll do next."

I don't think I've ever felt fury like this. It flows out to the tips of my fingers, curling them into fists. My body feels like it's on wheels, like I could roll over anyone and anything right now.

Suddenly I'm on my feet. My mouth is open and sounds are coming out and I don't think my brain ever gave the signal to talk or move. It feels instinctual, this call to protect my cub.

"What's your name?" I ask the woman. She jumps at the sound of my voice.

"Clarissa Hastings."

"Clarissa, I'm Josephine Shelton, and—"

She interrupts me to say, "It's nice to meet you," in a saccharine voice. She's as fake as the long nails on her fingers.

"I cannot say the same of you."

She gasps and flinches. I keep going. "That 'troublemaker', as you so rudely called him, is my son." I hear it, the shocked intake of breath from around the room. I know it's bold, to make a statement so publicly, but now that he knows he's mine, I want everyone else to know it too. "He is not here to attend the ranch. He is going to work on it with me. I am the owner of Wildflower. And there is nothing wrong with my ranch."

The owner of the feed store stands up. "You're inviting trouble into this town."

"Yeah."

"Exactly."

"That's what I think!"

I don't know who's saying it all, but the words fly up into the air like flares.

"You're all wrong." The statement is made by a deep, gravelly voice. Low, but far-reaching. A voice that, when it wants to, crawls into your throat, wrapping around your voice box and stamping out your ability to speak.

Beau Hayden.

He stands only a few feet away. I never saw him come in. His arms are crossed, his stance is wide. He leans back onto his heels slightly, turning up his chin and looking around the crowd. His gaze remains impassive, as though there isn't a chance in hell any one of the people sitting there could ever solicit a single emotion from him.

"You." He points a stiff finger at Waylon first. "If you're so worried about this town housing delinquents, you should put up a for sale sign in your front yard and move along, because you're as delinquent as they come."

Before Waylon can respond, Beau sets his sights on someone else. A man the same age as him, someone I don't know. "And you. Do you need to be reminded of what you did the summer after senior year?"

The man chuckles uncomfortably. "Now, Beau, I don't see why—"

"Shut up," Beau instructs. "You're done talking."

A different man speaks up. "Beau, you can't walk in here and—"

Beau interrupts him too. "Don't you even start with me or I will lay your shit bare, Griffin."

I look at Wyatt, his eyes are as wide as mine. I bet there isn't a person in this room who isn't wondering what the hell Beau Hayden has on Griffin, a dairy farmer who has been around nearly as long as the Haydens.

He looks out, leveling every single person with his stony stare. "None of you should be walking around acting high and mighty, because none of you are above reproach. Me included. So how can you sit here and say all that you have? You walk around acting like you know, but you don't know a damn thing. You think Wildflower will bring in problems"— Beau's eyes flicker to Clarissa, the snotty Phoenix woman, and she shrinks—"but problems are already here. A woman walked among you all for a long time, and none of you saw the bruises on her. You sure did manage to gossip about her though, didn't you? How about those two newcomers claiming to be Mrs. Calhoun's grandsons? They're raking the town, looking for potential customers."

"Customers for what?" Sheriff Monroe asks, clambering to his feet.

"Drugs, Monroe." Beau reins his tone in a little. He and the sheriff go way back, or so I've heard, and he probably needs to keep things amicable between them. "I don't want to hear another damn word about Wildflower from a single one of you. What happened in Tucson was terrible, but that didn't happen here. Bad things happen everywhere, whether you're aware of them or not"—his gaze flickers to Wyatt, who nods at his dad—"but you're still living your life. Since I came in here, someone somewhere died in a car accident, but every one of you will drive home in your car after this meeting. A shooting in Tucson does not guarantee a shooting here. What we know is that there are worthwhile kids out there who were dealt a shitty hand, and their hand is only going to get shittier the longer nobody reaches out and gives them a chance. Shame on all of you who are trying to insulate this town. You just might miss out on something really good because you're too busy turning your head." Beau holds his eyes on Wyatt for a long moment. Something passes between them, but I can't say for sure what it is.

Someone coughs. Another person adjusts themselves in their seat. Mayor Cruz steps back up to the podium.

"Thank you, Beau." He nods at Beau, still standing in the back of the room. "Does anybody have anything else to add?"

Not a single hand lifts.

"As mayor, I've decided to set aside the concerns of the town in an effort to continue the plans for Wildflower Ranch. Should it become clear there is a problem in the future, we will reconvene."

The nerves in my stomach melt away. Wyatt takes my hand, and Travis grabs the other.

Mayor Cruz is still talking. "Thank you all for attending today, and caring about Sierra Grande enough to open an uncomfortable dialogue. Part of what makes us great is being honest, and I believe we are stronger because of it."

"Is he trying to get reelected?" Wyatt whispers in my ear. I laugh.

Everyone files out, leaving us alone. Travis looks at me. I think he feels bad for what he caused, but he's still very angry with me. It must be so confusing for him.

"I'm really sorry, Jo."

"I know you are, Trav. I'm really sorry too. And I know it's going to take a long time for you to trust me again."

Travis nods, then gets up and walks out, leaving Wyatt and I alone. Wyatt palms my cheeks, leaning forward and pressing the tip of his nose to mine. "You did it, baby. You stood up for yourself. And your ranch. And your son."

His voice swims with unfettered pride.

"You believed in me."

"Always." He presses a gentle, swift kiss to my lips. "Let's get out of here."

41

WYATT

My dad's waiting beside my truck when we walk out from town hall. He has one arm propped on the tailgate, his thumb worrying his chin as he rubs it back and forth.

I squeeze Jo's hand. "Would you mind giving us a second?"

She gives me a relieved smile, and I'm thrilled to see her burdens have been lessened this morning. "You bet," she replies. "Travis and I will grab something from Marigolds."

Marigolds is a stone's throw from here, so she won't have to go far. "Thanks," I say, kissing her temple.

She walks away, Travis in tow. I continue on to my dad.

I stop next to the bed of my truck, perpendicular to him, and rest my forearms on the edge. "Hi," I say. My voice is gruff, but not because I'm upset. I'm so damn confused. Still, I know enough to thank him for what he did back there. I keep my eyes on the dirt and hay stuck in the corners of the bed. "Thanks for everything you said in the meeting. You must really believe in Jo's ranch."

"No, Son. I don't." My startled gaze meets his steady eyes.

"But you said—"

His head shakes, eyes crinkling at the corners. "I know what I said. All of it was true." He changes position, mirroring my posture. "Jo's ranch will introduce new people to the town, good and bad. The same way Dakota's restaurant brought in visitors, and Tenley's presence brought in all sorts of people. I think the concerns of the townspeople are valid. You've always had a gift for seeing deeper into people, and a greater capacity for letting them be human." The skin between his eyebrows furrows. "Your God-given gifts are different than your brothers, Wyatt, but they're no less valuable. If you say Jo's ranch is right for this town, then I believe it, because I believe in you. Simple as that."

I've never been short on words, but right now they escape me. My dad's next question blows my mind even further.

"Can I hug you?"

I stare at him. "You want to hug me?" I point back at myself. "In public?"

He shrugs, more from discomfort than nonchalance. My reaction makes him uneasy, I can tell. He coughs. "I'm an old man now, I don't have to worry about my tough-guy image so much anymore." His grin is lopsided. "That's Wes's job now."

My chuckle moves my shoulders. "Yeah, old man. You can hug me."

I won't say it's not awkward. It's been years since I've hugged my father. His palm slaps my back twice, not too hard, and when he steps back he says, "I love you, Son."

I break eye contact and look at my boots. The sudden pouring of emotion is almost too much for me, like a dessert that's too damn sweet. "I love you too, Dad."

"You know, I thought all this time you've been out fucking off, and ignoring the HCC. But I've been asking around, and it turns out you've had a hand in the goings-on of this town. You might've been a little wild when you were younger, but folks around here have nothing but good things to say about you now." His voice thickens. "Warner told me what you've been doing for Mrs. Calhoun. You're a good man, Wyatt. I'm proud of you."

I swallow down the shock. "Thank you, Dad. I appreciate it."

"Since I'm doing all this *talking*"—his lip curls on the word—"might as well tell you I think Jo is good for you. I've always liked her." He squints into the sunshine pouring down on us. "Not sure how she's got a kid, though."

"Maybe she'll tell you sometime. It's not—"

"Wyatt." Sheriff Monroe's brisk voice cuts in. "Just got a call about two idiots rappelling Devil's Canyon. Something went sideways and they fell. Lucky for them the rainwater from the high country washed in early. Just not enough of it."

When the water flows freely, it can be high enough to cushion the fall. A person could still die, but not with total certainty. The water gives them a chance they wouldn't otherwise have, and if they're lucky they'd be carried downriver, and crawl out somewhere past the canyon, where it's shallower and the terrain is kinder.

Not enough rainwater means they fell onto rocks covered by the equivalent of a prison mattress. Maybe nature stepped in and took care of the Marks brothers for me.

I cross my arms. "Why're you telling me?" I have no business in the matter.

"You know this place backward and forward. If there's a way we can get into that canyon besides helicoptering in, I need to know it. High country rain is headed our way now, and I don't want to put my men in harm's way if there's a better approach. I need your help."

I stop myself from telling him the people he's rescuing aren't worth putting good men at risk. Everyone should go home, crack open a beer, and watch the thunderstorm from the safety of their front porches.

But I've never been given a chance like this, never been so important to anybody but Jo. And having my dad as an audience to it makes all of it that much sweeter.

"Let's go," I tell the sheriff. "There's a little shelf on the north side of the canyon that can be accessed from a short hike. You'll have to pick through a shit ton of prickly pear though, so make sure everyone covers their skin or they'll be sorry."

I look at my dad. He nods at me to go. I'm nearly to the sheriff's car when Jo calls my name.

"Wyatt, what's going on?" she asks, jogging the last few feet to reach me. Behind her, Travis holds two brown bags and looks like he's not sure if he should be worried.

"There's a rescue in the canyon the sheriff needs my help on. Everything's fine."

Relief falls like a curtain over Jo's face. "Thank God," she breathes.

"Wyatt, let's get a move on," Sheriff Monroe calls from his police SUV.

I kiss Jo, short but passion-filled. "I love you."

"I love you."

She steps back until she's in line with Travis. With the midday sun on their faces, they look just alike. If he'd grown up here, if Jo's mother hadn't spirited him away, their secret wouldn't have stayed secret for long. Splinters have a way of working themselves out of the skin.

We speed off. Sheriff Monroe turns on his lights and glances at me in the passenger seat. "Bet you've never been in that seat before. You're used to being back there." He inclines his head to the back seat.

I grunt a laugh and adjust the visor to block some sun. In the distance, the sky is dark. "There's that rain you talked about."

Sheriff peers out over his steering wheel, then presses down on the accelerator.

I feel obligated to tell him who he's racing to save. "You know those guys my dad was talking about back in the town hall meeting? The ones looking for customers? That's who you're going to save right now."

The only way I know he's heard me is a small tic along his jaw. "You saying I should call off the rescue?"

"That's not what I said."

"What are you saying?"

"That maybe the people you're going to save aren't worth a whole lot of saving."

"I know you like to do things your own way, Wyatt, but I'm a law man. I believe in justice just like you, but in the kind that plays out in the judicial system."

I snort my disbelief. "Sure, Sheriff. Sure."

His snapping fingers get my attention. He holds his hand next to his chin and points down at the tiny body camera clipped to his shirt. "The judicial system is in place to remove the burden of responsibility from the citizens."

I nod once. "Gotcha."

"What do you think they were doing out there? Doesn't seem like a typical hobby for guys like that."

I shrug. "Fuck if I know. Maybe they were looking for a good stash spot."

He nods, considering. After a moment, Sheriff changes the subject, asking, "How'd Jo end up with a son none of us knew about?"

"You'll have to ask her."

"Nah, that's okay. Not my business." He brushes dust off the top of the dash. "I expect you to thank me at your wedding. As far as I see it, you and Jo are together courtesy of me."

I smile. "How is it you think *this* is your business?"

"Everyone loves love, Wyatt. You'll see. People will be all over your business now."

The sheriff's words make me think about the concept of marriage. I never saw it for myself. Never saw a wife and kids, like my brothers. I assumed I'd always be the fun uncle. Until Jo.

She makes me see different paths for myself when all I saw before were roadblocks. With Jo, the entire world is within my reach. She makes me better, simply by existing.

The sheriff takes the bumpy turnoff for Devil's Canyon, and I focus my thoughts on what we're setting out to do.

THE COUNTY SEARCH AND RESCUE POSSE PULLS IN SECONDS after us. Six people climb out of the black SUV, all wearing red T-shirts and threading their arms through packs that they secure into place with clips on the front of their chests.

They are all volunteers and highly organized. Backgrounds in military, security, and medical environments have qualified them for this team, but it's really their desire to do good in this world that makes it possible.

I know this because I looked into the requirements once, thinking it sounded like something I'd be interested in. Turns out, I have the desire but not the background.

Sheriff Monroe hops out and begins barking orders. I creep closer to the edge and peek over. Sure as shit, down at the bottom are the prone forms of Ricky and Chris Marks. Still clipped into their harnesses, they lie on their backs. From this distance, I can't determine their injuries.

"Wyatt," Sheriff hollers. "Show search and rescue where you think they might be able to get in. And hurry up, the storm's not going to hold off on our account."

I hurry to the group with the red shirts and SAR emblazoned on their chests. After a short nod of acknowledgment, I start explaining where I think we can enter the canyon without rappelling or needing a helicopter. "There's a spot on the far side, almost like a hiking trail, but you have to be careful because it drops off quickly. But if you stay pressed to the canyon wall you can follow it and it leads to a bit of a shelf about halfway down. It'll be a lot easier and safer to rescue from there instead of up here."

"Got it," a large, bearded man says. "Show us where it starts."

As one, we jog to the spot. Like I told the sheriff, it isn't easily accessible. Prickly pear cactus grows between us and the place where the small dip into the canyon begins.

I eye SAR's T-shirts. "Do you have more to wear than that?"

Without responding, each person removes a long-sleeved shirt and gloves from their pack and puts them on. The bearded man gives a hand signal and they fall into line. He leads them into the cactus, and they pick their way through. It's not dense like a jungle, but it's not pleasant to walk through, even with a layer protecting the skin.

All this for two guys who are rebuilding a meth lab and cherry-picking potential customers. Not to mention preying and capitalizing on an old woman's mental illness.

When SAR pulls Ricky and Chris out, I might shove them back in.

In the not-too-far distance, a lightning bolt fractures the sky. I hustle back to the sheriff and tell him the team is descending. The way the canyon is situated, with the recesses and grooves, it's difficult to see the team.

"Who called for help?" I ask, just now realizing I don't know any details of what actually happened.

"One of them boys down there. Lucky as hell one of them was able to reach their phone."

"Do you know how they fell?"

"Best I can tell, they anchored in around that tree"—he points back at a thick-trunked, mature Bald Cypress, much like the ones behind Jo's house—"which seems like a perfectly good idea. The locking carabiner is still in place, too. But the rope is missing, which leads me to believe they made a mistake in knot tying."

I know nothing about rappelling, so I nod at everything he says and accept it as fact. A deputy I don't recognize comes over, turning up his radio so the sheriff can hear. The buzzy sound of a voice crackles through.

"We've made it to the shelf, but the water's rising quickly. There's nothing to anchor to here, so we're going to free climb."

"No," the sheriff barks. "It's too dangerous. I'll call in the chopper."

"We can reach them, Sheriff."

"I said no," he bellows. "Get back up—"

A crack. A tremor. Booming, roaring, the sound like a swarm of bees. We stare, frozen, as water pours from the mouth of the canyon.

"Move, move, mo—" The garbled instruction punctures the cacophony, then stops. I lie on my stomach and crawl to the canyon's edge. Every couple seconds I catch sight of the color red, a swift and fleeting movement, as the team scrambles to climb up the steep canyon wall. I push back and stand, my shirt covered in burnt orange dust. Everything inside me is at a standstill, my breath stuck in my throat, as I wait for the first person to come up the tiny trail I led them to.

And then they do. One by one, they appear, and I count each person. After four, there is a lag and my stomach knots. Seconds that feel like hours tick by, and finally a fifth person appears, supporting the weight of the sixth. They make their way back through the cactus, and the emergency responders who were waiting for the rescue turn their attention to them.

Sheriff peers over the canyon, then looks back to the many who gathered to save the few. "The rescue has become a recovery," he announces, his voice even.

Heads hang, grief automatic, for those who don't know who it was they were working to save. The sheriff meets my gaze and gives me a tiny, imperceptible nod.

I need to see for myself, so I walk to where the sheriff stood. The water, powerful enough to lift trucks in a flood, easily lifted the broken but alive bodies of the Marks brothers and swallowed up what life was left. Now they both lie face down, unmoving but for the flow of the water. What came in with so much strength has simmered as it found an exit out of the slot at the end of the canyon. This will flow on and on, eventually feeding into the river that passes near Warner and Tenley's newly rebuilt home.

"It's called Devil's Canyon for a reason," I hear the sheriff saying. He's talking to the bearded man, the person I've come to assume is the leader of SAR. The person who was helped off the trail seems to be okay. A medic bends over them, wrapping their ankle.

I tuck my hands in my pocket and look one last time at the lifeless bodies below me. They were gearing up to unleash havoc on Sierra Grande, and I can't find it in myself to be too upset about their passing. I'd call it poetic, to have it be their own mistake that ended their lives.

I look down, say a quick prayer thanking God for taking care of people in his own way, and turn to leave. The sun is nearly gone, the gray clouds blocking it out, but there's a sliver of a ray passing the exact place on the ground where my gaze passes. It's all I need to see it lying there.

Bending, I dust off the toe of my boot. But, of course, I'm not dusting at all. My fingers close over the cool metal, tucking it into my grasp.

Without anybody noticing, I slip the gold bracelet with the green four-leaf clover charm into my pocket.

42

WYATT

The sheriff took me back to my truck, then went on to the station to wait out the thunderstorm. On the ride back, he'd explained that the helicopter would be fine in rain, but there was no need to go up against lightning and thunder. Especially when the situation was no longer life or death. When the storm passes, which won't take long according to radar, they'll retrieve the bodies.

"We'll have to notify next of kin. Poor Mrs. Calhoun," he muttered.

"Uh, yeah. You don't have to worry about that." I paused when I stepped from his SUV, my hand tented above my head to keep the rain from getting in my eyes.

"Why's that?"

"They were lying. They're not related. They knew Dixon and they were taking advantage of her diminished mental capacity."

The sheriff studies me. "And you know that how?"

I shrug. I'm not ready to share my secrets, so I say, "I have my ways."

The sheriff smirks. "You ever consider a career in law enforcement?"

I shake my head. "I prefer to bend the law, not enforce it."

Sheriff snorts a laugh. "Wyatt Hayden." He shakes his head and says my name like it's amusing. "You are a son of a bitch." He speaks with affection, so I know he means it as a compliment.

"I'll be sure to tell my mother you said so." I wink and close the door, keeping my head down as the rain starts up a little harder.

I call Jo, and she tells me she and Travis are at Warner and Tenley's house. It's not what I'm expecting to hear, and she explains that Tenley called and invited everyone over.

When I arrive, everyone is in the house. I hear country music, something old and soulful, Tenley's favorite kind. It's also Wes's, not that he'd ever admit it.

I climb the steps of the front porch and pause, a hand on the house, as I toe off my boots. They're muddy as hell after walking around in the rain. It looks like all my siblings had the same idea. Boots are lined up in a row, so I grab mine and set them down beside Wes's, using my foot to slide his over to the right to make room for mine. When I do that, a slash of terra cotta earth dirties the floor. I grab one of his boots and turn it over, then run the tip of my pointer finger across the bottom. I repeat the motion, this time across the front of my shirt, where a similarly colored dust discolors the fabric.

"There you are." Jo's voice breaks into my thoughts. "What are you doing?"

"Nothing," I murmur, puzzle pieces shifting. I put Wes's boot back in place and stand. Jo makes a face at my shirt. "Maybe you can borrow a shirt from Warner?"

"Good call." I unbutton my shirt and turn away, shaking it out. Warner keeps a clean house, he'd probably tan my hide for bringing in all that red dust. It's not cold out, but between the rain and wind, goose bumps rise on my skin.

"How did everything go?" Jo asks. Her head tips sideways, her eyes the beautiful shade of blue I can't seem to get enough of.

"They weren't able to make the rescue," I answer. Jo gasps and her hand comes to her mouth.

"I know it sounds terrible, but it's not. They were the kind of people who hurt others. They gave those firecrackers to Travis and walked away without giving a shit. Those firecrackers could've blown off his fingers, and they didn't care." I don't need to be mad anymore. The threat is gone, but still the indignation creeps in. "They were the same guys who were trying to bring meth back after Dixon died, and they're not really Mrs. Calhoun's grandsons either."

Jo squeezes her eyes closed and shakes her head quickly back and forth. "How do you know that?"

"I have a guy, a computer genius. And a hacker. He helps me out with information in exchange for me never telling Tenley he's the one who stole and was selling her underwear online."

Jo gasps again. "Wyatt," she hisses. "You should tell her."

"Hell no. That's my meal ticket. I never would've known about the Marks brothers or Sawyer Bennett." Thunder rumbles across the sky when I say his name, making it seem more ominous than necessary.

Her eyes narrow. "What about Sawyer Bennett?"

"Circle B, as in B-ennett. His family owned it."

Her hands run through her hair, gathering it over one

shoulder. "I don't understand. Why would they sell it to me, and then agree to invest in it?"

"That," I say, rubbing my forearms, "is something I don't know."

"I'm going to ask him."

"Can you hold off on that? I'd like to gather more intel before we show our hand."

"Are we playing a game?"

I shrug. "Who knows?"

Jo rubs her temples with two fingers. "This was a lot for one day."

I put my arm around her shoulder, picturing the water rushing into Devil's Canyon. "No kidding."

We walk inside, and I'm still shirtless. Wes and Warner both scowl at me. To irritate them further, I flex my chest muscles and do that thing where I make them pop one at a time. Dakota pretends to catcall me, and Wes mutters, "Fucking Christ," and throws up his hands.

Warner brings me a shirt and throws it at me. "It's not that kind of party, little brother."

Jessie sits on a barstool, her elbows propped on the kitchen island. I walk over and sit down beside her. "You're quiet," I say, reaching for a handful of grapes from a fruit platter.

"I'm good," she answers, taking a grape from my palm and tossing it in her mouth.

"You sure about that?"

She nods. I reach into my pocket and set the bracelet on the counter, using one finger to slide it over to her. "Missing something?"

Her gaze grows wide and her hand flies to her mouth. I

look up to find Warner's eyes on us. When he sees the bracelet on the counter, he looks away.

Jo comes up behind me, sliding her hands over my shoulders and hugging me from behind. I reach up and grasp her forearms. "Where's Travis?" I ask.

"In the living room playing video games with Peyton and Charlie."

"He better be sitting at the opposite end of the couch from Peyton," Warner growls.

"I'll make sure he knows better," Jo promises.

I reach around for Jo, guiding her onto my lap. "Make sure he knows one day they'll be cousins."

The movement in the kitchen stills. Tenley, the only person still doing something, stands up with a sheet pan she's pulled from a cabinet and makes a racket when she sets it down on the stovetop. "What was that?" she asks.

"I don't know why any of you are acting surprised. I'd be a damn fool to let this one get away." I cup the back of Jo's neck. My next words are meant only for her. "I spent a long time feeling like a person who wasn't quite right. Nothing in this life felt like it fit. And then you came along, and I understood why. A car can't run without oil, and that's what you are in my life. You are what I need to make everything else work. I could live without you if I had to, but damn, I don't want to. I want you, and Travis." Her eyes have begun to shine, the moisture beading at her lash line, and I offer her a smile I can feel in my heart. "Will you be my wife, Josephine?"

The tears spill over now and she laughs in disbelief. "Yes," she whispers. All around us, my siblings and their significant others erupt into applause. I kiss Jo, long and hard, and then the kiss deepens, and everyone around us groans. Dakota says, "Get a room," and Tenley jokes, "Let's keep it PG."

Beside me, I see Jessie holding up her phone. "Are you recording?"

She presses a button and puts the phone back in her pocket. "One day you will thank me for that."

Tenley takes food from the oven and tells us all to dig in. She's made my mom's tater tot casserole, and I'm glad she made so much because suddenly I'm ravenous. Warner takes three plates into the living room for Peyton, Travis, and Charlie, and Dakota pulls apart pieces of tater tot and lets Colt do his best to pick them up from her flattened palm.

While we're eating, I catch Jo's hand and hold it up. "What kind of ring do you want?"

"The kind that doesn't mind hard work," she answers.

I kiss the space on her finger where a ring will soon be. When we're finished eating, Jo and I go find Travis. We tell him I proposed and his only response is, "Cool." I think I see him tap his fingers against his leg in excitement, but it's hard to know what that really means.

Jo gives me a side-eye on the way out of the room.

"Cool," I mouth, and she laughs.

Jo hangs back in the kitchen helping Dakota clean up, while Tenley says she's going to feed Lyla. Unlike Dakota, Tenley is less comfortable breastfeeding whenever and wherever.

The storm continues outside, not quite as ferocious as the day Jo and I took shelter at her ranch before we got together, but close to it. I step out the front door and find Wes, Warner, and Jessie sitting on the porch. Colt sits on Wes's lap, his whole body slumped back against him. I walk over and hand each a beer, hesitating when I get to Jessie.

She swipes it from me and gives me a challenging look. "I'll be twenty-one soon, asshole."

I wink at her and take the last open seat, which happens to be between Warner and Jessie. I wonder if they did that on purpose? We're sitting in our birth order.

Lightning appears, and the thunder that follows sounds like the crack of a whip. "Beautiful storm," Wes comments, his ankle crossed over his opposite knee.

"Sure is," Warner says, taking a pull from his beer. I feel his gaze on the side of my face. "Heard you got called out to help rescue some people from Devil's Canyon. How'd that go?"

"They drowned when a bunch of water from up the river filled the canyon."

Nobody speaks, and then Wes asks, "Do they know how they fell?"

"Sheriff believes their knot technique is to blame."

We're quiet again, watching the storm from the safety of the front porch with a beer in our hands. The rain slows, the clouds part, and a rainbow shines over the sky. I hear Dakota and Jo laughing in the house. Wes and I glance at each other, and I wonder if he's thinking the same thing I am.

He made it. I made it.

Away from that place where I spent so much of my life, living in anger and shame and sadness that directed my thoughts and actions. I'm still a person who thinks rules are flexible, and prefers justice served in unconventional ways, but the tornado inside me is gone. Jo helped to quell it, and this morning, my dad eliminated it.

This family of mine isn't perfect, we each have our wounds and scars, but they're mine. And today, they showed up at Devil's Canyon and showed me I'm theirs.

When it's time to part ways, I surprise the hell out of them by hugging them. "Dad hugged me earlier today, so be ready when you see him next. It might be your turn."

Jessie says, "Dad hugs me all the time," and earns a dirty look from all three of us.

"Oh, by the way." I stop beside the lineup of boots outside the front door. "Thanks for getting red dirt on the bottom of your shoes. Don't forget to wash them."

Nobody says a word, and we never speak about it again.

EPILOGUE

Six Months Later

Wyatt

The kitchen counter is loaded with groceries. I think I've purchased everything a hungry teenage boy could want. We're on our own tonight. Jo, in an effort to be traditional, insisted we spend the night before our wedding apart from one another. I'd argued, but she got her way. She left about an hour ago with an overnight bag and a departing kiss. I'd told her to tell Shelby I said hello.

So now it's just me and Travis once he gets home from school. I'd called Tenley earlier for advice. She's the only stepparent I know. She'd pointed out it's not the same, because Peyton and Charlie still have their mom, and Travis has never had a father.

Which got me thinking. What did my dad do for me that I would've missed if I'd been raised by a single-mother?

This is how I ended up with a truck full of stuff. We're

going to grill. Camp. Shoot. Toss a football. All things my dad did with us.

Travis walks into Wildflower twenty minutes later and places his keys on the hook Jo has on a wall in the kitchen. He's only been driving for a short time, and Jo looks like she's swallowing nerves every time he drives off, but it was important to me to make sure he had a way to get around. After all he's been through, I want to keep him on the same general timeline as his peers. The truck was a gift from the Hayden family, an old beat-up thing that each Hayden boy drove when the time came. Not Jessie, though. She got a shiny new car, of course.

"I hope you're hungry," I tell Travis, taking steaks out of their packaging. I set them aside to allow them to come to room temperature.

Travis eyes the food. He grabs a bag of potato chips and opens it. "Starved," he says, shoving in a handful.

"So look," I say, striding out of the kitchen and into the living room. Jo has done an incredible job decorating. Everything is warm, inviting. Bookcases with books from every genre, overstuffed chairs the kids can sink into and get lost in a story. Sawyer found old maps from the days when Wildflower was Circle B and operating as a working ranch. Now they are framed on the walls, alongside a large sign that says *The World Needs You.*

As far as Sawyer is concerned, I don't think he's a threat. I confronted him about what I learned, and he told me he'd come to town to sell the ranch, and stayed because he'd lost his wife and being here reminded him of a time when he was a kid and felt truly happy. If that shit doesn't make a man emotional, he's a robot. He also said he'd picked Jo to buy the ranch because she had the best plan for it. I left him alone after that.

I pick up two of my purchases off the couch. "On my last night as a single man, I have a few requests, and I need a wingman. Are you up for the task?"

Travis's eyebrows lift. "A BB gun?"

"I assumed you've never shot before, and it's a good place to start."

He nods. "Okay. Yeah." He's trying to play it cool, but there's excitement hiding in his nonchalance.

"Also," I lift up the second box, "I want to camp."

At this he makes a face. "I've never camped before."

"There's a first time for everything. Grab a box and follow me."

It doesn't take too long to get all our stuff out back and situated. The tent is a bit trickier than I expected, probably because they're aren't at least four of us putting it together like when I was growing up.

"Are you sure you don't want Wes and Warner out here to be your wingmen?" Travis struggles to drive the stake into the ground.

I grunt as I drive my stake into the hard earth. "Screw those assholes."

Travis laughs and wipes a hand across his forehead. We finish the job, and later, when we're watching the flames from the fire pit twist up into the night sky, I hand him something I worked hard to sneak out of the house.

"A fishing pole?" he turns it back and forth.

"Have you ever fished?"

"No." He pretends to cast. I smile. His technique is as bad as mine was when I first started. That's what I'm here for. To teach him. Not just about how to fish, but to show him the beauty in being outside. Cultivating the art of patience. The appreciation for nature. All invaluable lessons taught to me.

"Travis," I start, sorting out how to say everything I've been thinking about. "I want you to know I'm not just marrying your mom. You're a part of this, too. A package deal. I understand all this has been a lot for you, and things haven't been simple. I want you to know we can be as much of a family as you want to be." I cross my ankles, my hands stuffed in the pockets of my sweatshirt. "I will be there for you in whatever capacity you allow, and I won't let you down. Ever."

Travis's eyes are trained on the fire. I don't blame him. I don't know a teenage boy who responds enthusiastically to emotional declarations. But then he looks up at me. Firelight jumps around in the shine in his eyes.

"I want you to adopt me. I know I'll be an adult in a couple years, but"—Travis lifts his shoulders to his ears and drops them—"I want to feel like I belong to someone. Like I have parents."

I reach over, place my hand on his shoulder. One squeeze. Two pats. "It would be an honor, Travis."

He may or may not see the tear rolling down my cheek. I don't make a move to wipe it away. In addition to teaching him how to fish and shoot, I'm going to show him it's okay for men to have emotions. I'm going to take every good thing my dad taught me, and add to it.

Jo

"You look stunning, darling." My mom puts her hands on either side of my face and kisses my forehead. I smile as best as I can and accept the love she's trying to show me. Years of hurt cannot be replaced with her apology, but the fact that she gave custody of Travis back over to me without a fight was a huge step in the right direction.

My wedding dress is ivory satin, with a lace overlay. I didn't think I'd opt for something so feminine, but when Tenley brought it to me during our girls' wedding dress weekend in Phoenix, I humored her by trying it on. Then I fell in love with it.

But not nearly as in love as I am with Wyatt. That man once drove me crazy, and he still does now, but in an entirely different way.

Dakota comes in and tells me it's all set. Colt kicks his legs to get down out of her arms but she holds fast to him. His behind-the-ear hearing aid is hardly noticeable, and his loss of hearing hasn't stopped him from turning into a headstrong toddler.

I take one last look in the mirror. Travis comes forward, extending his bent arm toward me. He will walk me down the aisle.

My son. When it comes to him, I'm filled with regret. I can only hope time heals us, that we form new memories, and use those as our foundation. Like my own mother, the apology doesn't replace the pain, but as long as we spend every day trying, we'll get there someday.

The music starts up, and that's my cue. I walk toward the chapel where Dakota and Wes married, and Warner and Tenley. It must be good luck to follow those two couples.

Fairy lights are woven into the flower garlands that wrap

around the columns of the chapel. A long white runner extends out the open doors and down the steps. Candles flicker in tall candelabras on either side. Dakota decorates the same way she lives life. With so much love.

"You ready, Mom?" Travis asks. He's been calling me Mom for a few months. I didn't say anything when he started it, fearing it would make him stop. Every time he says it, it's like my heart gets a little hug.

"Let's do it."

Dakota hired a string quartet for the ceremony, and she gives them the signal to start playing my wedding march. The first notes fill the air, and the small crowd turns around. All eyes are on me, but there's only one place for my gaze.

Wyatt, at the end of the aisle. Wyatt, with his dark hair slicked back, so handsome in his tux. The man my heart gravitated toward for years, who had his own demons to slay before he could love me.

I'm halfway there, halfway to him, when he wipes a tear from his face. It prompts my own. I can't believe the journey we had to go on before we were given to each other.

We reach the end of the aisle, and when the pastor asks who is giving me away, Travis says, "I'm giving my mom away," and kisses my cheek, and it's everything I can do not to break down.

Wyatt and I promise to love each other through it all, to honor and cherish one another. We exchange rings, we say *I do*, and he kisses me in a way that is appropriate for the given audience but promises more later.

Later, after pictures and cocktails, Wyatt leads me out to the pecan trees, past the point where the lights reach. The food will be served soon, so we don't have more than a few minutes, but we make the most of it.

"You are so beautiful tonight, Jo," Wyatt whispers against my skin.

I giggle. I've already had two glasses of champagne. "You've said that twenty times, husband."

"Be prepared to hear it twenty more," he growls into my ear, dragging his teeth along the outer edge.

I make an incoherent sound. "Take me home."

"I think we'd be missed."

"Fine, we can stay."

He laughs and kisses me senseless, until I'm certain my lips are bruised. When we rejoin the party, Shelby gives me a knowing look. She picks at my hair. "You literally have bark from the pecan tree in your hair."

"Oopsie," I sing.

She laughs. "You're not even drunk enough to be acting like that."

"Drunk in love," I remind her. Two arms encircle me from behind. I look down and spot Wyatt's newly appointed gunmetal gray wedding ring on his finger.

Shelby gives him a look. "I have something interesting to tell you."

"Oh yeah?" His deep voice tumbles over me. "What's that?"

"Your buddy Dan Howard was fired from the force yesterday. Someone anonymously sent the sheriff photos of Dan having himself quite the party."

"I hope it was worth it," Wyatt responds.

"You wouldn't happen to know anything about that, would you?"

"Are you asking me in an official capacity?"

"No."

"Then..." Wyatt draws it out. "No. I don't know anything about it."

Shelby throws up her hands and walks away.

I turn around and slide my hands up his neck. "What did you do?"

"Dan was in bed with the Marks brothers. I can't confirm it, but I'm positive he was looking the other way in exchange for a cut of the profits. So I made a way for Dan to let off some steam a few towns over, and then I made sure someone got pictures of it."

It doesn't even surprise me. This is what Wyatt does.

"What kind of party was it?" I ask out of curiosity.

"Hookers and cocaine," he says matter of factly.

I try not to show my shock. "Um, well. I guess Shelby was right. Quite the party."

Wyatt lifts my hand and kisses it. I do him one better and kiss him on the mouth. The rest of the night is a blur. I dance with every Hayden man, including Gramps. We laugh. We eat, we drink, we're as merry as can be, which is good because tomorrow I have to get right back to work. Wildflower Ranch won't run itself, and all the campers arrive next week. We are fully booked and fully staffed. I'd spent many nights awake and worried I wouldn't be able to entice a psychologist to the small town of Sierra Grande, and then, like a miracle, it happened. I sat at Marigolds drinking coffee one day and in walked a woman. She came straight to me, smoothed her pressed navy blue skirt, and slid her résumé across the table.

Sara Schultz. Psychologist with a focus on family and behavioral health. I hadn't a clue. I hired her on the spot.

I needed her desperately, as that was my only empty position, and she needed me too. With Mickey completing rehab and in anger management, she needed to support her family.

Wyatt drives me back to the ranch in his truck that's been decorated with tin cans. He pulls over as soon as we're far enough away from The Orchard and rips them from the truck and tosses them in the bed. The whole way home we hear them rolling around. Travis is going home with Beau and Juliette tonight.

Since we only have this one night alone, I'm planning to make it good. Tenley gave me the most beautiful lingerie at my bridal shower, and I'm wearing it under my dress.

Wyatt appreciates it, but not for long. He devours me the second I step out of my dress.

Afterward, he runs a bath for us, this time with real running water. My heart swells as I watch him testing the water temperature. He gets in first, and I sink in after him, settling between his legs. He rubs soap in his palms and washes my arms and my breasts, kneading my shoulders and my upper back. "You're perfect, Jo. I love you."

I lean back into him, relishing the feel of his warm chest on the back of my neck. When I was younger, I didn't expect much from my life because I was told not to. When I was older, I didn't expect much because I didn't think I deserved it.

Then Wyatt showed up and taught me how to fight for myself. For my hopes and dreams.

I used what I learned, and I fought for him.

I lean back and look up at my husband. "You're a person worth loving, Wyatt. And I'll make sure you never forget it."

Jessie Hayden's determined to break free from her nickname. Convincing her oldest brother of her place as his right-hand woman on the ranch is her only goal. Until she meets the son of her dad's old enemy.
Read the jaw-dropping conclusion to the Hayden Family series.

WANT MORE HAYDEN FAMILY? VISIT JENNIFERMILLIKINWRITES.COM to read a Hayden family prequel novella.

SNEAK PEEK AT THE CALAMITY

"I figure if a girl wants to be a legend, she should go ahead and be one."

- Calamity Jane

PRESENT DAY

It smells like wood. Rich mahogany. Deep and spicy.

The dean of Arizona State University is late for our meeting. A meeting he called me to, mind you, not one I sought out and certainly not one I wanted to attend. Lack of choice is why I'm here, sitting in this tufted leather seat across from the gleaming desk, waiting on someone I'd rather not meet face to face.

My stomach sank when his assistant, Rosemary, called my cell phone. My first mistake was answering. I should've let it go to voicemail. My second mistake was telling her I was available to meet the dean. I should've said I was back home at the Hayden Cattle Company. *Bad reception out here on the ranch, crackle crackle I think I'm losing you.*

But if I dare to be honest with myself, the real mistake

occurred when I did the thing I'm assuming I've been called here for. What I'd really like to know is who told on me? The number one rule of my operation is that nobody is allowed to talk about it. I guess I can't trust anybody in the age of cell phones and instant gratification. Assholes.

The door behind me opens. I sit, my back ramrod straight, and wait for the dean to approach. In my peripheral vision I see his charcoal gray slacks, his matching jacket. He rounds his desk and pulls out his chair. His hair is thinning on top, and on his hairline beside his ear is a large mole that matches his skin tone.

The creaking protest as he settles in his seat is the only sound in the room, and it seems to bounce around the walls. He folds his arms in front of himself and leans back. More protests from the chair. "You've been busy, Miss Hayden."

I smile. "My studies keep me very busy."

His lip tugs like he wants to laugh. "Right. And your extracurriculars? Do they keep you busy as well?"

"Maintaining a 3.9 GPA makes it nearly impossible for me to have extracurriculars." This little game is... well, to be perfectly honest, it's fun. "Perhaps next year I won't take so many demanding classes."

He nods slowly. "Are you aware it's against university policy to gamble on campus?"

I do my best not to react. I knew this was coming. "I'm not sure what you mean?"

"Miss Hayden, we know you've been operating a weekly poker game from your dorm room."

I palm my chest. "Me?" I'm great at many things, but lying isn't one of them. Like my brother Wyatt, I see rules as flexible. I view outright lying as offensive. It's something I try not to do.

"Dean Mueller," I begin, forming the beginning of my defense, "I am not a woman who goes into anything blindly. I did my research, and learned an unlicensed poker game may still be legal if the game is played in a residential building. Hence, it was played in my residence hall." Leaning forward, I remove my palm from my chest and place it on the desk in front of me. "Moreover, I do not profit from hosting the game, and I keep the buy-in very low. All of which makes it acceptable."

It's immediately obvious to me that, while impressed, Dean Mueller is out for blood. The contrite expression in his eyes tells me everything I need to know. An example will be made of me.

My fingers shake, and I slip them under my warm thighs to hide them. The rest of me is still, my back remains straight, as I prepare to hear my punishment.

"Miss Hayden, due to offenses that are, quite frankly, illegal in the state of Arizona and punishable by law, I have no choice but to ask you to withdraw from Arizona State and vacate your dorm room immediately."

My stoicism breaks. A gasp slips between my teeth. "Withdraw?" My voice cracks. "From college?" I thought I'd get a slap on the wrist. Be forced to volunteer in some capacity that benefitted the campus. "Isn't there something I can do? Volunteer?"

The dean watches me react, then says very simply, "No."

"How about..." What I'm about to say is a risk, but who really cares at this point? "Restitution?"

His eyes squint. "Are you suggesting a bribe?"

"Not at all." I shake my head vigorously. *But also, yes.* "I'm simply suggesting compensation or repayment for the hurt I've caused. Like, maybe I can fund a gamblers anonymous club on campus?" I have no idea if that's a thing, but if it's not, I'll make it one.

Dean Mueller shakes his head slowly from side to side. "Withdraw immediately, Miss Hayden." He rises to his feet. "You're lucky I'm giving you the option to do so. If I find you haven't withdrawn by the end of tomorrow afternoon, I will kick you out."

I grab my purse from the floor beside my sandaled feet and wind my arm through the straps. I swallow back my tears. "Of course," I say. Standing, I step from the desk and make my way to the door. As I grip the handle, the dean says my name and I turn back.

Behind him is a large window overlooking campus, and the sun streaming in backlights him so that he looks oddly ethereal. The god residing over this institution, deciding on who stays and who goes. I could fight his decision. Make an appeal. Call my dad, ask the big, bad Beau Hayden to step in and make a donation. It's not that I'm above doing that, but I overheard him when I was home for Jo and Wyatt's wedding. The HCC is struggling, though I wasn't clear on why.

And, at the end of the day, Dean Mueller isn't wrong.

He addresses me now. "Miss Hayden, you're a bright young woman. You have something my mother called 'moxie'. More often than not, that will serve you well. Every once in awhile, it may turn out otherwise. This happens to be one of those times."

I nod and thank him, then slip from the room. Avoiding the gaze of Rosemary, the assistant with the kind eyes, I make my way out of the building and into the warm sunshine.

Moxie. The word rolls around in my mouth, balancing

precariously on the tip of my tongue, and I tuck it back into my cheek, like a squirrel with an acorn.

My family calls me 'calamity'.

The dean says I have moxie.

I cannot figure out if these are good things to be.

<u>Continuing the Hayden Family series:</u>
The Calamity

AUTHOR'S NOTE

Since The Patriot and The Maverick, I've been setting the stage for Wyatt and Jessie.

You've just read Wyatt's story, and (fingers crossed) you felt his journey was satisfying. Full disclosure, Wyatt was the most difficult male protagonist I've ever written. Considering his personality, this may not be too surprising. Wyatt demanded I dig for his story, so I pulled out my writer toolbox and began to sift through his past. Though he didn't make it easy, writing his character was extremely fulfilling. I love giving my male characters deep emotions, and Wyatt was ripe for the opportunity.

Next up is Jessie's story, and I hope I've made the wait worth it. She's fierce, and strong, the kind of woman we'd all like to have in our corner. Buckle up, she may be the wildest Hayden yet.

ACKNOWLEDGMENTS

To my dear, sweet husband. I love you more than you'll ever know.

My son. You have a Hayden Family sticker on your school water bottle, bless your heart. You're one of my biggest fans.

My beautiful daughter. You contributed to the character of Jessie in so many ways. I hope you're always confident enough to be your own person.

Readers. Where would I be without you to love my stories? You made space in your hearts for the Hayden family and I am forever grateful. Every day it astounds me that you allow my words into your hearts and minds. Thank you, thank you, thank you.

My beta readers. You make me better. You help me to improve my stories, working with me to polish them until they shine. I have so much love and gratitude for you.

Thank you to Ellie at My Brother's Editor, Sarah at Okay Creations, and Darlene and Athena at SisterGetLit.erary for working with me on the Hayden Family series.

And…to the entire crew at Valentine PR, thank you for helping me spread the word and get my work into the hands of readers.

ABOUT THE AUTHOR

Jennifer Millikin is a bestselling author of contemporary romance and women's fiction. She is the two-time recipient of the Readers Favorite Gold Star Award, and readers have called her work "emotionally riveting" and "unputdownable". Following a viral TikTok video with over fourteen million views, Jennifer's third novel *Our Finest Hour* has been optioned for TV/Film. She lives in the Arizona desert with her husband, children, and her dogs Liberty and Magnus. With nineteen novels published so far, she plans to continue her passion for storytelling.

Visit jennifermillikinwrites.com to sign up for her newsletter and receive a free novella.

Printed in Dunstable, United Kingdom